I Think She's Trying to
Tell Me Something

I Think She's Trying to Tell Me Something

DAN GRAZIANO

AVON
TRADE

An Imprint of HarperCollinsPublishers

HarperCollins books may be purchased for educational, business, or sales promotional use. For information please write: Special Markets Department, HarperCollins Publishers Inc., 10 East 53rd Street, New York, NY 10022.

FIRST EDITION

Interior text designed by Elizabeth M. Glover

Library of Congress Cataloging-in-Publication Data

Graziano, Dan.
    I think she's trying to tell me something / by Dan Graziano.—1st ed.
        p. cm.
ISBN-13: 978-0-06-077875-0
ISBN-10: 0-06-077875-X
1. Sportswriters—Fiction. 2. Commitment (Psychology)—Fiction. 3. Rejection (Psychology)—Fiction. I. Title.

PS3607.R399I15 2005
813'.6—dc22   2005000565

05 06 07 08 09 WBC/RRD 10 9 8 7 6 5 4 3 2 1

For Andrea, of course.
And for Danny,
because everything is for him now.

Acknowledgments

I have to thank Steve Lawrence, who was the first one to try and convince me I could write for a living. It didn't make sense to me in the tenth grade, but it did to him.

That writing career couldn't have happened without Chip Scanlan and the crew at Poynter, without Tim Burke, Nick Moschella and Pat McManaman in Palm Beach, or without Chris D'Amico and Kevin Whitmer, who brought me back home.

But the book was always the real dream. Thanks to Ed Price and Mike Vaccaro for their first-draft readings and suggestions. Thanks to Burt and Joan Rubin and Carin Mehler, the world's best in-laws, for unwavering support. And thanks to David Eckstein, Francisco Rodriguez and the 2002 World Series champion Anaheim Angels, without whom I would never have had the time to write this thing.

In several very important and surprising ways, this book could never have happened without Sweeny Murti, who's the kind of friend who'll do anything for you.

My agent, Bob Mecoy, has been more than I could ever have hoped he'd be—helpful and enthusiastic from first draft to last. And Selina McLemore at Avon Books deserves thanks for putting up with the nonstop questions of a first-time author.

My brothers, Jim and Jon, are more than supportive, more than just the kids I used to push around. They're two of the most impressive men I know. And thanks to my parents, Dan and Dot Graziano, who've always made me feel like I could do anything I wanted to do.

Finally, to Andrea. There's no way I could do any of the things I do without knowing you're there to back me up. You're the greatest wife and mother that the little man and I could imagine. Thanks for changing my life.

"I had this dream last night," Jeff says, and for some reason I ask him what it was about.

"I dreamed that I killed every dog that lives on my hall."

Coming from anyone else, this would sound weird.

"I had set these traps, right outside my door," he goes on, "and whenever one of the little bastards came running past, yelping and barking and doing all the things that keep me from getting to sleep every night, he would get yanked right back into my apartment through a trapdoor. And then, once I had him, I drowned him in the bathtub. It went on for about four or five dogs."

"What about their owners?" I ask, after a gulp of my orange juice. "Were they pissed?"

"They weren't in the dream," he says, momentarily puzzled. But then he continues. "It's not that I hate dogs—"

"You do hate dogs," I say.

"Okay, I do hate dogs. But at least with most of the dogs in this city, I respect their right to live. Not these dogs. These little buggers I hate the way Bernie hates salad. These, I think we'd be better off without."

Jeff is off on a rant, and all I can do is stand here, trying to remember if he's even told me why he has come to my apartment at eight o'clock in the morning to wake me up and tell me about his dog dreams.

He is stretched out on the sofa in the middle of my living room, his brown suede jacket still on but his shoes off. His very long legs are hanging over one end of the sofa, each one capped in a brand-new sweat sock as brilliantly white as a snowball, and his head is propped on a pillow at the other end. Jeff has very short, sandy brown hair that never looks messed up. He used to have a goatee, but he shaved it off, and this has had the effect of making him look even skinnier, which I never thought was possible.

Another thing I never thought possible was that I would be up at eight o'clock this morning, listening to a story about dogs. Dream dogs, at that.

"When I signed the lease, it said in red letters, right at the top of the page: No Pets Allowed," Jeff says. "And I thought, 'Great, no pets in the building.' But instead, it turns out that the only apartment in the whole building that's not allowed to have pets is mine. Turns out every other apartment in the building actually *came* with a dog."

It's at this point, groggy and barefoot in my big blue bathrobe, that I finally decide to cut Jeff off and ask him what the hell he's doing in my apartment so early on a Friday morning. But before I can swallow my current mouthful of cornflakes and get the words out, he has changed the subject.

"So," he says, swinging a pair of blazing white feet onto the floor and folding himself into a seated position that brings his knees too close to his chin. "Tell me about this chick you met at the Fairway."

And I am totally blown away.

How in the world could he know about the girl at the Fairway? It's been about sixteen hours since I met the girl at the Fairway, and I'm not even sure I've told anybody about her.

"Bernie told me," he says, before I can say anything. So apparently I told Bernie. Still . . .

"She hot?" comes the inevitable question, and the answer is yes.

To sum up:

Yesterday afternoon I was in the express line at the Fairway supermarket on Broadway between 74th and 75th streets. The place was mobbed, of course, as it is every day, and I was about sixty-seventh in line, cradling a half gallon of orange juice under one arm and holding a pint of Ben & Jerry's Phish Food in my other hand. From behind me, I heard a woman singing.

"How you gonna do it if you really don't wanna dance . . ."

Surprised, I turned, found her smiling at me, and told her she sounded good. But I guess I mumbled. I do that sometimes.

"What?" she asked. "It didn't sound good?"

"No, no," I said. "I said it did."

"Oh," smiling again. "Thanks."

She was dressed all in black—black leather jacket over a black turtleneck, short black skirt, black stockings and black boots. She even had a pile of curly black hair to top it all off. Then she asked me a question about my coat, which led to a conversation about what we both did for a living (long line, remember?), and before I knew what was happening, she had taken a CD out of her purse, opened it, written her phone numbers on the inside of the liner notes and handed it to me.

"Call me," she said, "and let me know what you think."

It was her CD, and by that I mean she had recorded it. Her picture was on the cover, along with her name, which was Linda Lane, and she had given me a CD of her own music to listen to. And her phone numbers—home and cell—to call and let her know if I liked it.

It was a dazzling experience, and the kind that perfectly il-
lustrates the difference between merely visiting New York
City and living your actual everyday life here. For every
oblivious jerk who stops in front of you to let his dog relieve
itself, there's a pretty recording artist just dying to give you
her phone number while you wait in line at the grocery
store.

"Gotta love New York," Jeff says upon hearing the story. "So,
you gonna call her?"

"Of course I'm going to call her," I say. "I'm not exactly in
a position to turn down offers like this."

"You listen to the CD yet?"

"Not yet."

"Sweet," Jeff says, bouncing off the couch and heading, in-
explicably, for the door.

"Hey, where are you going?" I ask.

"I'm going back to my place, catch a few more hours
sleep," he says.

"What?"

"Yeah. I just woke up and I had to hear this story. But I was
out till four. I gotta get some more sleep."

"Whatever, man. Drop in any time." Trying to make a joke.

"You know I will," not getting it. "And by the way, here's a
free tip."

"Yeah?"

"You liked the CD."

"Thanks," I say. "I probably could've figured that out on my
own."

My building has a Pakistani doorman who thinks I play for
the Yankees. I do not play for the Yankees. I don't even work
for the Yankees. Being a sportswriter who covers the Yankees,

I happen to go to almost all of their games. Yousef, the door-man, sees me leave at two o'clock in the afternoon, and he sees me come home after midnight. Some days, he sees me lugging suitcases out the front door as I head to the airport for a road trip. I don't know how many hours a week Yousef works, but it seems like he's always there.

When I leave for the game, he wishes me good luck. When I come home, he asks how I did. A long time ago, I stopped trying to explain to Yousef that I don't play for the Yankees. Now, when he wishes me good luck, I thank him. And when he asks how the game went, I always say it went great. He must think the Yankees win every single game.

To be fair, Yousef's green marble desk in the lobby does not have a television on which he could watch the Yankees, so he's never seen me play. (Or, more accurately, never seen me not play.) And it's doubtful that he collected baseball cards when he was a kid growing up in Pakistan. So it's pretty easy to excuse Yousef for not knowing anything about base-ball. Truth be told, it's nice to have somebody wish you good luck on your way to work every day.

On this particular Friday—the one that began with Jeff in my apartment quizzing me about Fairway Girl—there is no base-ball game scheduled at Yankee Stadium. That's because it's November, and the baseball season has been over for weeks. As usual, the Yankees dragged it out for an extra month, going all the way to the seventh game of the World Series before fi-nally making it interesting for a change and losing to the Ari-zona Diamondbacks.

Usually, once the baseball season ends, I need a few weeks before I can feel normal again. This year, those weeks started later than usual, and it's only now that I'm back on my feet, shaving semiregularly and ready to rejoin society. On this day, I need a haircut, but first I need cash, so I actually have to walk three blocks past the haircut place to my bank, get cash from the ATM, and go back to get my hair cut. And while this doesn't sound like much of an effort, you must understand. When you live in a neighborhood in which everything you could possibly need is within a three-block radius, three blocks can sure seem like a long way. Especially when you're in your third week of baseball hangover.

I plod down three flights of stairs because the elevator is out again. In the lobby, Yousef is arranging letters on the message board and, of course, smiling.

"Mr. Jackson!" Yousef speaks in exclamation points. "You have a game today?"

"No, Yousef. There's no game tonight. The season is over."

"Oh," he replies, with uncharacteristic understanding. "Okay. You have a good day now!"

The barbershop is tiny and smells strongly of shampoo, mousse, and take-out falafel. There are four chairs and three stylists, and I have never seen another living customer in the place. My best guess is that they stay in business by overcharging and by giving thousands and thousands of haircuts during Yankee road trips, when I am not around.

It's the kind of place that really brings home the inadequacy of the chain haircut places—those stale suburban assembly lines with names like "UltraCuts" where the people cutting your hair would just as soon be trimming the hedges in their backyard. A place like this one, complete with the barber pole hanging by the front window and a perpetual pile of hair being swept up from around the chairs, makes you feel like you're really in a barbershop.

My barber is a young Italian guy named Paolo. And by "Italian" I mean "from Italy," not "of Italian descent." His sense of style, both in his clothing and his own incomprehensible haircut, give the impression that he woke up this morning in Europe and caught a train into Manhattan for work. Today, for example, he is wearing bright red jeans with a chain hanging out of one of the pockets, a grungy black T-shirt, and red and blue streaks through the one side of his hair that isn't shaved down to the skin. I once told Paolo he could cut my hair any way he wanted to cut it, so long as it didn't look like his. He laughed, but then again, he always laughs. That's probably because he's very friendly and neither one of us understands a single word the other one says.

I'm not kidding. It's a miracle my hair doesn't come out different every single time. I sit in that chair and I tell him what I want, and he nods, in spite of the blank look on his face. It's a fascinating relationship, really. We're in each other's company for a half hour once a month. He says something, I laugh. I say something, he laughs. At the end, my hair looks okay, I give him thirty bucks, and we part. He couldn't be nicer, although I guess he could be cursing me and calling me awful names the whole time and I'd never know it. He could actually be telling me he snipped a two-inch gash in the back of my neck and that I needed an ambulance, and I'd never know that either.

But every now and then Paolo communicates to me an unmistakable sentiment. Paolo's window faces 75th Street, half a block off Broadway, around the corner from the aforementioned Fairway grocery. And whenever a nice-looking girl walks by the window, the haircut stops so that Paolo can enlist me in his leering.

"Eh! Eh!" is the sound that immediately follows the cessation of the snipping. "Youzie uh? Youzie uh? Vurranace, eh?"

And of course I agree, because he's smiling and nodding his head as he says whatever it is he's saying.

And of course this is exactly what happens today. This time the exclamations are accompanied by a violent shaking of Paolo's right hand, as if he'd just jerked it back from a stovetop burner. I play along, looking out the window and spotting young Miss Linda Lane, striding down 75th Street, unaware of her audience, dressed all in black and with headphones in her ears, singing as she walks.

My reaction sparks something in Paolo, who asks, "Eh? You noehr? You nodis gul?"

"I met her yesterday," I reply, assuming I know what he said. "In the Fairway."

"Eh? In eh Furray? Disgul? Vurranace. Vurranace."

"Yes, very nice."

"You gonna tiggerat? You go at widur?"

And I really don't know what the answer is.

Strangely, I do know what the question is. But apart from being flabbergasted at my sudden ability to decipher Paolo, I really don't know if I'm going to take out Linda Lane. In spite of what I told Jeff, I really don't know if I'm even going to call her.

See, things have been a little weird lately.

I've been seeing ghosts.

Relationship ghosts, I call them. Eerie visitors from my romantic past. Women I never thought I'd see again. Some women I never wanted to see again. In the past three weeks, I have had random encounters with three different women with whom I once shared some sort of serious emotional relationship. Some of them appear to want something, others don't. But as you can imagine, it's starting to get weird.

So I ponder Linda Lane. I marvel at the story itself—that someone would give me her phone numbers on her own CD just minutes after meeting me in line at the Fairway. I go through all the usual questions: Why did she like me? Did I like her? Am I interested enough to pursue this? Is this music as bad as I think it is? And I wonder what I'll say when and if I call. But on top of all of this usual stuff there is another, new concern. One brought on by the relationship ghosts of the past few weeks. And because of that, I worry.

Even more than usual.

It all started at Midway Airport in Chicago, at six o'clock on a Monday morning. I was on my way home from Arizona after Game Two of the World Series, hustling to make a connection, brushing past I don't know how many hundreds of people waiting in line for other flights, to Cleveland, Nashville, Jacksonville, New Orleans . . . when I spotted a golden mushroom cap of blond hair that I'd once known very well.

As I plowed ahead through the masses (what were so many people doing here at this insane hour?), thoughts bounced around in my head like ping-pong balls. Thoughts like "It couldn't be her" and "Should I go back and say something?" and "Nah, it's just a coincidence."

But New Orleans was the key. The hair was in line to board a flight to New Orleans. And the last time I'd heard from Mary Ann, three years earlier, she had just taken a job in New Orleans. Between that and the hair, there was no doubt. It had to be her in line for that flight.

If not for the hair, I never would have given that line a second look. Nobody else wore her hair like that. Nobody else would have spent so much time and so much money to make it look exactly like that every time. It was her, all right, and that's why going back made so little sense.

But there I was, sitting and staring at a sign that said GATE C8, an hour and twenty minutes before my scheduled departure, and I decided for some reason that I had to know. I had no idea what I would say if we made eye contact. I had nothing in particular I wanted to say to her. We hadn't parted on good terms, and I've never wished we had.

Still, I went back.

Now, I am not a superstitious person. I'm not a big believer in fate or destiny or some otherworldly element that predetermines the outcome of my life. I believe to some extent in luck, but I think that actually jives with my views on fate and destiny, since it acknowledges a randomness not governed by any outside forces.

What I really believe, though, is that every now and then, when the universe takes the time to try and tell us something, it's our responsibility to hear what it has to say. And while it wasn't entirely bizarre (since I travel so much) to walk past Mary Ann in an airport three years after we'd said our last bitter words to each other, it wasn't as if I was always bumping into old girlfriends in strange places.

At least not back then.

So I went back. I went back to the line for New Orleans, coming at her head-on this time, and once I caught a look at her sleepy face I knew for sure that it was her. I also knew, all of a sudden, that I wasn't going to say anything to her. I don't know why, but that's the decision I made, and for a few seconds I felt pretty good about it.

Problem was, just as I thought I would get through it without having to engage in actual conversation, there was eye contact. Yessir, we looked right into each other's eyes. And as I picked up speed and cruised past her, I heard her say, "Jack?"

It took everything I had not to turn around, and the only thing that saved me was the fact that I was prepared for this and she was not. I ducked into the alcove in front of the men's room and hoped she would decide she'd made a mistake. It dawned on me that she could follow me this far, so I actually went *into* the men's room, where I spent the next fifteen minutes standing around, getting funny looks from the few people who were in there at that hour, wondering if I could have picked a hideout that smelled better, and flipping through the Cliff's Notes version of my relationship with Mary Ann in the short time it deserved.

I never really liked Mary Ann, which sounds weird considering we dated for more than a year. But sometimes you can trick yourself into things, especially when someone's smiling back at you.

Mary Ann and I went out because I asked, and because we found each other attractive, and because we enjoyed having sex with each other. But I never really *liked* being with her all that much. She was a snob. She was self-centered. She had a dog.

We met at a party thrown by a guy I worked with in Boston. She was an old friend of his, and we happened to get introduced. We had a pleasant enough conversation during which I discovered we shared a mutual love of food. She won me over when she asked me what was the most disgusting thing I'd ever eaten.

The question caught me off guard. Even now, I'm not sure of the answer, because it may well be something my memory blocked out. A small fly that flew into my mouth? A piece of earwax I mistook for a crumb of pizza crust? So I hemmed and hawed and smiled, eventually telling her I had no answer for her. Smiling back through a face that always seemed slightly crooked under that gold-mushroom hairdo, she blurted out, "Mayonnaise and grape jelly on saltines."

Which, I had to admit, was gross.

But hey, she was opening up. It was charming.

A couple of days later I called and left her a message. She didn't call me back for almost two weeks, during which time I had two very bland dates with a nice but uninteresting girl named Tina who actually picked me up in a bar. When Mary Ann did call, she once again caught me by surprise. I was home, on a Thursday night, watching Duke play North Carolina and thinking about whether I ever wanted to call Tina again. She called, apologized (but offered no reason) for not calling sooner, and we talked for a long time. I know it was a long time because the game was over by the time we hung up and I had no idea who'd won.

Our first date was a Red Sox game at Fenway Park, which was strange for me because at the time I was covering the Red Sox for the *Boston Herald* and not in the practice of going to games on my days off. But having learned I was interested in baseball, Mary Ann pressed me to take her to a game. It was the first and last considerate gesture she made while we were dating, and I quickly discovered that it was a hollow one. Mary Ann had no interest in baseball, and she never made an attempt to develop one. That may be one of the main reasons it didn't work out for us. Not the fact that she didn't like baseball, mind you. By no means would that have been a deal breaker. It's just that it's hard when you want to talk about your day at work and the person you want to talk to has no interest.

Or it could be that I just, as I've already said, didn't like her.

Our breakup was bad, but I think we both wanted it to be. She was leaving in two weeks for the new job in New Orleans. Months earlier we'd talked about the long distance thing, but by this point neither of us really wanted to see the other again, let alone talk for hours on the phone. Because of my schedule, following the baseball team around the country, we'd already spent enough time on the phone to know we didn't enjoy it. So we had a clean split. After the night we broke up by phone, we never spoke to each other again.

I was on the road, in Toronto. I had a day game and a dinner reservation, and the phone call that came in after the former meant the latter was biting the dust. After about four hours that generated a whopper of an international phone bill, we hung up, neither one of us in tears. The next day, as I flew to Chicago, she went to my apartment, removed all of her stuff (plus three of my CDs), left the key on the dinner table and walked out of my life.

Three years later I found myself at Midway Airport at half past you've-got-to-be-kidding-me in the morning, hiding out in the bathroom because I didn't think it would be a good idea to talk to her. It was possible, considering the tone of the last phone conversation we'd had, that she'd been saving up for three years to slap me. It was possible, considering the way I felt about her, that the first words out of my mouth would not have been charitable ones. It was possible that we would have a nice, if uncomfortable, conversation about how things were going and how the past three years had been.

Anything was possible, really. But I have no idea how that conversation might have gone, because I chickened out. I stayed in that airport men's room as long as I thought it would take Mary Ann to get on that plane, and when I came back out, she was gone. The universe may have been trying to tell me something, but I didn't want to hear its opinion on this issue.

So, as I settled into my first-class seat, I was overcome by an unfamiliar concern that I had misplayed some cosmic opportunity. Why would she have been there at this moment, a month before my thirtieth birthday and a month after my live-in girlfriend had moved out? What if she had something important to say, and now I'd never know? What harm could it have actually done to stop and say hi, ask how she was doing?

Mary Ann? Yeah, it's me. Yeah, it's been a while. So, are you still crazy?

Or something like that.

But I didn't stop, didn't talk, didn't find out, and now it seems to have started something very disturbing. Mary Ann appears to have been my Marley's Ghost, and I'm starting to wonder how many spirits will be visiting me in the coming weeks, months, and years.

"Man," Bernie says, wiping the Guinness foam out of the bushy black hair on his upper lip. "That's weird."

I've just finished telling him the story of almost bumping into Mary Ann at the airport, and he's processing it. We're at the Dublin House on 79th Street between Broadway and Amsterdam, finishing up a Saturday night that's already gone on way too long. We started out watching a basketball game across the street at Blondie's, but we came over here because the game was a blowout, the Golden Tee machine at Blondie's was in use, and the Dublin House is home to New York City's coolest bartender.

The bartender's name is Mike. He's a short, white-haired guy from Dublin, complete with the accent, the friendly handshake, and the uncanny ability to drop into easy conversation with any other human. He knows the name of every person currently seated at his bar, and we're now at the point in the night where he's handing out free shots of Jameson's Irish whiskey with every other round of beer we order. Soon he'll start drinking it with us.

Were it not so beloved by the residents of this neighborhood, Mike's place would have to be called a dive. Even when the patrons are only one-deep at the bar, it's hard to squeeze between the stools and the old wooden booths along the opposite wall to get back to where the bathrooms and the jukebox are. When it's crowded, forget about it. Beyond the dingy corridor that is the bar area, there is a room in the back that looks as if it were recently unearthed by archaeologists who started to set up for a picnic but then quit. There are ramshackle booths barely attached to the walls and a couple of scattered tables and chairs in the middle. The heavy wooden beams on the ceiling draw your attention because they look as if they are about to fall and crush you. There is no emergency exit door in the back room, which means in case of fire you'd have to try and fight your way to the front door, which means you would die. Almost no one ever sits in that room, because the Dublin House employs no wait staff. If you want beer and you're in the back room, you have to get up, go see Mike at the bar, and bring the beer back. And that can take all night.

But there's something about the place, and it's probably Mike's personality. No matter how crowded it looks when you go in, he always waves you down to some miraculously empty spot at the bar, where he shakes your hand, asks how you've been and processes your drink order as if it's the thing that gives him his life's greatest joy. The place also has plenty of Springsteen, Tom Waits, and Irish drinking songs on the jukebox. And if you come during the week, it's all locals and regulars, which is nice.

On this particular Saturday night, Bernie is engulfing the stool next to me, all three hundred pounds of him, and I'm waiting for his reaction to my ghost story. Bernie always has a reaction, and an opinion, and the latter is always worth hearing. He's staring past me now, maybe looking at the TV way down at the other end of the bar to get a hockey score or something, and he takes another pull of his Guinness. He is, as always, impeccably dressed, complete with the ever-present sport coat, perfectly shined shoes, slicked-back hair, and a manicured goatee. Bernie is fat—tremendously fat—but he is anything but sloppy. And in spite of his physical dimensions, Bernie is what you might call a chick magnet. This is a rare night, actually, because it's three o'clock in the morning and he's sitting here with me, in a bar practically devoid of women, instead of home with some new blonde. But I guess when you're Bernie, you have to take a Saturday night off every now and then.

I guarantee you've never seen anything like Bernie with women. He's the best I've ever seen—a wonder to me and an absolute idol to Jeff, who, in spite of his own New York Smooth Guy act, is totally in awe of him. Jeff will sit with Bernie for hours, talking over the big man's latest conquests. Jeff will never make a move with a new girl without checking it out with Bernie first. Of course, Jeff also refuses to introduce a girl to Bernie, for fear that she will fall immediately under his spell and forget him forever. He asks Bernie for tips, advice, stories, leftover phone numbers. Jeff can't get enough. Bernie is his *sensai*, and Jeff is the eager grasshopper, desperate for knowledge as he aspires to greatness.

The amazing thing is that it all comes so naturally to Bernie. Some guys were born to play baseball. Some were born to play jazz. Bernie was born to woo women, and to watch him work is to watch Jeter turn a double play or to listen to Coltrane.

He doesn't actually do much, because he doesn't have to. Women are drawn to Bernie. When pressed, they say it's his confidence. They call him charming. They call him warm.

And I once had a woman tell me that Bernie was the best sex she'd ever had. This I cannot picture—will not picture—for Bernie cannot possibly look good naked. I do, however, like to watch him at a bar—the effortless way he has of greeting his admirers, of buying them drinks, of letting the runners-up down easy and of closing the deal with the night's winner. He's class all the way, and his quiet confidence is obvious even to those who aren't attracted to him.

He does not have a technique to emulate, and it would be impossible for him to teach anyone the way he does it—he just does it. He humors Jeff, and I think he enjoys being worshipped, but he knows Jeff will continue being Jeff, and successful in his own right. When Jeff is down about women and reaching out for Bernie, I pity Jeff, for I know what he does not—that he'll never be Bernie, no matter how much he learns or how hard he tries. I know this about myself too, and it is for that reason that I am generally not in the business of asking Bernie for advice about women.

But this time I believe I've brought him something new. And since this is his passion—since he has studied the fairer sex as deeply as Newton studied gravity and Darwin heredity—I figure he'll at least get a kick out of what's been going on in my life.

"And how many more did you say there have been?" he asks, after a brief moment alone with his thoughts and his beer.

"Two, counting Connie."

"So three altogether."

"In three weeks."

"In three weeks, yes," he says, fingers tented in front of his lips, like Socrates processing the answer and preparing his next question.

The longer he thinks, the more I start to believe there's

some great wisdom coming. Bernie, as I said, always has an opinion. But this time, after another long minute of waiting, Bernie comes through with a pretty disappointing answer.

"That's weird, man," he says again, and has another sip.

"Yeah," I say, disappointed but playing it cool. "So I'm figuring, this girl I met at the Fairway, I can't really be taking her out when I'm already trying to figure out what to do with these other ones and I'm terrified that my senior prom date is lurking right around the corner."

"Nah," he says. "You should definitely take her out. The Fairway girl, I mean. Not the prom date."

"You think so?"

"Yeah, man. Absolutely. I mean think about it. For the rest of your life you're going to tell people this story. About the chick you met at the grocery store who gave you her numbers on her own CD. It's a great story, man. I mean, great. And whenever you tell it, people are going to ask you, 'So, did you call her? Did you go out with her? What happened?' You gotta have something to say. The story's got to have an ending."

Beautiful. I came looking for advice, and the man has looked over the next forty years of my life and planned my conversations for me. I'm going to call her. I tell him this, and he nods.

"One more, then hit the road?" he asks.

"Sure," I say.

We clink shot glasses with Mike, drain our complimentary Jameson's, and head over to the video golf game with new, full beers. It will be an hour and a half before we go home, because home is a three-block walk and because I've never left the Dublin House before closing, but I got what I needed. I got my audience with the great man. And now, armed with his advice, I will wake up tomorrow afternoon and call Linda Lane. And see if I can fit her into my schedule.

*   *   *

It's twelve-thirty in the afternoon when I finally wake up, and my first thought is that Bernie must have spent the night sleeping on my head. It hurts that bad. Damn that Guinness.

Eyes open, and relieved to find Bernie absent from my apartment and thus nowhere near my head, I stagger to the refrigerator for a glass of water, a slice of cold pizza, and some Advil. Of the three, the only one in the fridge is the Advil. The water pitcher and the pizza have been left out overnight, and they have met in the middle at lukewarm. The Advil, of course, is freezing cold because some drunken moron left it in the refrigerator. I'm starting to think I need to go back to bed when the phone rings.

Who could it be? Nikki McGowan, my first kiss?

No, actually, it's Connie. A far more recent ghost. The Ghost of Relationship Last Goddamn Month. This one actually shouldn't count, but I've decided to lump her in with the rest of the phenomenon because I wish she were further back in my memory than she actually is.

"Jack?" she says, haltingly. "Did I wake you?"

"No, no, no," I say. *Silly girl. I'm not awake.*

"Oh, good. Listen. So, I know it's probably still weird. But I was wondering if you'd thought anymore about what we talked about. You know, the other day."

The other day was when Connie decided to return to my life after an unexplained one-month absence that was entirely her idea. We met at the dry cleaners. She had come into town to pick up some clothes she'd left there over a month ago. Clothes I refused to pick up and bring back into my half-empty apartment. It was my line in the sand.

Anyway, I got the impression she'd been in there for hours, waiting for me to come drop off my sweaters. I was stunned to see her, but she was composed. As if she hadn't taken off without warning and avoided me for a month. We chatted coolly for a few minutes, and when she suggested we get together, I failed to muster the nerve to tell her I didn't want to. I actually told her I'd call her. I do not, however, remember telling her to call me.

"Yeah, sure," I say now, not really knowing what I'm assenting to.

"Well, I was thinking EJ's. For lunch, maybe? Are you free tomorrow?"

"Connie, I gotta tell you . . ." I start, but then stumble.

"What? This is too soon?" leaving me an opening.

"Yeah, you know what?" I say, my head throbbing against the receiver. "I think it may be too soon. Or it may not be. I just don't know. I just need some time to, you know, process all this."

"Oh," she says, obviously disappointed.

"Look, you kind of sprung this on me, you know."

"Yeah, I guess you're right," she says. "I just—"

"Connie, look. I'll call you. I promise I'll call you. You just have to promise me you'll be home when I do."

"Oh, that's not fair," she says, but she's totally wrong. Based on her recent behavior, it is completely fair. And I get a pretty good kick out of being able to take such a shot so early in the morning . . . er, afternoon.

"Look, seriously," I say. "I will call you. It's just . . . I guess it's just going to be a little while."

"Oh," again, disappointed. "Well, all right then. I guess I'll talk to you later."

" 'Bye, Connie," and I hang up.

That actually felt pretty good.

I think I will call Linda Lane.

I think I'll do it right now. While I'm feeling good. While I'm standing in my living room, wearing nothing but a pair of pink boxer shorts with rhinoceroses on them, chasing cold

Advil with warm water and congealed pizza, pondering surgery for the pain in my head and feeling as good (emotionally, at least) as I've felt in weeks.

Now where did I put that CD?

4 ◇ A Brief History of Connie

In the spring of last year I met Connie from Connecticut. Cute,
huh? Well, she was.

We both lived in New York, but we met in Florida, and our
first date was a day trip to Walt Disney World. It was a somewhat spectacular beginning that would not be outdone until
a year and a half later, when we had our ending.

I was in Tampa, Florida, which is an especially seedy den of
sin to which I am consigned every year for a seven-week
death march known as spring training. This is the absolute
worst part of covering baseball, spring training, and the most
misunderstood. People think we fly down to Florida, hang
out on the beach, play a little golf, kick back and get a tan.
They are, of course, wrong. People almost always are about
my job.

No, spring training is a killer. It's seven weeks away from
home without any significant break. It's six A.M. wake-up
calls, fourteen-hour days that begin way too early and end
way too late for you to do anything but weep as you drive
past a beach or a golf course. It's standing around a back field
or a clubhouse in the fifth week trying to dig up a story and

hoping somebody back home will care, which they won't, because it's not baseball season yet back home.

But it was in this environment that I met Connie from Connecticut. She and some girlfriends were in Tampa on vacation. This is a big thing with the folks up North. They plan their vacations around spring training. They come for five days or so, have the time of their lives, and leave thinking I have the best job in the world. I want to shake them and say, "Think about it! Would you really want to spend six more weeks here? In Tampa? Sitting in traffic all day every day in front of run-down strip clubs and pastel shopping malls?"

But with Connie, there was no such conversation. With Connie, I was all charm, right from the beginning. Well, okay, not right from the beginning. At the very beginning I spilled marinara sauce in her lap.

It wasn't a whole lot of sauce—just the little bit they put in the little plastic dish that comes with the mozzarella sticks. I and a couple of the other beat writers had dropped in at Bennigan's after a Tuesday night game. We were hungry and we wanted a couple of drinks (the longer spring training goes, the more drinks you need), and as I was carrying the plate of food from the crowded bar back to the booth, the little dish of red sauce went tumbling off the plate and onto the white shorts of this adorable little blonde, who shrieked.

The beers I had already consumed were not enough to make me try and wipe the sauce out of her lap (fortunately), but they made me bold enough to think I should turn the mishap into an opportunity.

"Oh, my God!" I exclaimed, perhaps too dramatically. "I am so sorry. I can't believe I just did that. Are you okay?"

Her two friends (also blond, also cute) were laughing, which probably helped my case. After jumping up, swatting away the offending dish, and frantically dabbing at her shorts with a wet napkin, she actually managed to twinkle two pretty green eyes, throw a smile my way, and absolve me of guilt.

"Oh, it's okay," she said. "These are old anyway, and I just bought a new pair this afternoon. I was probably going to get rid of these."

I was sure this was a lie, but I may have fallen in love with her on the spot for making it up. We introduced ourselves, and after a few minutes of witty banter (he said proudly), I invited the three of them over to the booth, where six of us were all of a sudden crammed in and reaching over each other for mozzarella sticks and onion rings. My fellow writers were not thrilled with me for having brought three attractive women to the table to share in our postgame feast, but that's because they were married and they had no interest. Or it's because they were married, had plenty of interest, and were angry with me for flaunting my singlehood.

Anyway, I was locked in on Connie, who was charming and interesting, who had one dimple on the left side of her face when she smiled, and who was receiving from me the most profound and prolonged apology I have ever issued for a culinary accident. She continued to insist that she was okay and that the shorts were soon to be trashed anyway. I continued to insist that she allow me to make it up to her. Eventually, she relented on that last part, just enough.

"Well, we're only in town two more days," she said.

"Two more days is plenty!" I practically bellowed. "Tomorrow's an off day."

Indeed, the next day was the Yankees' only off day of the entire spring. And while I should have spent it working on the fifteen stories I had to do for the paper's special annual baseball preview section, I acted as if I had nothing to do but hang out on the beach, play a little golf, kick back and get a tan. I was sick of work, and the risk of something happening while I was off dallying with Connie from Connecticut wasn't high enough to worry me. (Again, the beers.)

"An off day?" she asked.

"Yeah, an off day. They get one every spring."

"I didn't know that."

"It's true," I said. "So, name it. What do you want to do?"

It was here that I caught a break. Seems Connie and her gal pals had been doing some spring training schmoozing a couple of nights earlier out at Frenchy's on Clearwater Beach. There, they encountered two members of the Philadelphia Phillies, who offered to leave them tickets to an upcoming game. The girls were planning to go watch the Phillies play the Blue Jays in Clearwater the very next day. But Connie, who acted disdainful of the practice of chasing ballplayers, saw my invitation as an opportunity to avoid a fifth-wheel situation she would have found awkward. Sure, it would have been just the three of them at the game. But afterward, as a return for the favor of the free tickets, their presence would assuredly be required at Frenchy's, and Connie claimed this did not interest her.

"So I don't know," she said, leaning toward me and smiling. "What's there to do here?"

"Here, not much. But we could go anywhere," I said. "We could go to Disney World."

I was kidding. She was hooked.

"Okay!" she said. "I've never been. How far is it?"

The answer was that Walt Disney World was about a forty-five-minute drive from the very Bennigan's in which we were sitting, and it was resolved that I would pick her up in front of her hotel at eight A.M. the next day and we would drive there. And just in case you're wondering—just in case you ever find yourself in a similar situation while you're within a fifty-mile radius of the Magic Kingdom—I'm here to tell you it was one hell of an idea for a first date.

She was standing in front of her hotel when I pulled up in a rented red Mustang convertible at eight in the morning, all five-foot-six of her with legs and shoulders freshly tanned. She wore a blue tank top and—wouldn't you know it—a brand-spanking-new pair of white shorts, bought the day before to replace a pair that would later be ruined by a clumsy sportswriter. She waved as I pulled up, and she bounced over to the passenger side door.

"Cool car," she said, and immediately followed with: "See? New shorts."

It was a cool car, actually. It was the only spring training for which I rented a convertible, and it's something I'd like to look into in the future. Made all the difference, really.

The shorts were cool, too, but mainly because they were on Connie's legs.

Anyway, we were off, and we got to Disney around nine o'clock, parked, paid (a lot, by the way. Disney is no cheap date) and began exploring the Magic Kingdom. I hadn't been since I was fifteen. She, as she had mentioned, had never been. It was like bringing a kid there for the first time.

Connie was into everything. She wanted to ride the big roller coasters, and we did. We rode Space Mountain twice, long lines and all. She wanted to do the corny rides like the Flying Dumbos, though we did that one only once. For a while she even put up with my obsession with maps, as I insisted we get one immediately upon entrance and use it to guide us as we roamed around from Frontierland to Tomorrowland. Later in the day she would tear it out of my hand and throw it in the trash, but I have to admit I appreciated her waiting until we were almost done.

"Let's just walk around," she said, twinkling again as she crumpled my lifeline and flipped it in among the disposable cameras and broken mouse ears. "Let's just see where we end up."

Terrified, I went along, largely because we found something we both enjoyed everywhere we went. We stopped at a refreshment stand to buy two massive turkey legs, and I stood stunned as she tore hers apart.

If you don't know about the turkey legs, I'm not making this up. There are vendors at Walt Disney World that actually sell massive turkey drumsticks that people walk around the park eating—just eating as they walk, as if they were holding a gigantic meat ice cream cone. But normally, the people you see eating them are the fat guys with kids or the kids themselves. There are very few pretty Connecticut blondes cruising around Adventureland tearing the meat off turkey legs like jaguars that have just felled their prey. Mine, I believe, was the only one.

I couldn't stop smiling.

We waited in line at dusk for the Pirates of the Caribbean, and once we were through there, we left the park. It was nighttime by now, and on the monorail that took us back to the parking area I got to feeling a little romantic. So there on the monorail, Connie and I had our first kiss. Just a little peck on the lips, mind you, but a nice one, and one that made both of us happy. The drive back to Tampa was nice, and there was more kissing when I dropped her off at her hotel. Instead of writing down her phone number and giving it to me, she took my cell phone from me and programmed the number into it. She told me to be sure to give her a call once I got back to New York, and that we would get together again. I assured her that she shouldn't worry.

We talked on the phone twice between the time she left

Florida and the time I returned to New York. Turned out she was still living in Connecticut, but not with her parents, and she was working as a paralegal in a New York City law firm. She commuted to the city every day, and said it would be no problem for us to meet for lunch, dinner, or anything else once I returned. As I always do, I returned, and for a while every day with Connie was Disney World.

Together, we explored the city. When I was in town and working night games, we would meet for lunch and always make a point of doing something New York. The planetarium. Central Park. The Empire State Building. I treasured the lunches at least as much as the serious, dress-up dinner dates we'd have when I was really trying to impress her. Before long there was sex, and that was great, too. Being with Connie was easy, and so was my decision, in January of the following year, to ask her to move in with me.

"I mean, I just think it makes sense," I said, pleased that her baby greens were twinkling at the suggestion. "Whenever I'm here, you're here, and there's no point in paying two rents if we can pay one. I have the space. I even have an extra closet."

"Are you serious?" she asked, ready to burst.

"Of course I'm serious!"

"Oh, I don't believe it!" she said. "I was going to suggest the same thing, but I didn't want you to think I was being pushy."

In truth, I had started thinking that maybe I would like to marry Connie. So, apart from the previously stated financial benefits of cohabitation, living together would let me know whether or not we could stand to spend that kind of time with each other. It turned out to be an even better idea than I'd hoped, because I soon found out that marrying Connie would have been a terrible one.

"Oh, Jack," she was going on, hugging me now. "I love you." And just like that, it was over.

It took a while for the whole thing to actually end. When you put in ten months on a relationship, it doesn't just break off because one person says "I love you" and the other doesn't say it back. No, that little misstep blossoms into nights and days and weeks and months of fighting, yelling, sulking, backbiting, and all kinds of the important little things that make the world go round. We were in for it, and we didn't even know it at the time.

To tell you the truth, I have no idea why I didn't say it back to her. I probably did love her, and up until that exact moment I had sort of been planning to say it to her. It's always so hard to say it the first time—to break that "I love you" ice. But once I heard it come out of her mouth, I don't know. It just didn't sound right.

I shocked myself by not saying anything, and it's safe to assume I shocked Connie too. An awkward silence followed her fateful words—the first such silence the two of us had experienced in each other's company—and I don't remember how it was ultimately resolved. I might have finally said something like, "Oh, this is going to be great." Or she might have hugged me again and started making a plan for which pieces of my furniture would have to be replaced with pieces of hers. But eventually we did move on, and we set about the business of moving in.

The day we brought in her sofa was the day of our first fight. It was about my coffee table, which she didn't like because it didn't have a shelf underneath the tabletop. My coffee table was just a tabletop, and what I used it for mostly was to put my feet on when I watched TV. Now, she wanted to bring in her big fancy new coffee table with the little shelf on the bottom for the magazines and whatnot, and what was I going to do for a footrest?

It was a silly thing to fight over, and therefore it was a silly fight.

I said something like, "Well, how much of your stuff are we bringing, anyway?" And she took this the wrong way. Or maybe she took it the right way.

"Listen, Jack, I thought we talked about this. My coffee table is much more practical." And then some sort of crack about a poster I had on the wall, and it was all downhill. Every detail of the move became a point of argument, and we seized every opportunity to argue. By the time the move was complete, I was two weeks away from leaving for spring training, and I don't think either one of us was too upset about it.

To her credit, she was diligent about those "I love yous." She kept at them. In our happier moments together, she'd drop one on me from time to time. But it was a guaranteed mood-killer, because for the life of me I just could not say it. I still wonder sometimes why I could never say it to her. I'd said it to other women I didn't love nearly as much as I'd loved Connie. But there was something about it that just felt wrong, and I can't explain it.

Because of this obvious failing of mine, you'd assume that our breakup was my fault. And to a large extent you'd be right. But there were other forces at work, and I think Connie ended up losing her mind. Granted, I didn't do a lot to help her find it, but I'm not sure it would have worked out for us even if I hadn't developed my specific three-word speech impediment.

I got back from spring training in April, and Connie was a wreck. She really wasn't used to living on her own, so far from her family. Nights alone in the apartment in New York

City had terrified her. We'd talked on the phone every day and night, so I knew she had been going through a rough time, but I didn't realize until I saw her how bad it was. Her hair had grown down below her shoulders, which wasn't a problem except that it looked sloppy. She didn't look as if she styled it anymore, and she offered no explanation for the change from her previous style. She also looked tired all the time. There had never been bags under those green eyes before, and now they were a permanent fixture. She was waking up every night from nightmares. More than once I woke at four A.M. and found her on the phone, talking to her mother.

It was a mess, and it got worse every time I went out of town. When I was home, Connie acted as if she didn't want me around. We fought. We ignored each other. When I left, she acted as if it was the end of the world. She cried, she begged me not to go. I began to develop powerful feelings of guilt, and I wondered if I and my lifestyle were driving her to a breakdown.

I would find out much later that it wasn't just me. I didn't know until we broke up that Connie had been involved in some way with one of the attorneys at her firm. I don't know how involved, though I don't think it was a simple affair. I mean to say, I don't think she was outright cheating on me, though that's possible too. Jeff, my link to Manhattan's Byzantine gossip network, said he had heard that one of the attorneys at the firm where Connie worked had been fired for inappropriate sexual conduct regarding female employees, and of course Jeff assumed the worst for everybody. Maybe if Connie and I do meet up for a meal or something in the next few days, I can get the real story. Maybe she'll never tell me. Either way, things turned ugly, and there was nothing I could do to fix them.

* * *

For a while I went hard to the flowers-and-jewelry well. I bought her roses for no reason. I spent a lot more on her birthday gift than I should have. But she didn't water the flowers and she didn't wear the necklace, and it started to become apparent to me that my increased affections were not helping. She was retreating. One time I came home from a road trip to find her sleeping on the couch in the middle of her workday.

"Connie?" I asked.

"What?" she replied, suddenly startled awake.

"Connie, it's two-thirty. Aren't you supposed to be at work?"

"Oh, shit," she mumbled, feeling around her wrist for her watch, which she was not wearing. "I didn't know I fell asleep."

"Connie, are you okay?" I asked. But she only said she was fine, and she cruised right back out the door and back, presumably, to the office.

By this point it was late August, and things were bad. But when we hit the anniversary of September 11, things got even worse. See, I didn't know Connie in 2001, and I never knew how deeply that day had affected her. I still don't.

In the days that followed the anniversary, Connie did not go to work. She sat on that sofa in front of that TV and never looked away. She slept on the sofa. She ate her meals there, on her coffee table. She relived every detail. I was worried about her, but I was at a loss. At one point I even called her parents to see what they knew, but they said she wasn't returning their calls either.

The baseball season was still in full swing, the Yankees were headed for Chicago, and I was going through my own panicked preparations when Connie got up off the sofa, turned off the TV, and went into the bathroom to take a shower. When she got out of the shower, she was totally transformed.

"It's awful, isn't it?" she asked me, and I honestly had no idea what to say.

"What's that, Con?" I asked.

"What happened," she said, standing there wrapped in a big green towel, her hair dripping on the hardwood floor. "The Trade Center. Everything. It's just so awful."

"Uh," I offered, still stunned.

"Oh, I know," she said, as if everything were perfectly normal. "I know, and I'm sorry. I really don't know what to do. I guess I should go back to work, huh?"

"Yeah, Con. That might be a pretty good idea. Do you some good."

"I think so," she said.

Then she came over to where I was packing and hugged me tightly.

"I do love you, Jack," she said. "I love you so much."

She hadn't said it in a while, but then she hadn't said much of anything in a while. Looking back, I guess she must have been giving me one last test, to see if I could say it.

I failed, of course.

To this day I haven't said it to her. Not even to spare her from a potential breakdown. I suppose it was my fault, though I do think her getting so weird during the summer didn't help very much. And whatever happened with the guy at her law firm, that couldn't have been my fault at all.

When I got back from the road trip, she was gone. Lock, stock, and coffee table. I was dragging my suitcase in through the front door of the building and I saw Yousef. His smile vanished as soon as he saw me, and I knew something had to be wrong. Yousef always smiles.

"I'm so sorry, Mr. Jackson," he said. "So sorry."

(Let me pause here to clear up a little Yousef-related mystery. My name is not Jack Jackson. My name is Jack Byrnes. But one time, shortly after I moved in, my mother came to visit and told Yousef she was here to see Jackson, in apartment 3C. Jackson is my full first name, and only my mother uses it. Well, my mother and Yousef. I've always been Mr. Jackson to Yousef, and I've never seen any reason to correct him. Anyway, back to the suddenly very extensive History of Connie.)

"What is it, Yousef?" I asked, braced for the worst.

"Missus Connie, she leave her key."

And Yousef handed me an envelope with Connie's key in it.

"Wow," I said, not a hundred percent surprised, but still. "Did she say anything?"

"She just say to give you this," Yousef said. "She took many furniture. So sorry, Mr. Jackson. I think she's gone."

"It's all right, Yousef. Thanks."

When I got to 3C, I found all of Connie's things gone. No note, nothing. Curious about her well-being as well as her reasons for leaving, I called her parents' house. They told me she wasn't in. I left a message.

Two days later I called again. Again they said she wasn't in. Again I left a message.

This went on for two weeks before I finally gave in to the idea that Connie's parents were running interference for her, and I stopped calling. Obviously she was okay, or they would have told me otherwise. And obviously she didn't want to say anything, or she would have come to the phone. Or at least left a note.

It hurt, but in a weird way. I felt as if I'd failed with Connie. I should have been able to hold on to her. I should have been able to keep things the way they had been when we first started. Had I been able to tell her I loved her, who knows? Had I not been on the road so much, who knows?

But things happen, even really bad things, and you still get up in the morning and go to work.

After all, not every day can be Disney World.

5

On the Sunday afternoon that follows the Saturday night at the Dublin House, I decide not to call Linda Lane right away, mainly because I can't come up with a good way to open the conversation. I know it'll come to me, but I also know I need some fresh air, and possibly some hot pizza. So I throw on a sweater, a pair of jeans, and a baseball cap and head out into the city.

As soon as I step out the front door of my building, I realize it won't be a problem to find pizza. Make that pizza, souvlaki, funnel cake, or cheap knockoff sunglasses. I'm in the middle of a street fair—a Manhattan summer phenomenon that has somehow invaded November. Sure, the weather is especially warm for this time of year, but still. I find it hard to believe they just threw together ten blocks worth of food and T-shirt booths on a moment's notice because the weather was good.

Squinting through the glare and wincing at the noise, I have to decide whether to fight my way through the crowds in search of fried ethnic food or walk a block to Amsterdam where things are normal. I decide on the former, because fried ethnic food sounds pretty good right now, and I plunge into the river of humanity.

I buy a gyro and begin stuffing my face as I continue downstream. I have no idea what I'm shopping for, though some of those sunglasses might be pretty helpful. Feels like somebody turned the sun on extra high today.

Anyway, I'm not three blocks from my apartment when a woman's voice stops me cold.

"Wow," she says. "Imagine meeting you here."

For a split-second I'm afraid to turn, lest I find Tina Monroe, the girl whose pigtails I pulled in the second grade. But then I realize that I know this voice. I used to live for this voice, before I spent years living without it. The voice belongs to Amy, my original Boston obsession, and eventually I turn to face Relationship Ghost Number Two.

"I almost didn't recognize you," she says, motioning toward the baseball cap on my head and the glasses on my face.

"Yeah, you know," I say. "Kind of a rough morning, I guess."

"It's the afternoon," she says, with a little giggle and a big smile, and I can't believe the way her eyes still get to me.

There have never been eyes the color of Amy's. That brilliant blue that pierces your gut the first time you see it. The blue that melts into pools when she's being sweet or sad, and hardens into ice when she gets angry, always the same color but never meaning the same thing twice.

But it's more than just the color. There is a life to Amy's eyes. It's as if an entire microscopic world could exist in each one. There are times when I believe I will never get over Amy's eyes, and this is one of those times. They stagger you. They paralyze you. The impression they make stays with you, no matter how much time and distance you put between them and your own life.

"You okay?" she asks, stirring me from my hangover reverie, and for a moment I'm embarrassed.

"Yeah, sorry," I say. "Just, you know, spacing out."

"You never called."

She's right. In the two weeks that have passed since I ran into Amy in the Barnes & Noble at the corner of 81st and Broadway, I have not taken her up on her invitation to call. She gave me a business card that informed me she was working for ABC-TV in the city, and she told me there was something she wanted to talk to me about. This sounded strange, because we hadn't seen each other in five years and neither one of us had any idea the other lived in New York, but it also sounded intriguing, and I meant to call her. It's just that, in those intervening two weeks, I had run into my insane ex-girlfriend and met a girl in line at the Fairway. Not to mention I was still getting over the longest baseball season in history and drinking a great deal more than I should have been.

"Yeah, I know," I say. "Sorry about that. I really have been meaning to call. It's just . . . I don't know. I've been busy."

"Do you have time right now?"

I do. I have no plans for the day except to call Linda Lane, and that can wait. Hell, if Amy is going to say the right things, Linda Lane can wait forever.

We cross the street and head into Starbucks, which in the early years of the twenty-first century is as good a place to sit and talk as any indoor spot in Manhattan. I order a huge café mocha, and Amy gets some sort of tea, and we take a seat at a table in the corner. Shrugging off her coat and draping it over the back of her chair, she begins.

"It was so nice to run into you like that the other day," she says.

"Yeah," I say. "It was nice. A nice surprise."

"I enjoyed talking to you. Felt kind of like old times."

Of course, this is exactly what I thought. But I have been trying not to compare any of this to old times. The old times were too painful.

"Anyway, I wanted to tell you," she says. "I'm getting married."

Yup. There it is. The kick in the gut. I remember this one.

What I want to say, but don't: *What the hell, Amy? You went five years without crushing me, so you see me in a bookstore and decide you have a new opportunity? You string me along for two weeks, letting me think there might be a chance for something after all these years, then you walk me into a Starbucks and tell me this? Are you actually related to Satan?*

What I actually say: "Really? Wow. That's great, Amy. That's fantastic."

"We met in Michigan, when I was working there," leaving me frantically trying to remember when I'd asked for this information. "His name is George, and he's moving out here in a couple of weeks. We're getting married next May."

"Wow," I say again, really meaning that part. "Congratulations."

So now here we are, sitting in a coffee shop on a Sunday afternoon, talking about her wedding to some guy she met in Michigan. All I can think about is how soon I can get out of here, how much my head hurts and how angry I am about these damn ghosts that won't leave me alone. Is this the part where Scrooge is staring at his own tombstone? Is Christmas morning coming? Soon?

"Anyway," Amy eventually says, looking at her watch and indicating that our time together may finally, mercifully, be at an end. "Anyway, I want your phone number. I want to stay in touch, now that we're both here."

What?

"Excuse me?"

"I said I want to stay in touch, now that we're both here," she says, looking at me strangely. "You don't still think it would be weird, do you? I mean, Jack. We were such good friends."

Yeah we were. We were good friends. Best friends, just about. That's what pissed me off so much.

"Yes we were," I say.

"I really don't know that many people in New York," she says. "And with George going back and forth between here and Dallas for the next year or so at least, it would be nice to have somebody to hang out with."

Don't be a sap. Don't be a sap. Resist. Say no. Don't be a sap.

"All right, I guess," I say.

Doh!

"Great!" she yelps, and pulls out a Palm Pilot.

I briefly consider giving her a fake number, but I guess I'm a masochist at heart. I give her the number. She makes sure I still have hers. We hug. We part. She walks north on Broadway, I head south, back into the street fair, beaten and confused.

I wonder, as I avoid eye contact with everyone on the street, are they laughing at me? Do they know what a fool I am? But even if they are laughing, who cares? They don't understand. They've never seen those eyes.

Now, I've got to get home. I've got to sit by myself and sort this all out. It's too much to keep track of. Mary Ann, Amy, Connie, Fairway Girl, my headache. I knew I shouldn't have gone outside today. There's football on. I should have stayed in and watched football. Back home. Back to bed. Turn on the TV and sit. Maybe do some thinking. Maybe not.

As I approach the door to apartment 3C, however, I can tell from the sound inside that my television is already on. I am not surprised, when I open the door, to find Jeff reclined on my sofa with his feet stretched out in front of him, an empty and open pizza box on the floor and the Giants-Cardinals game on the tube.

"This pizza tastes funny," he says. Jeff has never been big on formal greetings.

"I forgot to put it in the fridge when I got home last night."

"That would explain it," he says, taking another bite. "Hey, whatever happened to that coffee table you used to have?"

This is my own fault, of course. When Connie moved out, I needed to find somebody who could check in on my apartment while I was on the road. Jeff, who lives one block away, was the perfect choice. He agreed to collect my mail, water the plant, and check in periodically to make sure the apartment was still intact. As a result, he now has a key to the apartment, which he believes is a license to come in any time.

I wonder sometimes if he's bringing girls back here when I'm away. Jeff sees so many women, it's possible he needs a second base of operation. But this line of thinking doesn't make me feel better about anything. I have ignored the question about the coffee table and decide to take the conversation in an entirely new direction.

"My head is killing me," I say.

"Oh yeah? Rough night? You and Big Bern out on the town? Who'd he take home?"

"Nobody, actually. He was beating them away with a stick at Blondie's, but we left and went to Dublin House. By the time we left there, it was empty."

"I guess even the master needs a night off to catch his breath," Jeff says. "He help you out with your little problem?"

"Sort of," I say, flopping into the recliner across from the sofa. "He convinced me I should call Fairway Girl."

"Oh, that reminds me," Jeff says. "She called."

"She called?"

"Yeah, about a half hour ago."

"You're answering my phone now?"

"Yeah, sorry about that. Kind of an accident. I just picked it up. Reflex, I guess."

Unbelievable, but my mind has moved on.

"Wait a minute," I say. "She couldn't have called."

"I'm telling you, she called. You think I'm making it up?"

"Dude," I say. "I didn't give her my number."

"Yeah you did," Jeff says. "You called her last night. Apparently, you were drunk."

Oh God.

"Oh God," I say, jumping forward and out of the recliner. "Really?"

"Yessir. The drunk-dialer strikes again. It's cool, though. I guess you didn't embarrass yourself too bad. She said she thought you were cute. I think she thought I was your roommate."

Hm. I have no idea why she'd think that, since you picked up the phone in my apartment. As if you live here.

"Oh, shit," I say, slumping back now into the chair. "I can't believe I did that."

"Well, you did. But I'm telling you, she wasn't mad. She wants you to call her. Said you made a date for tonight."

"Tonight?"

"Yup. You better get in shape, my friend. Sounds like you have a date."

"You don't understand. I can't go on a date right now. There's too much other stuff going on."

"What do you mean, other stuff?" Jeff asks. And because he's an uninvited guest, he gets the whole rundown.

I tell him about Connie, and our phone conversation this morning.

"Sweet," he says. "Way to tell her who's boss."

I tell him about Amy, and our Starbucks experience.

"She's getting married?" is the reaction to that one. "Oh wait, is this the one you didn't actually go out with?"

I tell him I'm petrified that Trudy, the girl I slept with one time when I was visiting a high school friend in college and whose last name I forgot is going to knock on the door at any minute and yell, "Remember me?"

"Yeah," he says, laughing. "Or some girl whose pigtails you pulled in the second grade!"

"I'm glad you think this is funny."

"Dude, it's coincidence. That's all. It's no reason not to call Fairway Chick."

"It's just, I have a lot to figure out right now. That's all."

"So figure out how to get Fairway Chick in the sack," he says, grinning. "That'll make everything better."

"Whatever."

And for a while we watch the game in silence. The Giants are boring. The Cardinals are bad. It's 6-3 in the fourth quarter. Finally, I'm fed up.

"All right, that's it," I say. "You've got to go."

"I've got to go?" Jeff asks, incredulous.

"Yeah, you're out. You heard me."

"What are you talking about?"

"I need you out of here," I say, "so I can call Fairway Girl."

"Ahh," he says, smiling again. "All right, man. You go to work. I got laundry anyway. Call me and let me know how it goes."

"Thanks," I say as he gets up and heads to the door.

"Hey," he calls back.

"Yeah?"

"You're sober, right?"

"Very funny."

Turns out, Jeff was right. Linda Lane is not remotely upset that I drunk-dialed her at quarter to five in the morning. She herself was awake, apparently, having got in late from her own big night out with her girlfriends. Evidently, I exhibited a drunken sort of charm in asking her out, and she was impressed with my moxie. She actually used the word moxie.

So we're going out. Tonight. Initially, I toy with the idea of suggesting EJ's, just out of spite, since that was Connie's suggestion. But EJ's really isn't for dinner. I'm not even sure it's open for dinner. So instead we meet at the Ocean Grill—a nice seafood restaurant on Columbus Avenue across from the Museum of Natural History.

Once again Linda is dressed entirely in black. She's wearing a short black dress, black stockings, and shiny black high heels. Draped over her shoulders is a long black sweater that hangs all the way down past her waist. Her hair is a cascade of black curls from the top of her head down onto her shoulders and about halfway down her back. She's even got a curl poking out in the front, right at the top of her forehead. Every now and then, maybe when she's feeling nervous or shy, she tries to brush it back, but it never moves. She's a very pretty girl, and I imagine someday I'll find out why all the black. But for now I'm enjoying her smile and her conversation.

She tells me she's a professional dancer who is trying to become a singer and is unbelievably excited that she actually has a CD out. She confesses that one of the reasons she gave me the CD was that I work for a newspaper and she had publicity on her mind. This rattles me, but she also tells me she thought I was cute and that she wouldn't have scribbled her phone numbers on the inside of the CD for just any newspaper reporter. I guess this is encouraging.

We finish dinner and decide to walk in the park for a bit. It's a nice night, if a bit chilly, and we're really not done with the conversation. Linda is one of these people who likes to challenge you on the first date—asking the kinds of questions you wouldn't expect anyone to ask. She's got her arm hooked around mine, and every once in a while she rests her head on my shoulder, playfully, only for a second or two.

"What's the worst thing you've ever done to someone you were involved with?" she asks me.

"The worst thing," I repeat, thinking. "The worst thing. Well, I've never cheated on any of them, so—"

"Never?" She pulls away, disbelieving.

"No, really. Never. Actually, I think you'll find most of my romantic life has been pretty dry and uninteresting. No real dirty secrets."

Yeah. Everything's right there, out in the open. Walking around these very streets.

"Wow," she says. "That's amazing."

"I guess it was pretty bad that the last girl I dated told me she loved me and I never said it back."

"That is tough," she says. "How long did you go out?"

"About a year and a half."

"A year and a half!" I've stunned her again. She's released my arm and spun around to face me. "How long after she told you she loved you?"

"About ten months."

"No! You went ten months hearing her say she loved you and you never said it back to her once?"

"Well, after a while she stopped."

"I guess so!" Linda Lane, laughing now. "That's pretty wild."

"I guess," I say. "It just didn't feel right."

"Okay, your turn," she says. "Ask me one."

"Ask you one?"

"Yeah. Your turn to ask me a question."

"Oh, I don't know. I really wasn't prepared for this."

"Come on!"

"All right, all right," I say, fishing. "What was your longest, most serious relationship?"

"Longest or most serious?" she asks, grabbing my arm again, this time with both hands.

"What, they're different?"

"Sure," she says, with one short chuckle.

"Okay, give me both."

"Longest, I went out with the same guy in college for

three years. Most serious, I married the guy I went out with after him."

"You were married?" I say, maybe a little too loud. Guess it was her turn to shock me.

"Yeah, I got married. It's not something I usually talk about on the first date, but you were going on about your I-love-you girl, so I figured we were being pretty open and honest."

"How long were you married?"

"Five months and six days."

"But who's counting?"

"Right."

"Why so short?" I ask.

"Like you said," she says. "It just didn't feel right."

There's obviously more there, but it's not the right time to press it, and she lets me know right away by changing the topic.

"Okay, I've got one," she says. "Who's your One That Got Away?"

And I don't answer right away, but I could. That's easy. The One That Got Away. I had coffee with her just a few hours ago.

6 ◇ A Brief History of Amy

The One That Got Away would be Amy. The original Boston obsession. The girl I fell in love with only to discover that she was not in love with me. I don't imagine there's anybody out there who hasn't been through that one.

I had lived in Boston for two years, working at the newspaper and keeping a schedule that left little room for a social life. I met Amy at a pool hall, late one Sunday night when my roommate, Sam, and I were out having a few drinks after work. She was an old friend of his, since she was engaged to one of his best friends from high school. The friend was there too, I think.

Amy was absolutely dazzling. Straight brown hair—no, we're going to go with auburn, auburn hair—down to her shoulders, a sexy slim waistline with a pierced navel, a smile that always seemed to suggest something, and you already know about the eyes. In my memory, she floats into the back room of the pool hall and slouches in an overstuffed leather chair, the kind of girl who's immediately comfortable in any room. The kind who knows she looks good and enjoys the fact that people notice. She lights up a cigarette, which is usually an automatic turnoff for me, but I don't care.

We hit it off right away, perhaps because she was engaged to this other guy and there was no pressure on either of us. While I may have been trying to impress her, she was not in the business of being impressed by guys she met in bars. She was planning her wedding. We all had a nice time, chatting, drinking, playing pool, and we parted on friendly terms. Amy and her fiancé lived in the suburbs and were headed back there. I didn't see her again for six months.

Sam and I were in the newsroom one day and he happened to mention, while typing away in the cubicle next to mine, that his old friends Amy and Whatshisname had broken it off. That she was single.

The next thing he saw was my head popping up over the cubicle wall. He stopped typing.

"How'd you find out?" I asked.

"She called me the other night, while you were out at the game," Sam said, starting to smile.

"Well," I said. "Did you give her my cell phone number?"

He laughed, but I wasn't kidding.

You know the scene in the first *Godfather* movie, where Al Pacino is walking through the Italian countryside with his bodyguards and he comes across Apollonia, and one of the bodyguards (Calo or Fabrizio, I always forget) says, "You got hit by the thunderbolt?" Well, that was me. I had been hit by the thunderbolt that night at the pool hall.

In hindsight, I did pretty much everything wrong. The fact that we even became good friends was a miracle considering my intentions and the way I pursued them. Weeks went by, and Sam bumped into Amy at the grocery store or something, and she mentioned that she and a friend of hers were going out to a party. Would we like to come? Sam came home, correctly assuming that I'd bounce out the door at the mention of such an invitation, and we went.

We planned to meet at a bar first and go from there. When we got there, the girls had already arrived.

"Hey!" Amy, smiling, chewing gum, nursing a beer, wearing jeans. God, could she wear jeans. "Good to see you again!" And she actually gave me a hug.

We had seen each other exactly once before, so what the greeting told me was that I had succeeded in making an impression. It was all there in front of me now—the chance of a lifetime. That first night was magical. We danced. We talked. She asked those out-of-the-blue deep questions I seem to like so much.

"What do you think about true love?" she asked, and at first I laughed, because it seemed like such a ridiculous thing to ask. But she went on.

"No, seriously," she said. "Do you think there's really someone out there that we're destined to be with? Do you think it happens? Or do we all end up settling in the end?"

Of course, what I wanted to tell her was that yes, I believed in true love, and in fact I believed that I had found it, sitting right in front of me at the bar at that very moment. But that would have seemed a little forward considering the circumstances, so I sipped my beer and gave some high-minded answer about being a romantic and still thinking there was something out there. That it was too soon to give up.

The length and depth of our conversation aggravated our companions, who continued to come by and ask us if we were ready to go yet, telling us we were being "too serious." But somehow it always ended up the two of us, just sitting and talking. Getting to know each other.

This would become a routine. As the weeks and months went on, we all became close friends. The four of us would go out almost every night of the week. Dance clubs. Pubs. Parties. Diners for early morning breakfasts before sunrise, before we went to sleep. The girls would stay the night at our apartment, though nothing would ever happen. I'm not sure why they stayed except, as I would later find out, Amy was having trouble getting over her breakup and didn't like to be alone in her place. Her friend kind of went along for the ride.

Amy was, in fact, having a lot more trouble getting over her breakup than I thought. And my ignorance of that fact may have been my undoing. I might not have gone for it so soon if I'd realized what a fragile state she was in—had I picked up on any of the clues. She brushed off every guy that made an advance, preferring instead the company of me, in whom she demonstrated no romantic interest. She drank way too much. She didn't want to go home and be in her apartment by herself—the apartment she'd shared with her erstwhile fiancé.

But she also never talked about any of these things. When she did talk about more sensitive topics, it was always in hints and generalities—the way she brought up true love in our first one-on-one conversation.

So I was the pea-brained bull in the proverbial china shop. I only knew what I wanted, and I had no idea about the right way to pursue it.

Of course it didn't work out. No relationship based on weeknight drinking binges, in which your deepest conversations happen as the sun is coming up, is going to work out if the feelings aren't strong both ways. There came a point where I couldn't take it, where I put it all on the line for her. Either we take this thing a step or two forward, or we don't hang out anymore. I couldn't be in close proximity to her every day and keep my feelings back. I poured all of this out to her in a phone call one night, a call that lasted past three a.m., and she reacted by telling me, basically, "No chance."

The climax went something like this:

"What it comes down to is, I just can't do it anymore, Amy. I just can't."

"You're telling me you can't hang out with me because it's too hard?"

"That's what I'm saying."

"Why?"

"Because I'm in love with you."

A respectful pause, perhaps to collect herself, and then: "Excuse me?"

"Yeah, you heard me."

"Wow."

"Well, somebody had to wake you up."

"I can't believe you used the L-word."

"Yeah, well, life is short."

But nothing happened. I mean nothing. She wasn't going to give. Looking back, I guess I admire her resolve. She knew what she wanted—or, more accurately, what she didn't want—and she stuck to it.

My point, through the whole thing, was that I deserved a chance. Just a chance. We knew we loved hanging out with each other. We knew we cared about each other a great deal. Our friends all thought we should be together. It made too much sense to not at least try it.

But she wouldn't try it. And the closest I ever came to getting a good reason was when Sam told me this:

"She wants to give it a chance. She really does. She's just afraid she'll screw it up, and then you'll have nothing."

This I'd heard before, from other women, and it pissed me off.

"Well, somebody better tell her she's screwing it up right now, and we're about to have nothing."

We stopped talking and stopped hanging out, but I was a wreck. I did all the usual breakup stuff. I made sappy mix tapes. I hung around the house in my underwear, eating pizza and ice cream. I was a slug at work, where I had trouble concentrating. I complained nonstop to my roommate, who justifiably got sick of me and started spending time away from the apartment. Once, I got him to agree to intercede for me, to have lunch with her and find out what was going on in her head. But all that came out of that was the devastating knowledge that she had started dating someone else.

Of course, the two of us continued to go to most of the same places we used to go together or with the group, so it was no surprise that we kept running into each other. But it was no good, and I always ended up either leaving the bar or making a fool of myself and then leaving the bar.

It was no kind of life.

I guess there were lessons to be learned from Amy. I guess she was the one who convinced me, once and for all, that (and this is very important) *you cannot start out as friends and end up lovers*. Just won't work. I've never known anyone who's pulled it off. And while I'm not sure anyone has ever fallen as hard, repeatedly, on his face as I did in trying, I know a lot of people who have got beaten up pretty badly by just such an experiment.

I thought I'd learned this lesson in college, when I swore off the friends-with-girls thing and decided that was for losers. I used to be the confidant—the guy who got to hear all the sob stories about the boyfriend before the girl went running back to the boyfriend. The guy who always got the line about "I want to give it a shot, but I'm afraid I'll screw it up, and then we won't even be friends anymore." All the work, none of the sex. So I stopped doing that and swore I never would again. But the feelings Amy inspired in me took over, and old promises to myself went out the window. And all I could think, when I found out she was getting married, was that this new guy must have felt the exact same way—awed, overwhelmed, and helpless.

He was just lucky she was feeling the same way.

7

Monday dawns, stubborn and reliable as ever, and it's time to get back to work. Yes, I do work in the off-season.

Which reminds me.

Of all the uninformed questions a baseball writer gets asked about his job, the worst, without a doubt, is: "So, what do you do in the off-season?"

The answer is simple. In the off-season, I cover baseball.

I mean, if you really think about it, this shouldn't be that hard to comprehend. Anybody who follows baseball has picked up a newspaper in the winter to read a story about what's going on with the team. A big free agent signing, a trade, a new manager, something. Who do you think is writing those stories? That's right. Me. The baseball writer. That's what I do in the off-season, and I can tell you it's no fun.

Especially in New York.

There are eight newspapers that have a full-time writer assigned to the Yankee beat, and it's the most competitive sports beat in the country. Every day, no matter how well you think you did the day before, you wake up in fear that one of the other papers will have a story you didn't have. So every morning, before I even eat breakfast, I wake up, switch on my computer, and check the Web sites of all of the other seven papers on my beat. I need to know what the other papers had. I need to know if I got beat on a story, so that when my boss calls to yell at me I can be prepared to tell him what I'm going to do about it. Most days it's okay. But you live in fear of the day when it's not.

Once I'm finished with the papers, I make breakfast and begin my daily phone calls. On a good, busy day in the off-season, I'll probably make twenty to twenty-five phone calls. I call agents, players, team executives around the game. The goal is to find out as much as I can about what's going on, and every conversation is directed toward that end. Maybe an agent lets something slip about a client of his that's always wanted to play in New York. Then maybe I can call the team and ask if they have any interest in such a player. Then maybe I find out they not only have interest, but that they have in fact offered him a contract. This is a simple example, but I've already gone on too long about my job. This story is not about my job. This story is about my love life, which is approaching total chaos.

The date with Fairway Girl was nice. And no, I did not respond to her One-That-Got-Away question with the entire history of Amy. I smiled that one away and smoothly told Linda Lane that the answer would have to wait until a later time, "When we're both a lot more comfortable." She laughed at that, and the rest of our walk in Central Park was as pleasant as the rest of the night had been. We resolved to see each other again, and we parted with just a hug, no kiss. No idea what to make of that, but I have other things to worry about.

First of all, Amy now has my phone number, and can use it to cause me unheard of amounts of psychological torment over the coming years.

Second, Connie is lurking somewhere, and I just know it.

Something big is coming from that dark corner of my recent past.

But most important, all of this has started to make me wonder about myself. I'm starting to worry I've developed a pattern of falling into impossible relationships. I'm starting to wonder if this might be all my own fault, and that I have some flaw that prevents me from dealing with women in an adult and rational way. There always seems to be one missing thing that prevents the big one from happening, and as the Relationship Ghosts keep haunting me, I am starting to wonder if they're trying to deliver the same message in different ways. I'm starting to wonder how this might all have been different if I'd stopped and talked to Mary Ann at the airport.

As I hear a key turn in the lock to my apartment, I'm starting to wonder about some other things too.

Of course, it's Jeff, and this time he's got Bernie with him.

"Duu-uu-hude," Jeff practically sings. "We got breakfast."

Which is nice of them. The least you can do when you barge in uninvited before ten in the morning is bring some doughnuts. Krispy Kreme. Well done, Jeffrey.

"Don't you guys have anything to do?" I ask.

The two of them look at each other. At the same time, they both say, "No." And then they collapse into hysterical laughter.

Of course, they're right. Neither one of them has a thing to do. Jeff is living off an inheritance from a fabulously rich uncle or cousin who once visited him at college and had such a great time he decided to leave Jeff a chunk of his fortune. Pretty good story, really. Jeff swears he didn't even get the guy laid.

Bernie works, but sporadically. He's a writer, and the last book he wrote turned into a big hit Hollywood movie, so he's been living off that for a while until his next brilliant idea comes to him.

Must be nice.

"I mean, couldn't you have slept in or something?" I press on, but by now I'm smiling. They have flopped onto the sofa, flipped off their shoes and fired up the PlayStation. Their energy has brought unexpected life—not to mention doughnuts—to my otherwise dreary morning.

"Slept all day yesterday, I was so messed up from the night before," Bernie says. "Don't they know when it's time to close that place?"

"I've never left there before closing, I don't think," I say.

"That guy's something else," Bernie says reverently. We love Mike.

"Anyway," Jeff butting in now. "We came for the scoop. We came for the rundown. How'd it go? How was the big date?"

"Ah, the date," I say, grinning, and the two of them are immediately encouraged. "It was very, very nice. Very nice."

"That's it?" Jeff, the far more tactless member of the pair. *"Nice?"*

"Yeah, man. It was nice. We had a good time. I'll probably take her out again."

"That's cool," Jeff says. "Anybody else call? The teacher you had a crush on in seventh grade?"

I'm glad to see everybody's picking up on this.

"Yeah." Bernie, giggling along with his doughnut buddy. "How 'bout the girl whose pigtails you pulled when you were six?"

"We've already used that one," I say.

"So come on, man," Jeff says. "It's like seventy-five degrees out there today. We're going out. You coming?"

"Guys, I've got to work," I say.

"Come on, work," Bernie says. "You got a cell phone, right?"

He's right. I do have a cell phone. I've already made my calls to the East Coast agents, and I can't call the West Coast agents until noon anyway, when they start arriving at their offices. I can carry my cell, my organizer, and a little pocket notebook all over town if I want to, and I won't miss a thing.

"Where you guys going?" I ask.

"I don't know," Jeff says. "Let's just go."

I decide I'll go. I have to grab a quick shower, and they can amuse themselves with the PlayStation, which has emerged from exile since the departure of Connie. They're already set up for Madden football, and that means I have plenty of time for my shower.

Having no plan, we end up at Chelsea Piers, where we're going to hit golf balls. It's great. You hit them right at the Hudson River, into this huge net. It's a perfect day for it, and Bernie scores us a free extra bucket of balls by sweet-talking the girl at the counter, so we're set up for the rest of the morning and the early afternoon. It's strange to be in short sleeves this time of year, but the sun is toasting my arms and the only time it feels even slightly cool is when the wind gusts in from the river. The sky is an unbroken robin's-egg blue, and there isn't a cloud to be found. A day like this in November is a gift. I'd have been furious at myself if I'd spent it indoors.

Bernie doesn't play golf, but he loves the driving range. Even takes off his sport coat for the occasion. He's got a pretty good swing, considering the facts that he doesn't play and that he weighs over three hundred pounds, and he catches me checking it out during a break in my own practice session.

"You all right?" he asks, and I realize I'm staring.

"Yeah, yeah, yeah," I say. "Sorry. Just zoning out. Been doing it a lot lately."

"Jack, you can't let these girls get to you like that," he says. "You've got to play it cool."

"I don't think you understand," I say.

"What's not to understand?"

"They're in my face, man! Every time I go out of my apartment, one of them is there. I'm scared to turn a corner. It's crazy. And the more I see of them, the more I start to remember all the screwed-up relationships I've ever had, and I start to wonder if there's something wrong with me."

"Hm," is the response. Sometimes, Bernie can say just the right thing.

But I'm still going.

"You ever see *Broadcast News?*" I ask.

"Sure," Bernie says, Jeff now standing next to me and leaning on a rented seven-iron, looking interested. And a little worried.

"Well you know the scene where they're in Nicaragua, filming the revolution or whatever?"

"No," they say in stereo.

"Well, just before he heads into the line of fire, Albert Brooks turns to Holly Hunter and says, 'If anything happens to me, you tell every woman I've ever gone out with that I was talking about her at the end. That way they'll have to reevaluate me.'"

"Pretty good line," Jeff says.

"I don't remember that line," Bernie says.

"Well, that's what he says," I say. "And that's how I feel. I can't let go, for some reason. Every one of these past relationships feels like a failure, or feels unfinished. And the more I go over them, the more I start to worry. And I don't really want to be starting something new with some new girl if I'm worried I suck at this stuff."

"Wow," Bernie says. "You're really screwed up."

"Thanks," I say. "That's what I needed to hear."

After Chelsea Piers, we take the subway uptown a bit, and we decide to have lunch at the Manhattan Ocean Club. Nice place, especially if your two independently wealthy friends are picking up the tab. Bernie knows the hostess, so we get seated right away, and she looks at Bernie as if she can't believe her good luck.

"You got a story for us there?" Jeff asks Bernie.

"Not really," Bernie says. "Went out with her once. It wasn't that great. Stopped calling each other after a little while."

I am flabbergasted.

"I don't get it," I say.

"What don't you get?" the benevolent master asks kindly, tenting his fingers again.

"You just stopped calling her? You went out with her once? It wasn't that great? And here she is, fawning all over you as if you showed her the best time of her life. Like she's never met a cooler guy."

"Well," Bernie says, grinning, "I probably did show her the best time of her life."

Jeff requests and receives a reluctant high-five from his idol. Three guys in business suits shoot our table dirty looks.

"But don't they ever get mad at you?" I ask, still incredulous. "Don't you ever have one that ends badly? Do you ever have regrets?"

"Sure, I have regrets," Bernie says. "Hell, man. I thought I'd be married by now, maybe have a kid, tell you the truth. I'd love that, to be honest."

"Surely you've had opportunities," I say.

"I don't honestly know. I don't usually get to the point where I—or they—start thinking about those things. I don't think I've ever dated a girl for more than a couple of months."

Jeff's turn to be flabbergasted.

"And you're upset about this?" he asks. "You don't enjoy being the poontang king of Manhattan?"

"Oh, I have a good time, don't get me wrong," Bernie says,

sipping water as we continue to wait for someone to take our order. "It's just, the way you picture it isn't always the way it goes, that's all."

"What do you mean?" I ask.

"Well, like I said. Go back a few years, and I would've figured I'd have a wife and a kid or two by now. But I don't. My life's totally different from that. Which doesn't mean it's bad, it's just not how I pictured it."

The waiter comes. We all order seafood dishes. Jeff and Bernie order beers. I, still technically on the clock (though not exactly working my tail off today), order water and a Diet Coke. The waiter leaves. The discussion continues.

"So, what?" I ask. "Bernie the Great won't live forever? You figure you'll find the right girl, settle down—"

"Yeah, sure," Bernie says. "I don't know. I figure, yeah. Just hasn't happened yet. I haven't found a girl I thought was worth, you know, investing the time. Hey, look on the bright side. I don't have all these ugly breakups coming back to haunt me."

It's true, and I can't argue. Maybe that's my problem. Maybe it's my approach. Maybe I get too damn serious every time. Maybe I should try the Bernie technique. Say, with Linda Lane.

But I think I like Linda Lane.

But there's your problem, moron. You always like the girl as soon as you find out she likes you.

Which is true, but whatever. In a week I turn thirty. It'd be tough to change now.

After lunch, I finally beg off. I have to go home and get some more phone calls made. Jeff and Bernie argue, but I settle the issue by telling them I'll meet them out later, after dinner. They're planning to go to the Village—some dive where they have live music and no place to sit. I'm up for it, but I do have to do some work, so I hop in a cab and head back uptown.

No messages on the voice mail, but it does seem a call

came in. The caller ID shows a 504 area code, which is a Louisiana number, which is strange because I don't know anybody in Louisiana. Except, of course, Mary Ann, our Marley's Ghost. But that has to be a coincidence.

Doesn't it?

Work beckons, but it's a slow day. The Yankees are after the big free-agent slugger, but they've been dancing with his agent for weeks now and nothing's happened. No other team is pursuing this guy, since none of them can pay him what the Yankees can, so everybody in the world knows he'll sign eventually, and there's not much more to write about it until it happens. The few phone calls I do get returned add up to a short story updating the state of the negotiations. I write it while eating Chinese food before heading back out the door.

Jeff and Bernie have called to say they're at Down the Hatch, which is not a place for live music but is within a two-block radius of about fifteen such places. I believe they have been at Down the Hatch since I left them, because they sound absolutely wasted. That would usually convince me I didn't want to go join them, but on this night I feel like getting absolutely wasted. And if you think that sounds like a disturbing trend these days, you're right. I think I'm drinking to help me ignore my problems.

I arrive at Down the Hatch, have one beer with the drunkards, do a shot of something pink that Bernie has the nice-looking female bartender make for us, and then we head out for our club of choice. It's a Monday night, so it's not insanely crowded down here, but it's still Greenwich Village.

The place we end up is called The Slaughtered Lamb. The sign out front says, NIKKI STACK, EVERY MONDAY NIGHT. $5 ROLLING ROCK PITCHERS.

"This is it," Jeff says. "This is our spot."

So we go in, find a dark corner with a table that's too small for the three of us, order a pitcher of Rolling Rock and sit back to wait for the music to start. Nikki Stack is a one-woman show—just her and her acoustic guitar. She's wearing jeans, brown cowboy boots, and a white T-shirt. Her brown hair is cut very short—shorter than any of ours—and she smiles at her audience between every song, emitting only a quiet "Thank you" before easing into the next melody.

She seems almost out of place here, since the place is the kind of dark, wood-paneled beer joint where you'd expect to find drunken single people falling all over each other. And while this may very well be such a place on a Saturday or Sunday, on this night it is mellow, and the mellow sounds of Nikki Stack serve as a pleasant background for our conversation.

While we seem to have left the romantic trials of Bernie back at the Manhattan Ocean Club, it appears to be Jeff's turn to open up about his love life. I'm enjoying all of this because it's taking my mind off my own problems. And Jeff's love life is always interesting. He's no Bernie, but he does see a variety of women. They all stick around long enough to generate a good drinking story or two, but no longer.

Now, though, it seems Jeff has been seeing a new girl. Her name is Anna, and to hear him tell it, she's the most beautiful creature who has ever walked the earth. And he's not saying this to brag. He's saying this because he can't believe his luck.

"I'm telling you guys, you have no idea what this is like," Jeff says. "She literally causes accidents just by walking down the sidewalk. You see guys bumping into each other because they couldn't stop staring. Yesterday, I saw a woman slap the guy she was with because he couldn't take his eyes off her."

Jeff appears to be in awe of this woman, and that's not something Jeff generally allows himself to do. Modeling himself after Bernie, Jeff claims to prefer the surface relationship—

the one that rewards you with sex and the cool confidence of the upper hand. Jeff is fond of telling me he broke up with a woman because she got "too into it."

But this is clearly something new, and it clearly has him scared. Anna has some power over Jeff, and he is very uncomfortable with it.

"Tell him about the couch," Bernie says to Jeff, and I realize this is a conversation that began at Down the Hatch, while I was still at home.

"The couch," Jeff says, staring into his beer glass. "She made me get a new couch."

"She made you what?" I ask.

"She made me get a new couch. She didn't like my futon. Said the cushion wasn't thick enough. Hurt her to sit on it. So I actually went out and bought a real couch."

"Wow," I say. "This sounds like a good thing."

"I don't know. I guess," Jeff tells his beer. "But then, as soon as I brought the new couch home, I had to call her. I mean, I had to call her right away and tell her I got a new couch. I wanted her to come over right away and sit on it, just to make sure it was okay. I mean, I don't get it."

"Wow," I say again, looking up to see Bernie with a huge grin on his face. "That's really something."

"Jeffrey's in lo-o-o-o-ve," Bernie then starts to chant. "In lo-o-o-o-o-o-ve."

"Oh, that's nice," I say. "What grade are we in?"

Jeff, however, is acting as if he hasn't heard Bernie. He continues to stare into his beer, like a condemned man staring at the phone from the electric chair, hoping the governor will call. He seems down, or morose, or simply thoughtful. Then again, he is stone drunk.

"Thank you," Nikki Stack says to her microphone, and sets the guitar down for a short break. She wanders over to the bar and orders a drink. And frustrated by the lack of table service, I get up to get our pitcher refilled. So I'm standing at the bar next to Nikki Stack, Every Monday Night, $5 Rolling Rock Pitchers, and she turns to me and says, "Jack?"

No way.

No freaking way.

This one, I swear I don't know. No way, no how.

"Jack Byrnes?"

Okay, so she's got both names. Something is up. Somebody's playing a trick on me. I look back at the table, expecting to see Bernie and Jeff laughing. But Bernie has gone to the bathroom, and Jeff is still studying his beer.

"You are Jack Byrnes, right?" Nikki Stack is asking. "Hello?"

And I realize I've spaced out. But I also realize I have no idea what to say. I have no idea who this girl is except that she plays here Monday nights and comes with five-dollar Rolling Rock pitchers.

"Yeah, that's right," I say, hoping to convey my utter confusion.

"Jack, it's me, Nikki. Nikki McGowan."

Oh, right. Nikki McGowan. Who I kissed when I was thirteen years old. My first kiss.

8 ◇ A Brief History of Nikki

This won't take long.

It actually wouldn't be worth doing at all, it's all so silly, but for one thing. It seems as if every woman who has ever hurt, disappointed, or confused me is planning on making an appearance in the coming weeks, and I just want them and everybody else to know about the one they'll never beat. No, that's right, Mary Ann. No chance, Amy. Connie? Forget about it. None of you will ever touch Nikki.

Nikki, after all, was the first.

The first, as everybody knows, is the worst, because you don't know it's all going to be okay. When you're thirteen, there is no portfolio of breakup experience with which to reassure yourself. When you're thirteen, you just feel stomped on, and there's nothing you or anybody else can do about it.

When I was thirteen, I played soccer, as did all of my friends. Those of us who had to wait for our rides home played after school, on the back fields that nobody was using at the time. By thirteen you're starting to take these things pretty seriously, and the competition after school could get heated.

By thirteen, though, there's also another element, and it's

called breasts. The girls, who just yesterday functioned only as your friends' annoying sisters, were suddenly, and in a very tangible way, interesting. And when they assembled along the sidelines to stand around and pretend to not watch us play soccer, it added another element to the game—showing off.

Nobody would dare admit to noticing them. It was all too new and terrifying, and we weren't about to share our communal fears with one another on the soccer field. It just wasn't done. It would have been like having a summit to discuss why our voices had been changing or what these little hairs were doing all of a sudden, you know, down there. No, all we did was go at each other with special, newfound vehemence, in the unspoken hope that we would impress one of the girls.

The problem was that we were not in charge of the situation. By that point, our teachers were already telling us that girls matured faster than boys did, and the girls took this as validation. They held it over us, acting as if they'd been around this and every other block. So it wasn't as if we could knock each other out for hours on the soccer field, then just march off and pick one to walk home with us. They would have shoved us away, possibly screamed, and definitely looked at us as if we were crazy. No, we had to wait for them, and when they came to us it was always a surprise.

So surprise is the best word to describe what I felt that one day when I was leaving the locker room with my friends and found Tracy Carter standing in the hallway. Tracy was part of the same clique as Nikki McGowan and a couple of other girls who'd never spoken to me before. They were all cute, but of course none of us knew what to do about that yet, so we ignored them, they ignored us, and everything went along peacefully.

But that day, outside the boys' locker room, Tracy Carter changed all of that. At least for me, she did.

"Hi, Jack," Tracy said, leaving me helpless, completely stuck for what the proper response might be.

"Hi?" I ventured, and this seemed to work.

"I need to ask you something," she said.

She was wearing a short pink skirt. Tracy always wore short pastel skirts. It was kind of her thing, and from the standpoint of the guys who had just left that locker room, it was a good thing. For a second I thought maybe she was going to express her own interest in me, and my heart skipped a little bit at the thought. But that wasn't how these things worked, and I soon found that out.

I had no idea where she was going, and the next few sentences out of her mouth left me almost as confused as I had been when I started. The basic gist of what she was telling me was that Nikki "liked" me and wanted to know if I "liked" her. This was a big thing, and the right thing to do would have been to proceed carefully—to play it cool.

So I did the exact opposite.

I told Tracy that, sure, I liked Nikki. After all, Nikki was very pretty. She had long hair. Her sweater was beginning to expand in the right places. Her skin looked like vanilla ice cream. I didn't tell Tracy all of these details, but I let her know that I'd be receptive to Nikki's interest in me. Tracy said, "Okay," smiled and skipped away, leaving me to wonder what was supposed to happen next.

I didn't have to wait long. The next day, as we left the locker room, Nikki was standing in the same place Tracy had been the day before.

"Hi, Jack," she said, and this time I knew what to say. I'd practiced, just the day before, with Tracy.

"Hi," I said.

The other guys were looking back at me, whispering to each other as they walked away. I hadn't told them a thing about what had happened with Tracy the day before, and I was wondering what kind of gossip was going on about me and Tracy. Now, I was wondering what direction that gossip would take the next day, the guys having seen me with Nikki.

This time there would have been good reason for gossip.

Within two minutes Nikki had her arm around me and was leading me in a direction that was not where we needed to go to get our rides home. She was leading me toward a dark hallway where there was a cutout in the wall between lockers, and she had a mischievous smile on her face. Her long brown hair swayed back and forth as she walked, and when we got to the space between the lockers, she pushed me up against the wall.

I had seen movies in which people kissed, so I knew the basics—or so I thought. But when the lips of another person touch yours—with a purpose—for the first time, you panic. Or at least I did. My first thought was, Am I doing it right? The kiss couldn't have lasted long enough to answer all of my questions (Where do the noses go? Is that her tongue? Am I supposed to use mine? Is it supposed to be this warm? How long does it go on? Where do I put my hands?), but the fact that Nikki was still smiling when we pulled apart made me feel like I was at least competent.

She giggled and said, "We better get going," and she hopped up and headed back up the stairs and out to where our parents were waiting in their cars. When we got there, I got a bewildered look from Eddie McGowan, who was just about to go look for his sister and couldn't, for the life of him, figure out what she'd been doing with me. Nikki hopped into her mother's station wagon without another word to either of us, and Eddie followed her in, still looking quizzically at me.

I hollered, "See you tomorrow, Eddie!" but that didn't seem to make him any less confused.

I did not ask my parents about it, and I didn't tell a single one of my friends at school the next day. I decided to wait until soccer and see if it happened again.

It didn't.

That day's soccer game ended, and I was stunned to find no girl there when I left the locker room. I looked around. Not the coolest move in the world, but I didn't really care. I was after another kiss. It was fun. I wanted to try it again. And at this point I had no reason to believe it wouldn't.

But there was no Nikki. No Tracy to ask about Nikki. No girls at all from the group. Just a bunch of guys, walking away and whispering to each other stuff they didn't want to say to me. Eddie McGowan looking at me, looking angry. I was rattled, and confused again, but I tried my best to shake it off and head for the cars. Briefly, I hoped I would see Nikki at the cars, though I had no idea what we would do if she were there. I was disappointed when she wasn't, and I stood around and stared for a while until my mother called my name. I got in the car, went home, had some trouble getting to sleep that night, and arrived at school the next day looking for answers.

I thought for a second about asking Eddie, but made the surprisingly wise decision that it would be a bad idea. I went through the morning in a fog, and just before lunch I ran into Tracy Carter in the hallway. She saw me and turned around to walk the other way. I jogged and caught up with her.

"Tracy?" I asked.

"Oh," she said, faking surprise, as if she hadn't seen me. "Hi, Jack."

"Um," I said. "I was wondering . . ."

She said nothing. I went on.

"Has Nikki said anything about me?"

"What do you mean, Jack?"

"I mean, has she said anything to you . . . about the other day?"

"Look, Jack," she said, stopping and finally looking at me. Sliding her backpack off her shoulder and onto the hard marble of the hallway, she slouched back against a locker. None of this seemed to me like a sign that she was about to say anything good. She was a lot taller than I was. I'd never noticed that before.

I waited for what seemed like an hour for her to keep talking.

"Nikki doesn't like you anymore," she said.

I felt like my stomach had slipped into my right sock.

I mean, really? Was that even possible, that Nikki didn't like me anymore? Already? Had I fallen asleep and missed two weeks? Was I that bad a kisser? Was there anything I could do?

Fortunately, once again, my censor was working in the presence of Tracy, and I didn't blubber any of this stuff out loud. But she was waiting for me to say something, so I finally did.

"I don't understand," I offered.

"Well, she found out you liked Tina Cervasio."

"Tina Cervasio?" I blurted. "How did she—"

"So, you do like Tina Cervasio?" Tracy asked me, still leaning back against the locker, looking as relaxed as the attorney who knows she has the goods on the witness and can wait all day.

"No," I said, flailing, desperate, helpless against the forces of teen girl group warfare. "No. No. No."

"Well, that's what she heard."

"Who? From who? Who told her that?"

"Does it matter?"

"Of course it matters!" I was fired up now. "Whoever it was, they don't know what they're talking about."

"Did you ever tell anybody you liked Tina Cervasio?"

"No!" I shouted, but Tracy wasn't convinced.

Nor should she have been. I wasn't telling the truth.

About two months earlier Joey Marrone had asked me if I liked Tina Cervasio. And I'd said sure. I mean, basically, at this point, all of us liked any girl who would look at us, and Tina sat next to me in Social Studies. We talked a lot. We were friends, sort of. And sure, I wouldn't have minded if Tina Cervasio had been my first kiss. But shortly after that, Tina had begun dating an eighth grader whose name is the only one in this story I don't seem to be able to recall. I'd heard they'd recently broken up, but it really didn't matter to me. Especially once I'd been between the lockers with Nikki.

But the fact is, somebody (and there was no way to know whether it was Joey. Could have been somebody he told. Lots of gossip bouncing around those cold stone hallways back then) had told somebody else (didn't have to be Nikki. She could have heard it anywhere) that a while ago I had admitted to liking Tina Cervasio. And I was screwed.

"Well," Tracy said, "that's what she told me. And she didn't like it very much."

"Well, can I talk to her?" I asked.

"I don't think so, Jack. I think she's moving on."

Moving on? As if it were a soap opera. But "moving on" after one kiss? I was stunned, but I couldn't do much about it. Tracy had picked her backpack back up and started to walk away, her little lavender skirt swishing as she walked. I followed. But I had nothing to say. After a few feet I stopped walking, and she kept going down the hallway, her little black shoes clacking on the smooth marble. She never looked back. I don't think I ever spoke to her again.

I did speak to Nikki again, but not for long. This was about two weeks later, when I saw her walking down that same hallway with Joey Marrone.

Joey Marrone?

Really?

Joey Marrone with the leather jacket and the slicked-back hair? Joey Marrone who looked like Danny Zuko's wannabe kid brother?

Joey Marrone who screwed me over?

Yeah, it took a little while for it to dawn on me, but it finally did. It was Joey who'd told Nikki about what I'd said about Tina Cervasio. And he'd done it so he could move in on her. Once again I was stunned. They walked by, clearly trying not to look at me. Rage welled up. I wanted to kill Joey Marrone. I wanted to know how this had happened to me. I wanted to punch one of the lockers.

All I could do was shout out, "Nikki!"

It must have been loud, because she turned around. Joey, the weasel, didn't.

"Nikki," I said. "Why . . ."

And "why" what, I didn't even know. Nikki looked at the floor. She was wearing jeans, because it was Friday, and a pink sweater. I'll never forget it.

"You had your chance, Jack," she said. "You blew it."

And she walked away, with Joey, who still hadn't looked back, and that's when I kicked a big dent in one of the lockers.

After spending most of the afternoon in the principal's waiting room and the rest of it in her office, I headed out to the cars. Once there, I saw Eddie waiting by the open door to his mother's station wagon. No Nikki in sight. My own mother was there, but it took me a while to get into the car.

"Jackson?" she called. "Are you all right?"

But I was not all right. Not on this day. My heart in a thousand pieces, I dropped my head, terrified to look around for fear that the entire school was pointing and laughing at me.

I got mad at my mother when she spent the entire ride pressing me about what was wrong. I didn't tell her, but I spent the night in my room, and I think she and Dad guessed it right. Dad came in to try and talk to me about girls, I think, but I was unreceptive and he gave up.

When I woke the next day, I couldn't believe I had to go to school. I tried to fake being sick, but Mom wasn't buying it, so off I went, slinking in through the front door, desperate to hang myself before algebra class.

The first person I saw was Eddie McGowan, who looked at me for the first time in a week and said, "Ah, forget it. She's just a girl, anyway."

Resilience is a staple of the thirteen-year-old constitution, and by soccer that day I was feeling much better. Sure, I went at it with more ferocity than I ever had before. But when the time came to pick up my things and head out of the locker room, I didn't even look at the empty spot where Nikki had stood that day. I just walked with my friends, chatting away and laughing like nothing had ever happened. Sure, it was an act and all I was thinking was that if Nikki were at the cars I wouldn't even try to meet her gaze. If she wanted to say anything to me, my plan was to blow her off—not even look at her. Of course, she never gave me that chance, since she was back in that dark hallway with Joey Marrone or God Knows Who. But I nonetheless walked defiantly back to the cars without spotting her, and the process of getting over my first breakup was under way.

Now, Bernie and Jeff must be drunk, because they are dying. I mean, they cannot stop laughing. We're sitting at the table with Nikki, and I'm in my twentieth minute of explaining how she and I know each other, and Bernie and Jeff can't believe it. When I came to the table to introduce her, I didn't think they'd recover.

"Hey guys," I'd said. "This is Nikki. The first girl I ever kissed."

Jeff, maybe one drink away from passing out, stared up and blinked a few times. Bernie—I am not kidding—fell off his chair. I'd never seen anybody fall off his chair laughing, but Bernie really did it. It was some scene—a three-hundred-pound man in a sport coat tumbling onto the floor while his overwhelmed chair went skidding away and knocked over the microphone stand. Jeff was still staring, and Nikki and I were smiling, first at each other and then at the two of them.

"What's so funny about that?" Nikki asked.

"Wait a minute," Bernie said from the floor. "You were serious?"

"Yeah, man, I was."

And now it was Jeff's turn to lose it. He started slowly, the laughter bubbling up as if from inside a volcano, but he erupted sure enough, and within seconds he was bent over the table, pounding his fist so hard the menu and the advertising flyers slid off the table and landed on Bernie's face. The six other people in the bar were staring at us.

Nikki deserved and got an explanation—a brief one of how the first thirty years of my life had been throwing me a twisted birthday party-slash–*This Is Your Life* episode. She seems quite cool, and got a kick out of my retelling of our one-kiss relationship.

"I don't know," she says, still smiling. "I guess I should apologize?"

"Damn right you should!" I shoot back, only half serious. "You thirteen-year-old girls don't know the damage you do!"

"Yeah!" Jeff, chiming in. "He can trace his whole screwed-up love life right back to you."

"Well, I'll tell you what, guys," she says, rising to return to the stage. "Your next round's on me."

"Oh, right," I say. "Just what these guys need—another round."

* * *

Another set, another couple of pitchers. Jeff and Bernie are pretty much done for the night, but I'm hanging out, waiting for Nikki to come back to the table.

She's been the most fun part of this whole bizarre sequence, probably because she came so completely out of the blue. Also, there seems to be no chance of rekindling anything with Nikki—unless the kiss she shared with the attractive female bartender between sets was some sort of joke. Nikki seems very comfortable and very happy, and it's refreshing to talk to a woman from my past without having to wonder what she wants.

"So, anyway," she says, "give me the rundown on all these women who are coming back to haunt you. I think this is fascinating."

Ah yes. I guess it is time for a rundown. The whole thing's so out of hand that it's time to assess. To see if there are any patterns that can be determined. Who knows? Maybe we can predict which one will show up next.

Across the table, Bernie is rolling quarters down his nose in an attempt to bounce them into his pint glass. Jeff, I believe, is asleep. These guys appear in no hurry to go anywhere.

So I start with Mary Ann. I recount the airport scene, my decision not to talk to her, the fact that I didn't really like her all that much. The whole thing.

"You should have talked to her," Nikki says.

"You think?"

"I don't know," she says. "Seems like somebody might have been trying to tell you something. I mean, how often do you see people you know in airports?"

"Not very often."

"So I don't know. Might be fate."

"I don't believe in fate."

"Ha!" she snorts. "Well, Jack, I think it's time you started to rethink your position on that."

All right, all right. I go on. Relationship Ghost #2. Amy, the original Boston obsession. This is always a tough one to recap, because I still think, way in the back of my mind, that the feelings I had for Amy were more powerful than the feelings I had for any of the others. I still think that should have clicked into place, but it just never did. I still figure there was some mechanical failure or something.

For a second I wonder why I'm pouring all of this out to a complete stranger in a Greenwich Village bar at three o'clock in the morning. But five dollars is an awfully good deal for a pitcher of Rolling Rock in New York City, and it's possible I've had more than I should.

"Sounds like you never got closure on that one," Nikki offers, regarding Amy, and I think she may be right.

"Yeah, but she did," I say. "She never had a problem getting closure. That's what bothers me. How can you feel so strongly about a person and have them feel nothing in return?"

I have a lot of questions left over from that one.

"I don't know," she says. "I think we've all been through that one."

We move along to Relationship Ghost #3, Connie. Again, the long rundown, recapping my most recent relationship failure. Again, the same questions I always get.

"You say you did love her, right?" Nikki asks, leaning back in her chair, her hands folded in her lap.

"Yeah, I really believe I did."

"So why couldn't you say it?"

"I really have no idea. None."

"Weird."

"Yes," I say. "Yes it is. But then again, is it really? Maybe I'd finally reached a point where this was the only thing I could do to screw up this one."

"Wow," she says. "You sound pretty messed up."

"Thanks."

"You shouldn't take these things so hard. Everybody has breakups."

"You're right, I know," I say. "I don't know. Maybe it's turning thirty that's getting me."

"Yeah, thirty messes with your head," she says. "I had mine a month ago."

"I don't know," I say. "I guess I figured by thirty I'd be able to get one of these things right."

"I think your problem is you're looking at it all wrong," she says after a long pause.

"What do you mean?"

"I mean, just because a relationship ends, that doesn't mean it was a bad one. Sometimes they just end. The most you can ever hope for is to have one that lasts the rest of your life. If it's not that one, it has to end."

"I guess." I shrug.

"Your problem right now is that you're focused on the wrong thing. You're wondering why your relationships end. Try thinking about the good things. I mean, you did have good times with these women, right?"

"Of course!" I say.

"Maybe it would help you to think about those times," she says. "Maybe every relationship you've had so far has just prepared you for your Big One. If you don't learn something helpful from each one, then it basically amounts to a waste of time."

Pretty good, really. I didn't come here seeking advice, but I'm happy to have it. The conversation has been pleasant and the music was good, and all in all this has turned out to be the best night I've had in a long time.

*   *   *

They turn the lights on, prompting a groan from Bernie and a start from Jeff, who was definitely asleep.

"Well, I guess that's it, guys," Nikki says, sliding her chair back and standing up. "Jack, it was great to see you. I hope you guys'll come back in some Monday night, now that you know I'm here."

I promise her we will. We hug, and all of a sudden it's my job to get my two drunken friends home. It takes twenty minutes to find a cab, and once we get in we end up having to stop twice along the way so Jeff can get out and throw up. The cabdriver's shouting at Jeff not to puke in his car. Bernie's hanging out the window talking to women who may or may not be prostitutes. Jeff is yakking up a storm.

I'm sitting in the backseat, smiling. I just spent a day in the city with my friends, had a nice lunch, hit some golf balls, heard some good music, and ended up the night by getting advice on my love life from a guitar-playing lesbian who also happened to be the first girl I ever kissed. Now I'm in a cab headed uptown on Tenth Avenue while my two friends lean out the windows vomiting and flirting.

And I wonder:

Why would anybody live anywhere else but New York?

9

Nikki has opened my eyes to a whole new way of looking at my problem. Unfortunately, she may also have ruined my second date with Linda Lane, previously known as Fairway Girl.

I have had a difficult Tuesday, and not just because it was hard to get out of bed after all that Rolling Rock. Off-season baseball coverage is dependent on the number of phone calls you get returned every day, and on this day I didn't have too much luck. Either there's not much going on or I can't find out what it is. The frustration gets to you sometimes.

By three o'clock in the afternoon, I decided I needed to take a walk, because sitting around waiting for the phone to ring was starting to drive me crazy. I called Jeff, only to find out he was spending the day in bed.

So I grabbed my cell phone and headed out into the city. I walked to Central Park, where I saw some people running and remembered my own days as a runner, when I ran the New York City Marathon, back when I was in better shape. I miss running sometimes, especially running in the park. The park is a miracle, really, an impossible oasis of calm and civility set in the middle of the biggest and busiest city in the world. You can sit on a bench on a lawn in the middle of the park and see the skyscrapers towering all around. It's a great way to get a break from the noise and the bustle.

I was sitting on a bench, in a central section of the park, and I was thinking about my late night conversation with Nikki. Maybe she was right. Maybe all of these relationship ghosts were coming back to tell me something. Maybe I needed to stop looking at all my failed relationships as failed relationships and try to find a lesson in each one. I wondered if it might not be a good idea to meet with my ghosts, not for purposes of closure but to help facilitate this new resolution about reviewing the good times, of seeing my past relationships as constructive experiences.

I sat for a while, writing in a journal I'm semifaithful about keeping. I do more of my own writing (not work writing) in the winter, when the schedule is more permissive. The park was tranquil, the peace of a weekday punctuated rarely. An elderly couple, all dressed up for some reason on a Tuesday afternoon, walked past me on a footpath. A guy sitting on the bench across the way, his feet propped up on the seat of his bicycle, eating a banana, surveyed the scene while taking a break from his exercise. I always look around, taking in the scene, but the journal is the place where I write about whatever is on my mind on a particular day. On this particular day I filled fifteen pages with rambling ideas about Nikki and relationship ghosts in general.

After about an hour of walking around the park, I found myself on my way back home. On 74th Street between Columbus and Amsterdam, I ran into Paolo, the unintelligible barber, who had a gorgeous blonde on his arm. She was stunning, with long golden hair running down past her shoulders and a long overcoat that fell a quarter of the way down her perfect legs. In her high heels, she had to be six inches taller than Paolo, but that didn't seem to bother him. He introduced her, presumably giving her name (I have no idea what it was), and then he brought up a topic I hadn't considered all day.

"Hey," he said. "Wahapunwid at guhl? Thugullin the Furray? Wahapun? You tiggerat?"

"The girl from the Fairway?" I asked, shoving my hands into my coat pockets and wondering once again if it's a good thing that I'm starting to understand Paolo. "Yeah, actually, we did go out."

"Vurranace," he said, smiling. "Vurranace. Lavisgud, eh? Lavisgud."

Relief washed over me as I realized I had no idea what the last thing he said meant. I told him I'd see him around, and I mumbled something to his blond beauty about it having been nice to meet her. Paolo and I shook hands, and he winked at me. Odd guy.

But it turns out his question was timely, because when I got home my caller ID was blinking. The message was from Linda Lane, an aggressive young woman, as it turns out, and she was wondering if we might not be able to share another meal.

Delighted that somebody had called me back, even if it wasn't a helpful GM or other baseball source, I immediately returned Linda's call. I told her I would be free after seven o'clock (the time I had arbitrarily assigned myself for giving up on work), and I explained that, due to the nature of the baseball off-season, I would probably have my cell phone with me during our date.

"Should you stay home and work?" she asked. "Because we could do it another night."

"No, it's all right," I explained. "Pretty much every night's going to be like this, until February. I basically just live my life, and if work interrupts, I deal with it."

So we made plans to meet for sushi at a place on 69th Street, and here we are. And all I can talk about, for some reason, is my ghosts, and my new outlook on them.

"I mean, did you ever have a breakup where you spent the next month or so analyzing and going over and over every little thing you did wrong?" I ask.

"Sure," she says, through tight lips. We're in our second hour of this, and the flirty way in which she asked me relationship-related questions on our first date has given way to terse acknowledgments. She has mutilated five packets of sugar into twisted, folded, wrinkled sculptures that now rest by the side of her plate. She hasn't made eye contact in twenty minutes.

You're losing her, says a voice in my head, but damn if I'm listening.

"Me too," I say. "But I think we've got it all wrong. Ultimately, don't you want to learn from them, like you do everything else in life, even mistakes? Especially mistakes? In the end, wouldn't it be better to just be able to think about the good times, and just get past the bad? Wouldn't that be healthier?"

"I guess," she says, not even looking at me anymore.

She looks good, though I still haven't seen her in anything but black. Tonight it's a black turtleneck and a long black skirt. Her black leather coat is slung over the back of the chair next to her, and her pretty round face is resting on her fists as she leans forward with both elbows on the table. Her lips are painted a very dark shade of red, and she looks up at me with inquiring brown eyes and blatantly attempts to change the subject.

"So," she says. "Tell me more about your job."

My job? Why does she want to talk about my job? Isn't this other stuff fascinating?

"My job's not that interesting, really. Basically, I watch baseball games and write about them. I travel a lot, so I see a lot of the country, but that makes it tough too."

"Makes what tough?"

"You know, relationships."

And I'm off again, into another lecture that Linda Lane doesn't want to hear. She begins looking around for our waitress, in an effort to get her to bring the check. She hasn't even heard my latest question, and the reason I know that is because she answered, "Mm-hm," and it wasn't a yes-or-no question. By the time the check comes and she insists on paying it, I start to realize I've lost her.

Outside the restaurant, as we face each other awkwardly, I tell her I had a nice time.

"Me too," she lies, pulling the lapels of her jacket closer to her face.

"Oh," I say. "Here's a cab. Don't you need a cab?"

"Yes," she says, a little too quickly. "Thanks."

"Well, I guess I'll call you," I say.

"Sure," she says, and leans in for a hug. No kiss, not even a peck. Just a brief, uninspired hug and she bounces into the cab, possibly never to be seen again.

I walk back to my building, thinking I should have taken a cab myself, and Yousef greets me in the lobby.

"Mr. Jackson," he says. "You got a package."

As I'm signing for the package—a manila envelope from an address in Ohio that I don't recognize—Yousef asks me how my night was.

"Pretty good, Yousef," I answer. "I had a date."

"A date?" he asks, smiling broadly. "Yes. Good-looking young man in the city. You must go on many dates."

"Not too many, Yousef."

"Aw, now you are modest. I'm sure the women are chasing after you."

And I realize that Yousef, in his own way, is trying to help me out. See, he knew Connie, who used to live here, and in his mind my breakup with her is still fresh. He's trying to help boost my confidence.

"Thanks, Yousef," I say. "I appreciate that. Have a good night."

"Good night, Mr. Jackson."

I take the stairs up to the third floor, and as I approach the door to 3C, I hear the sound of a TV—my TV. I look at my watch, see that it's after ten o'clock, and curse Jeff under my breath. I really just want to be alone, and it's starting to annoy me that he just feels free to walk in any time he likes. As I open the door I'm getting ready to say something to him along these lines, but I can't get the words out.

It's possible that I can't even breathe, I am so stunned by what I see before me.

She's about five-foot-ten, with shoulder-length straight black hair and a face I swear I've just seen on ten of the fashion magazines at the newsstand downstairs. She's standing in my hallway, on the way to or from the kitchen, smiling a brilliant white smile through apple-red lips, and she says, simply, "Hello."

I say it back, but that solves nothing. I still don't know what the most beautiful woman I've ever seen is doing in my apartment.

It occurs to me that I've dropped my keys. She points at them and giggles. My knees buckle.

"Hey, man," comes a voice from my living room. "Hey, is that you?"

It's Jeff's voice, and suddenly things are coming together. Jeff appears over the right shoulder of our cover girl and explains it all in a few words.

"Jack, this is Anna," he says. "Anna, Jack."

Aha. Now I get it. This is the goddess who stops traffic and gets men slapped for staring on street corners. This is Anna, about whom Jeff was, apparently, not exaggerating.

"Ahhh," I stammer, before extending my hand. "Nice to meet you, Anna. Jeff's told me . . . about you."

She's smiling, as if she's seen it before, and Jeff actually lets out a chuckle.

"I think you dropped something, buddy," he says, pointing at the spot on the floor where my keys have fallen.

"Oh yeah," I say. "No, that's where I keep them."

They both laugh at that.

"Don't worry," Jeff says. "She has that effect on pretty much everybody."

They smile at each other, but she doesn't seem in the least way embarrassed by the compliment.

We adjourn to the living room, where I take my seat in the recliner and my uninvited guests sit on the couch. Actually, only Jeff is sitting. Anna is lying down, her head in Jeff's lap, and her legs, each wrapped beautifully in black leather, draped over the arm of the couch. A shiny black boot peeks out from under each leg of pants that seem to have been tailored specifically to her body. I try not to stare. I fail.

"So, what brings you guys?" I ask.

"Don't worry," Jeff says. "It's not like we were hanging out here all night. We were walking by your building and I pointed it out. Anna said she'd like to meet you, and so we came up. We've been here five minutes, maybe."

"The TV's on, Jeff," I point out.

"Hey," he says, holding up two hands. "The TV was on when we got here. That's why I was surprised you weren't in. I figured you left it on for the cat or something."

"He has a cat?" Anna asks.

"No, I don't have a cat," I say. "He's kidding."

"Do you not like cats?" she asks.

"Not particularly."

"That's a shame," she says. "They're great to have around."

"Really?" I ask, genuinely curious about how someone could possibly think that.

"Oh, sure," she says. "They can teach you a lot about love, and loyalty, and the pleasure of. . . . mmmm"—rubbing my friend's left leg now—"physical contact."

I may not be able to take much more of this. Not without some physical contact of my own, if you know what I mean.

"So I take it you have a cat," I say.

"Oh yeah," she says. "A beautiful white longhair. Jeff just loves her."

I look now at Jeff, who refuses to look at me. Jeff hates cats, possibly even more than he hates dogs, and for him to have this woman convinced he loves her cat means to me that he's completely over the edge. Sure, I can see why. He probably isn't the first man she's ever wrapped around her finely manicured finger. But Jeff, come on. A cat?

"Oh, I'm sure he does," I say. "Hey, do you guys want anything to drink or eat or—"

"No, we're fine," Jeff says. "So, tell us. Where were you tonight? Hot date?"

"Yeah, sort of," I say. "Fairway Girl."

"Oh yeah?" Jeff asks. "Again?"

"Yeah, you know. She called again."

"Wow," he says. "She must really dig you."

"Well, after tonight I'm not so sure."

"Who's Fairway Girl?" Anna asks, and Jeff tells her the quickie version of my meeting Linda Lane.

"Wow," she says. "Do you like her?"

"I don't know," I say. "I don't know if she likes me. We've gone out twice, and I don't know. No kiss."

"No kiss good-night?" Anna asks.

"Nope. Just a hug, both times."

"Ooh, that's not good."

"No, I know," I say. "But I think tonight it was my fault. I think I bored her."

"How did you bore her on a second date?" Jeff asks. "Usually it takes three weeks before they want to talk about anything but your job."

"I know," I say. "But I think I was going on and on too much about relationships. Kind of thing that doesn't belong on a second date."

"Yeah, that's a buzz-kill," Jeff says. "But you've got a one-track mind right now."

"You said it."

And this leads right into about thirty seconds of silence. We're all watching the TV; none of us cares what's on it. The conversation needs rescuing. It can't possibly degenerate into the same conversation I'm having with everybody these days.

Just then, Anna, as socially graceful as she is stunning, sits up and leans toward me. Bless her heart, she's changing the subject.

"So, what's your job?" she asks.

"I'm a baseball writer. I cover the Yankees."

"That sounds pretty cool," she says.

"It can be."

"You go to all the games?"

"Yup. I'm on the road pretty much all the time."

"I know some of the Yankees," she says, and Jeff starts to look uncomfortable.

"Really? Which ones?"

"Derek Jeter," she says, to no one's surprise.

"Yeah? How do you know Derek?"

"I went out with him a couple of times."

"What was that like?"

"I don't know. He was kind of boring. All he really liked talking about was baseball."

This I can believe.

"Well, anyway," Jeff says, eager for the next new topic, "I think we're going to head home."

"Oh yeah?" I ask, rising to let them out.

"Yeah, I'm still a little wobbly from last night," he says.

"You boys were out late, I'm told," Anna says. "Hitting on lesbians?"

"That's not exactly true," I say, smiling. "But close."

"Well, it was nice to meet you, Jack," Anna says. "I'm sure we'll meet again."

"I'm sure we will. Jeff seems to like it here."

Jeff laughs and calls, "See ya, buddy," as the door shuts, and finally I'm alone with my thoughts.

10

As I yawn and stretch my way into Wednesday, I am resolved to get to work on the ghosts. My plan is to set up meetings with Connie and Amy, in which my purpose will be to rehash some of the better parts of our relationships. I have no idea how to go about this, since I can't very well sit them down and say, "Okay, now, I have to learn and grow from what happened between us, so let's forget about the ugly breakup and talk about all the fun we had," but I resolve to call at least one of them today and set up a date.

The whole idea, as I see it, is to kind of erase the breakup. Too often the breakup is the part of the relationship that lingers—the only part we remember. And as a result, we end up thinking poorly of a person with whom we once shared very special feelings, and that just doesn't seem fair.

I've never been big about taking pictures, but I do save some things. On a shelf above my desk are a couple of ticket stubs from movies I saw with Connie. I reach up and grab them, and I smile as I remember the bad movies we saw together.

On the floor next to the desk is an old, gray, folded piece of paper. I know what it is without unfolding it. Years ago I wrote

Amy's phone numbers on it. I never threw it out. I guess I always hoped I'd need it again, or felt like it was some connection to a time when there was still hope there. Or something.

In a fit of empowerment, I crumple the movie tickets and throw them on top of the overflowing wastebasket under my desk. It doesn't feel as good as I thought it would.

I've got to do something about this. After all, why should a rotten ending (and they're all rotten endings, whether you want to believe it or not) overwhelm all the good that preceded it? Can't we learn at least as much—and probably much more—by dwelling on the positive things that happened before it all went wrong? Isn't that the stuff we should learn from?

I want to fix it so that our relationships end on positive notes, so that the only memories left over are the good ones. I don't know how these conversations are going to go, but damn it, I'm going to try. I look again at the gray piece of paper, still lying folded on the floor. I still can't bring myself to throw it out. Maybe tomorrow.

The morning begins with the usual phone calls to agents, who are not being helpful. The Yankees tell the agents with whom they negotiate not to talk to the media, because the Yankees themselves are terrified of what will happen if they talk to the media. This makes it very difficult to cover them.

My first breakthrough of the day comes courtesy of an agent who is not connected with the Yankees' situation in any way, but is friends with the agent I really need. He gives me a little nugget about the negotiations with the Yankees and where they stand, and this enables me to call people with a base level of information that may make them more willing to open up. If I know something, they might think I deserve to know more. It's a dance, but sometimes it works.

By six o'clock I have filed a story that says the Yankees are a day or two away from announcing the biggest free-agent signing of the off-season. I have no idea if one (or even all) of my competitors will have this story tomorrow, but I've done my job for the day. And if I don't have an exclusive, I can chalk it up to a hypercompetitive market in which exclusives are hard to come by.

I have yet to call Connie or Amy. It's hard to know which one to start with, since I don't particularly look forward to seeing either one. I could do them in order, but if I were doing that, I'd have to go back to Midway Airport and start with Mary Ann. I can't escape the feeling that she was the key to the whole thing and I blew my chance at finding out what all of this was really about. After all, this new theory is basically Nikki's, and it could be completely wrong. It just happens to make more sense than anything else I've been able to come up with so far.

I pick Connie, mainly because I know her number by heart. I dial, secretly pleased that I might be calling during dinner, and Connie answers the phone.

"Hello?"

"Hey, Connie," I say.

"Jack?"

"Yeah, it's Jack."

"How are you?"

"I'm good, Connie. How are you doing?"

"Good. Everything's good here."

This is a bit uncomfortable, and I'm starting to wonder if I'll regret calling.

"I didn't interrupt dinner, did I?" I ask.

"No, not at all. My mother's cooking."

Damn.

"Well, anyway, listen," I say. "I was thinking about what you said—about getting together to talk?"

"You were?"

"Yes, I was. And I think I'd like that."

"Oh really?" she asks, sounding excited. "That's great Jack. Oh, I'm so glad you called."

"So, anyway, what's a good day for you?"

"Well, I'm not doing anything tomorrow," she says, apparently playing hard to get. "Could we have lunch?"

"Sure, Connie. Lunch sounds great. What time's good? I'm pretty flexible."

"I would say around one o'clock, but it might have to be downtown, if that's all right."

"That's fine," I say. "Should I just meet you outside your office at one?"

"Okay," she says. "And we'll find a place."

"Sounds good, Connie."

"Okay," she says. "Well, I'll see you tomorrow, then. I'm looking forward to it."

"All right," I say, not looking forward to it, and we hang up.

Now I can't get to sleep, which is a problem I often have when I'm going over plans in my head. I lie awake in bed, in the dark, envisioning the conversation with Connie. I flick on the light and open a book, hoping I can read myself to sleep. But that doesn't work, and before long it's seven o'clock in the morning, the sun's peeking around the blinds, and I know it's going to be a rough day. When sleep finally comes, it comes too late. My alarm clock rings at nine-thirty, jolting me off my pillow. I'm exhausted, but I'm determined. I'm going to tackle these ghosts head-on, no matter how unpleasant it may be, and I'm going to start today.

What I don't realize, as I dress and head out the door, is that this is the day it will really get complicated.

I have to be in midtown at eleven A.M. because Mariano Rivera is hosting some event for children. Rivera isn't likely to say anything interesting during his public appearance, but our access to the players in the off-season is so limited that we have to seize every opportunity.

The event lasts an hour and a half, and Rivera does stop to talk to the five reporters who have shown up. We go over Game Seven of the World Series again, and he remains disappointed. But he really wants to talk about these kids and the money he's donating to the nearby hospital to help them. At the end, we all shake his hand, he thanks us for coming, and I head out onto Sixth Avenue to try and find a cab in the middle of the day.

This is no easy task, and it's complicated even further by the fact that it's raining today. I mean, it's pouring. I'm holding a folded-up newspaper over my head to keep my hair from getting wet and trying to hail a taxi with the other hand. No luck, but the good news is only one leg of my pants got soaked when the last cab blew past me and splashed me with the water from the pothole it hit.

As I try in vain to clean up my left pant leg, I see a cab pull up right in front of me to let someone out. This is a huge break, and one I'm prepared to seize. As soon as the cab discharges its passenger, I will slide in and direct it downtown to Connie's office, where I'll be content to wait in the warm, dry lobby if I happen to arrive early.

But then the cab door opens and the world changes.

Her hair is a deep, rich, hot-chocolate brown, and it ends just north of her shoulders. She wears it in bangs, which point right down to a very cool pair of brown eyes. She's dark-skinned and slim, and as her pretty face looks up at me, I realize I must be staring. But instead of correcting the situation, I instead set about the task of freaking out a perfect stranger.

All this woman is trying to do is get her umbrella open as half the population of Manhattan brushes by on a midtown sidewalk, and here I am, staring at her camel-colored rain-coat, her knee-high black boots, and her gorgeous hair, and before I know what's going on I'm holding out my hand to introduce myself.

"Hi," I say. "I'm Jack."

The look on her face is one of fear, and I begin to realize what I may have done. If this is her first time in New York City, I have probably scared her out of her mind. New York-ers have a reputation for many things, but none of them has anything to do with introducing themselves to strangers.

But once she realizes I am talking to her and not asking for money, she actually smiles. It's a sincere, natural smile that brings out the dimples in her cheeks, and her glittery brown eyes actually seem to smile with her. There's a soul behind this smile, and it's easy to spot even on a first encounter.

"Julie," she says, shaking my hand. "Julie Gordon."

I am in a daze, and the conversation we have is, as a result, fuzzy. It's as if I'm outside the conversation, watching it take place. There are words coming out of my mouth, but I have no idea who's thinking them up.

"Is this your first time in New York?" I ask after introduc-ing myself with a soggy handshake.

"Yes, actually," she says from under her umbrella, looking like she's trying to suppress a laugh. "It is."

"So," I say, as if it weren't pouring rain, as if we actually knew each other, "what brings you?"

"Well, since you asked," she's looking around now, maybe for the candid camera. "I'm here to interview for a job. At *People* magazine."

And she points to the large beige building behind me, which I can only assume houses the offices of *People* maga-zine.

I am not oblivious to the fact that Julie is in a big-time hurry to get (a) out of the rain and (b) to her interview. But something is telling me not to let this conversation end. This is a feeling I've never had before, and it's dragging me along. I'm not even in control of my own mouth.

"Well, let me be the first to wish you good luck," I say. "And if you don't mind my asking, how long are you in town?"

"A few days," she says, still smiling, convinced she's playing along with some game, still looking around.

"Do you have any plans for dinner?" I ask, though I can't believe it.

"Actually, no," she says. "I don't know anybody in New York."

"Well," I say, with a raindrop clinging to the end of my nose, "may I offer you an official Welcome to New York dinner? Some night this week?"

"That sounds interesting . . . Jack?"

"Yes, Jack."

"That definitely sounds interesting," she says. "And I must say I'm a little overwhelmed by the hospitality. They don't say anything about this in any of the guidebooks."

Oh, this couldn't have gone better. Not even if it had made any sense at all.

Since I always forget to carry business cards, I fumble in my coat pocket and find an ATM receipt, on the back of which I scribble my phone number. I hand this precious document to the beautiful stranger, who declines to give me hers (can't say that I blame her), and she shouts over her shoulder that she promises she'll call me.

Then I stand in the rain with a thousand new thoughts shouting at each other in my head.

At first I panic. I wonder if I said the right things or if I'd come on too strong. I wonder about the general etiquette of the situation. Is one permitted to do what I have just done— offer his phone number to a stranger on her way to a job interview in a strange city?

I decide that my actions have at least made me memorable—maybe I am now to her what Fairway Girl was to me, and maybe she'll be energized by the sheer, out-of-the-blue lunacy of my introduction. I commend myself for that before moving on to different worries.

It is raining, as I believe I have mentioned, and very windy. What if the receipt blows out of her hand? What if the rain washes the ink off the back of it? What if she just decides I'm some lunatic, wants nothing to do with me, and throws the thing in the wastebasket in *People* magazine's lobby? There would be no way to find her. I have no idea where she is staying, how long she is staying, or where she's headed when she leaves town. For a second I hatch a plan whereby I will call the editors of *People*, pretend I'm a reporter (which shouldn't be too hard, since I am) trying to find Julie Gordon, and get them to tell me where she's staying or where she's from.

But then I figure that would make me a stalker.

How about waiting outside the building until the end of her interview? That's a plan for a few seconds too. But then I figure that too would make me a stalker.

At this point I realize I'm soaking wet, having left my umbrella back in my apartment because I'd neglected to look out the window before leaving home. But for the last few minutes I've been bouncing up and down concrete steps like a little kid. I wonder if I've just experienced Love at First Sight, because what other force could cause a grown man to dance in the rain pondering stalking techniques and not even realize he was getting wet?

I walk a block and duck into the 50th Street subway station and head uptown. It's not until the train is passing the 66th Street station that I begin to recover my senses. I realize I've missed Columbus Circle, where I should have changed trains. I also remember Connie.

Connie.

Jesus Christ, I was supposed to meet Connie for lunch.

I look at my watch and see that it's five minutes until one. Even if I hop out here, get a cab right away (not likely), and get downtown without traffic (even less likely), I'm going to be insanely late. Even if I had a helicopter, I'd be insanely late. I ponder all of this as I elbow my way up the stairs to the street level and start looking for cabs. I fumble for my cell phone, thinking I'll call Connie and tell her I'm going to be late, but then realize I don't remember her work number. I am screwed.

Strangely, though, I can't stop smiling. As I stand there in the rain, headed for an unavoidable case of pneumonia, I'm smiling the biggest smile I've ever smiled in my life. I don't remember the last time I felt like this, and it's great.

Julie.

Julie Gordon.

Man, I hope she calls.

Taxi!

11

My head just isn't where it needs to be. It's that simple.

I got the cab without any trouble. Problem was, when I got in, I told the driver to take me to my apartment. I hopped out of the cab in front of my building and raced inside and up the stairs (that damn elevator's still out). I unlocked my front door, shook the water off my clothes, hung my jacket on the doorknob and collapsed into my desk chair. Now I'm staring up at the framed photograph of Mookie Wilson's grounder going through Bill Buckner's legs in the 1986 World Series, and within two minutes my cell phone rings. It is, of course, Connie, and she's pissed off.

"Jack?" she asks, trying to fake polite.

"Yes?" I answer, still clueless.

"Where are you?"

"Oh, shit. Connie."

"That's it?" fake politeness now gone. "That's it? 'Oh, shit, Connie?' That's your explanation? I've blown half my lunch hour, Jack, and you didn't even call?"

"Connie, I'm sorry," I say, scrambling for an excuse. "I . . . I just got so hung up, and I lost track of time, and I don't know—"

"Where are you now?"

"Uh . . ." debating the merits of honesty here. "I'm in my apartment."

"You're in your apartment?" she just about shrieks.

"Yeah," I say. "I was running around in midtown in the rain, and I wanted to come back and change, and I guess I just didn't know what time it was. I am so sorry."

"No, no, no, no, no," Connie says, up several octaves from the start of the conversation. "You know what I think this is, Jack? You know what I think? I think this is a way of getting back at me. I think you call me up, make a lunch date, and deliberately blow it off, just to screw with me. That's what I think."

"What?" I ask, suddenly offended.

"This is some sick way of trying to get back at me, which is really twisted, Jack, because I didn't do anything to you that you didn't deserve."

I really had wanted to get into these issues over lunch, and I still do. I think hashing all of this stuff out is a key element to the Nikki McGowan/Jack Byrnes Theory of How to Get All These Women Off My Back. But not on the phone. Not when Connie's this upset. This isn't right.

"Look, Connie—" I start.

"Don't give me that crap, Jack! You tell me right now. Are we going to get together or not? Because I need to move on. I need to know."

"You need to what?" I ask, again incredulous at the conversation's latest turn.

"I need to move on," she says, and I wonder if she's calling from her desk or a phone in her lobby.

I actually ponder this for a few seconds, then smile as Julie Gordon's face pops back into my mind, and I miss some of Connie's rant.

". . . so you need to be honest with me Jack, because—"

"Look, Connie, stop," I bark, cutting her off. "I'm sorry. I screwed up. But I'm not trying to get out of seeing you. I really do want to get together."

"Prove it," she says.

"All right. How about dinner? How about dinner tonight?"

"Tonight?" she asks. I really don't think she expected this.

"Yeah, tonight. Eight o'clock. Gabriel's, on 60th, by Columbus Circle."

The phone is silent for a moment, but Connie recovers quickly, thinking she's calling my bluff.

"Okay, fine," she says. "Gabriel's. Eight o'clock. I can make that."

"Great . . ."

"But Jack, I swear to you, if you stand me up again, I will not take it well."

Oh, I'm sure of that.

"Don't worry, Connie," I say. "Don't worry. I'll be there."

"Okay," she says, softening for the first time since she called. "Eight it is. I'll see you then."

And we hang up.

That was no fun.

Can't wait for dinner.

Ah well. Nikki never said this was going to be easy. The whole point is for it to be effective. If things go well, Connie and I can part after a nice, albeit expensive, meal (why didn't I just pick some cheap Chinese place?) with both of us feeling better about our failed relationship. If things go well, we'll never see each other again, never speak to each other again, and most important, never wonder what might have been. I'll have attained closure on at least one of these relationship ghosts and be armed with a plan for dealing with the others.

Of course, if things don't go well tonight, I'll be back at square one and may have to head back to the Village for some more Rolling Rocks with Nikki Stack.

Hey, there are worse things.

* * *

I've decided not to tell anybody about Julie, which is a new way to go. I usually blab to everybody I see about the latest girl. Maybe I'm feeling superstitious about this one. Or maybe it's like the *Seinfeld* episode where George decides to do everything opposite the way he's always done it before, because it's never worked out for him. He ends up getting a date with a pretty girl, getting his job with the Yankees, and yada yada yada. You get the idea.

So Julie will be my little secret, and boy is she a fun one. Sure, I wish there had been a message from her on my machine when I got back from meeting her this afternoon, but I dismiss such aspirations as unrealistic and decide to hope for a message on the machine when I get back from Gabriel's.

It's seven-forty, though, and if I want to make it to Gabriel's on time I've got to get going. Who knows about the subway, and it wouldn't hurt to be there early, just to save a little face from this afternoon. I really want this conversation to go well, and there's no point in spending the first half hour of our dinner trying to apologize while she pouts.

I slide on a gray sport coat, no tie, and snatch my keys from the corner of my desk. But just as I take my first step toward the door my eyes stop on the package I picked up yesterday from Yousef in the lobby. Bulky manila envelope with an Ohio postmark. Why haven't I opened it before? Must have forgotten. Can't imagine why . . .

For some reason I stop what I'm doing and head back to the desk, where I tear open the envelope.

And within one minute I realize I shouldn't have done that.

It's a book, which is no big deal. I get lots of books in the mail—baseball books, from writers or publishers who want me to read and review them for the paper. I usually toss them aside, and I almost never read the form letters folded and tucked inside the front covers. But this book is no baseball book, and I see that right away. This book is called *Picking a Shade*, and it's a novel. Its title is written in bright pink letters on a white cover, on which a cartoon woman in fishnet stockings is surveying a glass case full of cartoon guys. It's one of those books for women, by women, about women's relationships with men. It's one of those books I would never buy but that some girlfriends of mine read exclusively. And as I wonder why it was sent to me, my eyes wander down to the bottom of the cover.

There, in bright pink letters, is the name of the author.

Danielle Hall.

That's right.

Another ex.

Resisting the temptation to throw the book against the wall, hide under the covers of my bed and scream the night away, I look at the letter that was inside the envelope, hoping it will explain.

It doesn't. It's a form letter.

But for some reason, I flip open the front cover of the book, and there, in red ink, is the following handwritten inscription:

Jack,
See if you can guess
which one is you?
Hope you're doing well,
Love, Danielle

Love?
Love, Danielle?
What the hell is that?
Come to think of it, what the hell is any of this? A ran-

dom package containing a book by a woman I haven't seen, talked to, or thought about in almost ten years? A personalized inscription, indicating that I may *be* one of the characters in her book?

It could be a gag, right? Could be Jeff and Bernie setting me up? But no. How would those guys know about Danielle Hall? No, this is for real, and the way things have been going lately, I'm not surprised.

What I am is late. Late again for Connie, and that's not going to happen twice in one day. No chance. In seconds I somehow recover myself and make two decisions. First, I will put this book down, pretend nothing ever happened, and make every effort to cope with its consequences upon my return from Gabriel's. There. It's back on the desk.

Second, I need a cab. Subway won't be quick enough, not if I want to avoid pissing off Miss Unstable Connecticut, and I need to run to get that cab.

The cab gets locked up immediately in Lincoln Center traffic (rookie mistake, scheduling dinner at eight near Lincoln Center. Inexcusable), and by the time I get to Gabriel's it's ten after eight. But Connie's not there yet. I am spared. She walks in five minutes later, stunning in a black business suit with a knee-length skirt as she shakes herself out of her raincoat, and I keep to myself my suspicion that she was late on purpose. I smile, take her coat and offer her a drink as we wait for our table. She smiles back, and things seem pretty civil.

But all I can think about is Danielle Hall and that book.

Damn you, Danielle, you've even made me forget about Julie Gordon.

Well, for a few minutes, anyway.

We're sitting at our table by eight-thirty, and we order a bottle of red wine. I planned on drinking because, well, I'm on a binge these days, but also because I figured it would help loosen things up. We have a lot of things to get out in the open at this meal.

I've spent a good amount of time trying to figure out the best way to begin this very important conversation, and what I've come up with is that I have no idea. That's why I'm thrilled when Connie starts talking.

"So," she says, flipping her blond hair to one side and tilting her head. "Why the change of heart?"

"Excuse me?" I ask, terrified that she may have the wrong idea.

"You know," she says. "Why, all of a sudden, were you so eager to get together? You must have something to say."

Relieved, I give her a nonchalant shrug and respond, "Nah, not really. Just figured . . . I don't know."

"See?" she says, suddenly annoyed for some reason. "There's the problem. You never told me what was really on your mind. That's why we broke up."

Ooh. Okay. She's on the offensive. That's fine. This'll be easier to get into than I thought.

"No, Connie, that's ridiculous," I say.

"Excuse me?" she responds. She always loved it when I called her ridiculous.

"That's ridiculous," I repeat, to make sure she knows I know what I'm saying. "I always told you what was on my mind. I am the all-time king of telling people what's on my mind. That's not why we broke up."

"Okay, smart guy," she says. "You tell me why we broke up."

And here's the beauty part. She's sitting there expecting me to put this whole thing on her. But that's not what's going to happen. That's not part of the Byrnes-McGowan plan. This is my perfect chance to take this conversation to a new level, full of possibilities for depth and soul-searching and, yes, closure.

"The reason we broke up," I say, "is because I couldn't say 'I love you.'"

And it works. She's flabbergasted. Speechless. There's no way she saw this coming, and that's just the way I wanted it.

To make things even more perfect, the waiter shows up with the wine just as I finish my bombshell. Like a movie. He shows me the bottle (like I have any clue), and I nod. He uncorks it, pours a bit into my glass. I taste it, nod again. He pours her a full glass. He pours me a full glass. And all this time she's just sitting there, staring. Her face is blank except for her pretty green eyes, which are staring *into* me. The eyes seem to be the only part of Connie that realizes what has happened and what must happen now. The rest of Connie will soon follow, and hopefully so will my brilliantly planned discussion. But for now I take some satisfaction, as I stare back at those eyes, in knowing that it's all going perfectly.

"I mean," I say, once the waiter is gone. "Don't you think?"

"Yes," she says. "Yes. That's exactly why we broke up."

"I know."

"You know?" she says, coming back now into herself. Trying for indignant but still stuck in confused. "You know?"

"I know."

"But then . . ." and I worry she's trailing off before she comes back with, "But then, why didn't you say it?"

"Connie, to tell you the truth, I don't know. I have no idea why I never told you I loved you. I probably did love you. And it's not like I'm scared of the words. It's not like I've never said it to anybody else. But with you, I don't know. I seriously don't know why I couldn't say it."

Once again she has no idea what to say. The merlot is good, I discover, and I wonder if she's planning to try hers anytime soon.

"Look," I continue, realizing that she's forgoing her turn in the conversation. "A lot of things messed us up. It got bad. And no, I wasn't happy with you just walking out the way you did. But I know it was me, and the I love you thing. I know it all started when I couldn't say it back to you. I never intended for things to go wrong. I just . . . I couldn't say it, and I still don't know why."

And now she's crying. Which, I guess, was to be expected. She dabs at her eyes with the white cloth napkin, and I wave over a waiter who's alert enough to know to bring tissues. She takes a tissue, thanks the waiter and wipes her eyes, sniffling.

"I'm sorry, Connie," I say. "I really am."

"I just don't get it," she says, still crying, green eyes searching my face for an answer that isn't coming.

"I don't either, Connie, but that's what happened. And because of that, we didn't work out, you and me. But the way I see it—and I'm sorry if this upsets you—we weren't supposed to work out. If we were, I would have been able to say it, and we would have lived happily ever after. But we weren't, for some reason, and that sucks, because we really had something good. Once."

She's looking at me now as if I'm a math professor and she doesn't get how I've solved the problem on the chalkboard.

"So, what are you trying to say?" she asks, legitimately confused. "You want to give it another chance? Or . . . you don't?"

"No, Connie, I don't," I say, making sure to look right into the greenies to get the point across. "We're over, and I think if you really think about it, you know that."

She pauses, then gives a little nod, taking her eyes away from mine and casting them down at her hands.

"I just wanted you to know," I continue, "that I know it was my fault."

By now she seems to have stopped crying, but she still hasn't brought her eyes back up to mine.

"Oh," she says to her napkin. "It wasn't all your fault."

And that's it. Now we have it. I didn't plan the conversation out ahead of time, but if I had, it would have gone exactly like this. The tough part, I hope, is over. What logically follows now is that we ease, delicately, into the conversation I really came here to have, then part as friends, laughing and smiling, with an unspoken agreement never to see each other again. Maybe it's a crazy dream, but I really think it will help. And as the waiter arrives to take our orders (and we tell him we need more time to look at the menus), I really think we're headed in that direction.

Connie proves as receptive as I'd hoped. The awkward part dealt with, she puts her lingering sadness aside and engages me in a very enjoyable talk about the good old days. We talk about the marinara sauce at Bennigan's. We talk about Disney World. She tells me she's recommended Disney World as a good first date to a friend of hers who lives in West Palm Beach, and I think that's great. Memories pour back and forth across two oversized white ceramic bowls of pasta, and we order a second bottle of merlot. The tears are a thing of the past, and for the rest of the night Connie's green eyes anchor a smiling face. By the time we finish dessert and the check comes, I really think this has been great.

We get the coats, I help her on with hers, and we walk to the corner of 60th and Broadway, right at Columbus Circle across from the Trump building. She points to the kitchen of Jean-Georges, visible from the sidewalk. We remember the night we ate there—best meal I ever had in New York, which makes it the best meal I've ever had anywhere. One more nice memory for the road.

A cab pulls up, and we hug. She gets in, I close the door, and we wave as the cab drives away. And as I wait for the next cab to come by, I smile.

Is this what closure feels like? Does Connie feel the same way I do? That we've put a neat little bow on this thing? I sure hope so. Because I really believe I may have succeeded in erasing the breakup. I really believe that now, when I remember my relationship with Connie, I'll remember Disney World instead of the empty apartment and the missing CDs.

And really, that's the way it should be.

12

I love my alarm clock, which is saying something, because I'm not a morning person, and most people who aren't morning people do not have good relationships with their alarm clocks. But mine plays CDs, so I can wake up to any song I choose. It can be set for two different wake-up times—not as big a deal when you're single as it is when you're sharing a bed, but still a nice backup feature. It can give me the current temperature outside my apartment—*outside*—so I know what to wear before I even get out of bed.

But as nice as my alarm clock is, I am starting to think it will soon be totally worthless to me. I no longer need its help. I now have Jeff. The human alarm clock.

"Anybody home?" comes the too-familiar voice as I sit straight up in my bed in the next room. I'm still not used to this, so I'm still startled when he does it. Not satisfied with barging in the front door uninvited, my good pal Jeffrey now opens the door to my bedroom—a previously inviolable sanctuary—and begins my day for me.

"Oh," he says, holding a bag from Krispy Kreme in one hand and a paper coffee cup in the other. "There you are."

"Dude!" I practically shout as I rub the crust out of my eyes.

"What?" he asks, chewing, a spot of jelly on the side of his mouth.

"You just walk in to my bedroom now?"

Blank stare.

"I mean, what if I had a girl in here or something?"

"I thought you went out with Connie last night," he says, then his eyes get big. "You didn't bring Connie back here, did you?"

"No!" I bark back at him. "I didn't bring her back here. I didn't bring anybody back here. I'm just saying, what if? You know?"

"I gotcha, boss. No problem. From now on I'll wait in the living room."

It's a step.

"So," he says. "How'd it go with Connie?"

"Not bad, actually."

"Cool."

"But there's something else," I say, and Jeff looks up.

"Oh no."

"Oh yes."

"Another one?"

"You guessed it."

I hand Jeff the form letter that came with the book.

"I got a kick out of this," I say. "Read it twice when I got home last night."

He reads it out loud:

"Ruby Gold has had her share of guys. Enough to know they come in all shades. From the wisecracking kid who had the crush on her in second grade, to the emotionally stunted writer who shared her bed as a college freshman, to the cheating husband of her early womanhood, she's tried them all and can't seem to find the one that complements her. Join Ruby as she picks her way through the cosmetics counter of life, looking for the shade that will suit her best. The one that brings out her eyes. The one that makes her feel beautiful. Will she find her perfect shade, or is life about settling for the best one you can find?

Danielle Hall's first novel is by turns witty, exasperating, optimistic, desperate, and laugh-out-loud hilarious, fueled by a main character whose lifelong search for love can't seem to find its target. Danielle inhabits Ruby Gold, infusing her with her own lifetime's worth of experiences—the good, the bad, and the totally ridiculous—and brings us along on her sometimes impossible but always hopeful quest."

"So," I say when he finishes and looks confused. "What do you think?"

"I don't get it."

"Danielle Hall was my girlfriend my freshman year at UVA," I say, like the magician who has just made the girl disappear. Oh, to be a magician.

"Oh, crap," my ever sympathetic friend Jeff says.

"Yep."

The letter is a brutally written piece of propaganda, by a P.R. flak named Angela Graves. Angela, according to the letter, is the one you're supposed to call if you want more information on the book, or if you want to make an interview request for the author. I tell Jeff I'm thinking of calling Angela, introducing myself as the emotionally stunted writer who shared Danielle Hall's bed in college, and putting in an interview request she won't soon forget.

But before I do that, I've got to read this thing. I don't care if all 287 pages are as bad as the first two (with which I read myself to sleep last night), I've got to read this. Because before

I confront Danielle Hall (and I will confront her—that's what I do now), I want to make sure this is really, truly, honestly a book that equates the males of the human species to lipstick.

Because that's what it looks like to me. That she's comparing men to lipstick. Which would, of course, be totally unacceptable.

But even we, the emotionally stunted, are capable of being fair-minded, and I therefore would never want to jump to a horrible conclusion like that based on a form letter by Angela Graves.

"You sure you want to read this?" is Jeff's response, and I, on a serious roll now, holler, "Hell, yes!" back from my kitchen, where I am preparing eggs.

"I don't know, man," he says. "This looks pretty bad. I had a girlfriend once who read all this kind of crap, goofy looking paperbacks with pink covers. All she bought, I'm serious."

"We've all had girlfriends like that," I say. "I'm guessing Danielle's a girl like that, although I didn't go out with her long enough to know what kind of books she read. But I'm guessing she's a girl just like that, who read enough of these books and decided it wouldn't be so hard to write one."

"Yeah, probably," Jeff says, in the kitchen now, sniffing around, about to ask me for an omelet, I just know it. "So, is she next?"

"What?"

"Who's next? I mean, assuming you knocked Connie out of the picture last night, who's next? You gonna keep after these chicks, keep talking to them like you talked to her, try and get them out of your life?"

"Ah, yes," I say, grateful for the question. "Amy. Amy is next. I'm going to call her, set up lunch, and bombard her. I'm going to do it either today or tomorrow. I'm on a roll."

"Sure," he says. "That's pretty clear from this letter. You're on a roll."

"Funny," I say, and keep beating the eggs, determined to make him actually come out and ask for an omelet.

As Jeff yammers on about something else, I drift off, thinking of Julie Gordon, prospective *People* magazine reporter. No, she hasn't called, and no, I'm still not planning on telling Jeff—or anybody else—about her. A week or two goes by and she doesn't call, then maybe I let these guys in on it. It is, after all, a decent story. Bernie will appreciate it even if nobody else does. And maybe it'll catch on. Maybe guys all over New York will start standing on street corners, waiting for beautiful women to step out of cabs so they can introduce themselves and give them their phone numbers without being asked. I could spark a new revolution in dating.

"Jack!" Jeff half shouts, and I realize my eggs are burning. That's just great.

"Oh, shit," I say, and race to the stove.

As I slide the burned eggs into the trash, I go into the fridge to get two new ones, and Jeff clears his throat.

"Yes?" I say.

"Oh," he says, feigning surprise. "You offering to make me an omelet?"

"Well, I really—"

"I mean, I had the doughnut, but it wasn't really much. Sure, I'll have one."

Do I know my guy or do I know my guy?

Omelets devoured, Jeff and I sit on the sofa playing a game of Madden football on the PlayStation. I have not done a stitch of work today, and I'm not a hundred percent sure I plan to. Doesn't seem like there's anything going on anyway. The Yankees won't do anything else until they sign the big slugger, and they're taking their sweet time with that the way they do with everything else. We've already written stories about the other guys they're pursuing—a new left fielder, a starting pitcher, a backup outfielder—but none of it's hot, and I have people who will call and alert me if something huge is happening. That's why, once the game ends— with a miracle touchdown catch by an animated rendering of Randy Moss and a disturbing live-action victory dance by Jeff—I kick my lanky friend out of the apartment and set about the business of ghost-busting.

Sure, I could sit here and wait for Julie Gordon to call, and I've considered that. But the fact is, she may never call, and I can't waste the time. Only a few days left in my twenties, and I've got to use them.

I know Amy gave me her phone number at the Starbucks. What I don't know is what I did with it. It's somewhere on my desk, but that doesn't really help. The folded gray paper won't help, because that's an old Boston number. And the way my desk looks right now, there could be plans for an intergalactic death ray on there and it would be years before I'd find them. So, figuring her last name hasn't changed yet, I look Amy up in the Manhattan phone book, and there she is. I call, and the answering machine picks up. Perfect. Just what I wanted.

"Hey, Amy, it's Jack. Jack Byrnes. Just giving you a call, seeing what's up, and wondering if maybe you would want to grab lunch sometime. Maybe talk about old times. Anyway, I think you have my number, but in case you don't, it's 555-4635. Hope to hear from you soon. Thanks."

I'm not thrilled with the message, particularly the part about "talk about old times." Why did I say that? That's supposed to be a surprise. And repeating my name, with the last name, not exactly the picture of smooth. But I've never known how to act with Amy, even when her eyes weren't around to throw me off.

* * *

It's a crappy day, so I figure I'm staying in. No problem, I can make a few work calls after all, and then keep myself busy with Danielle Hall's *chef d'oeuvre* for a while. I mean, it's mindless, but Danielle's really not a terrible writer. Reading this book only makes you wish she'd use some of her powers for good instead of evil.

I haven't got to the part about me yet, but I have read far enough to wonder what kind of inscription she wrote to her high school boyfriend, assuming we all got copies. Based on the description in the book, I'm guessing Joe High School got something like this:

> Dear Asshole,
> Thanks for ruining
> my life! This is all
> your fault.
> Love, Danielle

I mean, the way this guy comes off, it makes *me* hate men. Danielle's (or should I say Ruby Gold's?) high school boyfriend appears to have bullied her (physically) into giving up her virginity, impregnated her, forced her to get an abortion, refused to pay for it, and dumped her for a cheerleader. I'm waiting for the sequel, in which Joey has an affair with Ruby's mother and crashes his pickup through the bay window in the front of their house.

Yes, while *Picking a Shade* looks like a silly little novel about men, women, and relationships (and for the most part, it is), it is not without its darker elements. And I get the feeling that a lot of the issues with which Danielle and Ruby (and possibly Angela Graves) are dealing have their roots in Big Joe High School and his pickup.

So I'm encouraged. I mean, compared to this guy, I have to come off looking pretty decent.

The phone rings, interrupting my reading. I fold down a corner of the page and grab the phone as hopefully as I ever have. But it's not Julie. It's the Yankees. They're calling to tell me they're having a press conference at three o'clock. I couldn't be more disappointed.

I look at the clock, which tells me it's eleven A.M., and I figure I have a good two and a half hours of reading time before I have to get to Yankee Stadium. I pour a fresh glass of water and settle back into the sofa with my copy of *Picking a Shade*.

Thirty-five pages later, there I am. Not quite sure why it took thirty-five pages to get from high school to freshman year of college, but oh well. I am introduced to the members of Oprah's Book Club as Jim Barnes (she didn't even change my name that much, really), and I am pleased to find myself described as "devilishly handsome." A cliché, sure, but a flattering one.

It goes downhill from there.

Jim Barnes occupies eleven pages in Danielle Hall's first novel, and he is nothing short of a clown. He is portrayed alternately as insensitive, clueless, "charmingly naive," and downright stupid. Sure, some of the events in which I am depicted are based in fact, but I think it's fair to say much of it is exaggerated. For instance, I don't remember ever asking Danielle, who was from Iowa (as Ruby is), if all she ate as a kid was corn.

To tell you the truth, I think I was pretty good to Danielle. I think I handled her mood swings well. I made sure she always had an orgasm before I did (though Ruby claims to have faked a few with ol' Jimbo—another potential topic for my impending interview with the author). And I even dealt with her crazy family situation as best I could. Sure, I admit to being a little emotionally underdeveloped at age nineteen. But I would never say "stunted." I had plenty of room to grow, and Danielle could have found that out if we'd stayed together longer than two months.

No, I dispute Ruby Gold, who claims the reason she and Jim Barnes broke up was because he was too immature.

I believe, and always have believed, that the reason Danielle and I broke up was because Danielle was insane.

13 ◇ The Brief, Turbulent History of Danielle

She had red hair, first of all, and because of that—fairly or unfairly—I have been terrified of redheads ever since. Danielle's hair was long and beautiful. It framed an unremarkable freckled face that rarely smiled and it fell to her shoulders. Its color was rich and unbroken, as if she were a cartoon princess on the front of a medieval fantasy book. Or a romance novel.

Danielle and I started out as friends—a big mistake I used to make all the time. In the first three months of freshman year, she dated four different guys, all of whom lived on my floor. For this reason, she was around a lot, and she and I got to do a lot of talking. She was always clear about her lack of romantic interest in me, but we would talk a lot, and she didn't seem to mind filling me in on the details of her troubled life.

It was during this "friends" period that I learned about her family history, which was not good. Pick a major problem, and they'd had it. There were tales of divorce, child abuse, suicide—seriously, just name it. Her parents didn't speak to each other, and she hated two of her four sisters. She was very close with her brother, though she told me there was a story about him that she'd never tell (I wonder if he's in the book). We'd stay up late into the night, talking things over in the floor's lounge. More than once she fell asleep with her head in my lap. On every single one of these occasions, I got an erection.

See, Danielle had the kind of body that makes a hormone-driven freshman guy wonder if there was any other reason to come to college. Its star attraction was her rear end—still the most perfect one I have ever seen, bar none. Remember the children's board game "Trouble," with the little plastic bubble in the middle of the board that made a cute "pop" when you pressed it to roll the dice? Danielle's butt always made me want to do that—press it and see if it would make that noise. It was perfectly shaped, perfectly sized, and the topic of many, many conversations among the guys in my freshman dorm. Once word got around that I was going out with her, my friends literally congratulated me and couldn't refrain from comments about her ass. Usually it's bad form to comment on the ass of your friend's girlfriend, but in this case it couldn't be helped.

So it wasn't tough to figure out where I stood on the "friends" issue. I wanted to be more than friends. Don't we always? But I was good. I was patient, especially for a young man who would later be described as "emotionally stunted," and I waited it out. I had this bizarre theory that all the guys she was dating were assholes and that I would eventually look pretty darn good by comparison. And it turned out, I was right.

Well, not about those guys being assholes. Some of them were actually my friends.

But Danielle's pattern was pretty easy to discern. She'd date a guy for a while, either have sex with him or string him along and let him think she was going to have sex with him, and then wait for him to slip up. I mean, if this guy made the slightest mistake, she'd shut down. She'd cry. She'd mope. Eventually the whole thing would blow up into a huge shouting match and she would end it, probably spending more emotion on the breakup than she'd invested in the relationship in the first place.

She did this four times in the first three months of freshman year. Four times I heard all of the climactic arguments. Four times I heard both sides of the story. And yet, when my turn came, I took it anyway. I was as eager as I could be.

Come to think of it, maybe she's right. Maybe I was stupid.

It started at Thanksgiving, when Danielle informed me that she wasn't going home to Iowa because the flight cost too much and, well, her family wasn't exactly one she was thrilled to rush home to. Appalled, I insisted that she come home with me, on the much more affordable train to New Jersey. I insisted on this without ever checking it with my parents, and she accepted my invitation before I had time to call them and make sure it was okay.

My parents didn't like Danielle at all. My mother has never been thrilled when I have brought home a girl whose own family situation wasn't strong. She worries that I'll end up with someone who didn't have the solid family background that I had and therefore won't appreciate the importance of family in my life. My mother worries a lot. She is, after all, a mother.

But on Thanksgiving weekend, 1990, I was oblivious to such concerns. I saw this grand gesture as a way into Danielle's tight jeans, and I figured everything was going great.

Everybody put on a nice show. Danielle couldn't have been sweeter. My mother was just as sweet in return, and my father was a good host in his own, quiet way. We went to Thanksgiving dinner at my aunt's house, with no fewer than twelve members of my extended family in attendance, and Danielle handled it all brilliantly, with no hint of her fragility. On the train ride back to Virginia, Danielle slept with her head on my shoulder.

We continued on the friends track through December, though there was an increasing amount of physical affection being thrown my way, but when we returned to school from Christmas break, the rules had all changed.

We did what all college students are supposed to do on the first weekend back from vacation—we all went out and got drunk together. Because of this—and because of all the emotional soup in which we found ourselves, Danielle and I ended up lying down in the same bed together at the end of the night. Nothing crazy, we still had all our clothes on and everything, but we just collapsed together on the same bed. Then we kissed for the first time. Then we kissed for the second, third, fourth, fifth, and sixth times. And before you knew it, things got . . . well . . . escalated.

We had hazy, clumsy, drunken sex, at least twice. When we woke up in the morning, naked, in my twin bed (my roommate blessedly absent, off on his own romantic adventure), we did it again, just to make sure we hadn't dreamed it all. From then on, for the next two months, we had sex an average of four times a day. It was insane.

We'd cut class just to have sex on the bare stone floors of our respective dorm rooms. We'd have sex in her bottom bunk bed, quietly, with her roommate sitting on the top bunk and reading. I went to the bathroom at a party and she followed me in. We did it in classrooms. We did it at night on the lawn in front of the dorms.

It was the ultimate example of letting the little head do the thinking. My senses had all come together to focus, with ultimate power, on this one thing that was going on in my life. My grades got their ass kicked. I stopped calling home as much as I used to. When I had to do laundry, I ruined clothes because I left them in the dryer too long while we were having sex on a different dryer.

My roommate and all of my friends, weeks after the initial congratulations, tried to tell me I was an idiot for getting so heavily involved. Their position was that I'd have been better off using her for sex and discarding her before she did to me what she'd done to those four other guys on the floor.

My position was that they had no idea what they were talking about, that I was different from those guys, and that they could all go to hell.

I was in love, or so I thought. More like lust, really. Or porn. Pretty soon we didn't even talk anymore. We just had sex. We tried new positions. She tried different underwear. I mean, wow. I'm getting worked up now, just remembering it.

But of course, it ended, exactly the same way her relationships with those other four guys ended. I said something I thought was harmless, and she took it the wrong way. I tried to make up for it by telling her I loved her, and she looked at me as if I was insane. I chased her across campus, back to her dorm, pleading with her for one more chance. She was granite. I went back the next day. She was basalt. She stopped returning my calls. I went to her room late one night and saw another guy coming out. I was crushed. I retreated to my own room, blew off my own classes, fought with my friends.

She wouldn't see me, wouldn't talk to me, nothing. When I did catch her by surprise, she showed no regret, no sadness, not one single tear over the sad state of our relationship. Here I was, shredded, and she was just moving on, as if nothing happened.

She visited the floor once, months later. Apparently, she was dating another guy from the floor, trying to set some sort of record. I'd heard about it, but she'd been orchestrating her comings and goings so I wouldn't see her.

Fortunately, on the night when I finally did see her, I was drunker than I'd ever been, so I was able to articulate my feelings accurately.

I was sitting propped up against a wall in the hallway, babbling back and forth to my equally hammered friend about something—who knows what? And I remember her coming out of the door to Bill Jenkins's room. She'd dated Bill earlier in the year but was now dating his roommate, Jeremy. She spotted me and looked panicked, but it was too late. I'd already spotted her.

I don't remember the exact words that came out of my mouth. I do remember screaming loud enough to wake the entire floor as she sprinted—literally sprinted—to the exit stairs. I didn't chase her or anything—those days were over. I just spewed a string of drunken invective that must have made an impression, because we didn't see Danielle on the floor again all year.

The next morning, my head throbbing, I heard a knock at the door. Bill Jenkins knocked twice and entered, laughing hysterically.

"Dude," he said to me. "That was some performance."

"What?" I asked, honestly ignorant of what he was talking about.

"With Danielle, man. You really let her have it."

And again, I didn't remember what I'd said, so I was still confused.

" 'Unholy bitch?' " Bill said, laughing harder. " 'Go back to the hell you came from?' That's great stuff, man. Great stuff."

And Bill left. And I looked at my own roommate, Keith, who was sitting at his desk and just nodding at me with his own smile on his face.

I fell back to sleep, unconcerned about the impression I'd made on my floormates, but when I woke I knew I had some patching up to do. Not with Danielle, to whom I never spoke again, but with the aforementioned floormates, who'd only been trying to help. I'd been a real jerk, all because of a girl, and it was time for me to start apologizing.

That was my big freshman year lesson, and I learned it the hard way. When I have occasion to remember the whole affair, I view Danielle as the conduit to that lesson, and nothing more. I learned from her.

I learned never to date redheads.

I learned not to try to go from friends to lovers (though I broke that rule one more time).

I learned to take advice from well-meaning friends, especially ones who've already been burned by the very woman they're trying to warn you about.

What I didn't learn was that, apparently, when you have a bad breakup, it never goes away. Sure, it might lie dormant for a decade or so, but you're bound to run into her sometime down the road, even if it takes her sending you a copy of her novel, in which you're one of the characters, to bring you back together.

That's a nasty lesson, and it's one I'm getting pretty sick of learning.

14

The Yankees know how to throw a press conference. They bring you in, along with fifty or so of your closest colleagues and competitors, and they stuff you so full of food that you end up having to belch your questions. They have carving boards with two different kinds of meat, chicken fingers, pasta, finger sandwiches, and a beautiful tray of desserts from one of the nearby Italian bakeries in the Bronx. You stand around for an hour or so eating and drinking (water and soda, of course—we are, after all, on the job), and then they move you into the main room and bring in the star of the show.

In this case, the star of the show has with him his agent, his glittering fiancée, and both of his parents, all flown in on the owner's private jet from southern California. That's one side of the podium. The other side features the Yankees' manager, GM, team president, and, just because they can, Yogi Berra. They're all here to announce a seven-year contract worth $120 million, and it's hailed as a great and glorious day for baseball's most historic franchise. The big lug smiles for the cameras and even manages to spill a couple of tears. I mean, this is a show. This is the show George Steinbrenner puts on to make himself and his team look good for his fans, and to gloat in front of the twenty-nine other teams who couldn't afford this guy if they mugged Steinbrenner at the ATM. It's silly and forced and overblown, but one of the things the people love about sports is spectacle, so we're here to give the people what they want.

The reason it's tough for me to enjoy this whole thing is that my mind is, obviously, elsewhere. I'm plotting my big speech to Amy. I'm deciding whether or not to call Danielle before I finish the book, and therefore violate my earlier vow. And I'm wondering why, in the twenty-seven hours since I ambushed her on a rain-drenched midtown sidewalk, Julie Gordon has not dialed the smudged phone number on the back of that receipt.

A subway ride, a rainy three-block walk, and three flights of stairs (what is with that elevator, anyway?), and I am home. I can't even imagine how distracted I'd have been at the press conference had I known of the bounty that awaited me. There are four—count 'em, four—messages on my machine. I never get four messages. I doubt I even have four friends. This is something. Casting my waterlogged notebook aside, I press the button and hope.

Beep.

"*Hey, Jack, it's Amy, returning your call. I'm glad you called, and sure, I can do lunch. I don't know if you had a day in mind, but you can call me back at work if you want and we'll set something up. I'm actually not far from you, I don't think, over on Columbus and 67th. It's 555-4306, and I'll talk to you soon. Okay? Bye.*"

Beep.

"*Hey, dude, it's Bernie. Just want to know what you're up to tonight. I was gonna go over to Blondie's. I think Kentucky-Duke is on. Anyway, if you want to go, gimme a call. See ya.*"

Beep.

Silence, and that 504 area code on the caller ID again.

Beep.

"Um, yeah. I hope I have the right number. Jack, this is Julie Gordon. We met yesterday? On the street corner? Oh God, now I really hope I have the right number. Anyway, if this is Jack, and I hope it is, um, well, I told you I'd call you. I wanted to thank you for my welcome to New York. It was a lot different than I expected, but it was definitely interesting. And I'm sorry I didn't call sooner, but it's been busy. Anyway, I'm at the Marriott Marquis in Times Square, and I'm here until Monday morning. So if you want to call, give me a call here, and maybe I'll take you up on dinner. Okay? So, I guess I'll talk to you soon, maybe. And if this isn't Jack, I'm sorry to leave this rambling message on your answering machine. Okay. 'Bye."

Joy.

Sheer, unabated joy.

That is, without a doubt, the most exciting answering machine message I have ever received.

Another frantic flip through the Manhattan white pages, and I find the number for the Marriott. I dial it, ask for Julie Gordon's room and actually pump my fist when the operator says "Just a moment" and transfers me. The phone rings three times, and I start to panic, but it doesn't last long.

"Hello?" she says, and my smile is wide enough to swallow the phone.

"Hi, Julie?"

"Yes?"

"Julie, it's Jack Byrnes. From yesterday? The cab?"

"Oh, hey, Jack," she says. "Boy, that was quick."

"Yeah, I just got back home. Just got back."

Now it gets awkward. We are, after all, perfect strangers.

And since she probably hasn't been sitting around for the last two days planning our future together, as I have, a proposal is probably a little too forward for this, our first phone conversation.

"So," I say, swinging my left arm and pacing in small circles. "How did your interview go?"

"Oh, it was good, thanks. I think I'm going to get the job."

"Wow, that's great. What's the job?"

"I'll be a writer for the magazine. Write features on celebrities and stuff like that, you know. Silly stuff, but fun."

"No, it sounds great," I say. "Not silly at all."

"Well, thanks," she says, and I'm in love with her voice. Like honey pouring out of the receiver and drizzling down onto my shoulder. "I'm a little intimidated by the idea of living in New York, but I guess it's exciting."

"Where are you from?"

"L.A."

"Well, that's not exactly Iowa," I say. For some reason Iowa just popped into my head. "I mean, it's not like city life will be new to you."

"No, you're right," she says. "But New York is different, you know?"

"Oh I know."

"How long have you lived here?"

"About three years. Moved from Boston. Even that was a big adjustment."

"Oh, I'm sure."

"So this is your first time in New York?" I ask, knowing the answer. "You seen anything good?"

"No, I feel like a slug. I was so tired from my flight that I got back here after the interview and went right to sleep. Slept all night. I know it's lame."

"Well, it sounds like you've got a few more nights to make up for it, no?"

"Yeah, I really don't know what I'm doing," she says. "I guess if I'd been thinking ahead, I would have bought tickets to a show or something."

"Well, so now I know you're free for dinner tomorrow night," I say.

"Yes," she says. "Yes, I am totally free for dinner, and I'm looking for a New Yorker to pick me out an outstanding restaurant. *People* magazine is picking up the tab, so all you have to do is tell me where to be and when. Cheapest date you ever had."

"Wow," I say. "Sounds good to me. I'll call some places and see where we can get in. Any particular place or kind of food you had in mind?"

"I'll eat anything. And the swankier the better."

"All right. Well, I guess I'll call you tomorrow, then, when I know where we're going."

"Sounds good to me. I'll be around all day, seeing some sights, but you can leave me a message here at the front desk. I'll check back in for them."

Sure. I can't imagine she's ready to give me her cell phone number.

"I tell you what," I say, trying to make it easier. "Why don't you call me tomorrow, around two o'clock. By then I'll know where we're going, and you won't have to worry about going back to your hotel to check your messages."

"That sounds good," she says.

"Cool," I say. "So where are you off to tonight?"

"I'm going to see where the night takes me. Wander around New York a bit. I'm sure I'll find plenty to do."

"I'm sure you will."

"Okay, then, Jack, just call me tomorrow."

"No, you're calling me."

"Oh, right, I'll call you tomorrow. I'm looking forward to it."

"Me too," I say. "This time I'll try to look like I haven't been standing in the rain all day."

She laughs.

"All right," she says. "Sounds good. Thanks for calling."

"Thank *you* for calling," I say, and I want to tell her she made my day. But right now we're playing it cool. Or at least trying. "And I'll see you tomorrow."

" 'Bye."

" 'Bye."

And I hang up the phone and begin dancing.

Now, I've spent a good portion of my life being a lovestruck sap, so I know the signs. I understand that I have to calm down a bit and deal with the other aspects of my life. So once I'm out of breath from the soft-shoe on the hardwood floor, I take stock. I have to call Amy back. I have to write my story. I have to call Bernie, though I could probably just meet him at Blondie's. And Danielle Hall's book is still sitting on my desk, reminding me of all the work that still must be done.

Ideally, I'd clear all the ghosts out before I ever sat across a clean white tablecloth from Julie Gordon. I'd have a quick, efficient lunch to clear the decks with Amy, call Danielle to ask the lipstick question and maybe even hop a flight to New Orleans to surprise ol' Mary Ann. Then, I'd be free and clear for Julie, who deserves my full attention.

Problem is, she's leaving town in three days. And while she is moving back to New York, it wouldn't hurt me to establish a foothold. So I will have to go on my first date with the future Mrs. Byrnes with all of this other past-relationship stuff still hanging in the air. No problem. I can hack it. No chance of the Linda Lane episode repeating itself. I may be a dumbass, but I can learn my lessons.

I look at the clock. Four-thirty. I'm guessing Amy's still at work. I call and get her voice mail.

"Amy, it's Jack. Tag, you're it. I was thinking Sunday for lunch, and I can come to you, since my schedule's more flexible. So, call me back and let me know if that works, and what time. All right? Thanks."

I'd do the Amy lunch tomorrow, but tomorrow is Julie Day. She at least deserves the day all to herself.

Next, I call Bernie, who is home. No big shock there, since he has no job.

"Hey, man."

"Hey, what are you doing?"

"Yeah, I was out. Yankees had their press conference today."

"Aha. How was it?"

"All right. Dog-and-pony show, you know."

"Was his girlfriend there? I saw a picture of her in the *Post* this morning. She's hot."

"Yeah, she was there. And yes. She's hot."

"Sweet."

"So anyway, I've got to hack this story out, but yeah, Blondie's sounds good. You going to eat first or eat there?"

"Figure I'll eat there. Get some wings, a burger."

"Sounds good to me, man. If you get there first, grab a table. I should be there by the time the game starts."

"Cool."

"All right. See ya later."

"See ya."

And for a second after I hang up I wonder what would have happened if Bernie had gone to the press conference. I wonder if the slugger's fiancée would have fallen for Bernie. I've seen it before, of course. I've seen women leave the men they were with to go home with Big Bern. But I've never seen it happen with a girl whose fiancé just signed for $120 million. Got to think that'd be a pretty strong pull.

Everything filed for the night, I run a comb through my hair, throw in a dab of gel, slap on some cologne, and head out for Blondie's, where soon twenty-four small chicken bones, picked clean, are sitting between Bernie and myself. We're out of napkins, and the checkered tablecloth bears stains of hot sauce and bleu cheese dressing, but Blondie's wings are good, and we're actually discussing whether we should order more.

"Well, let me ask you this," says Bernie, who downed a cheeseburger and fries before I even showed up. "How late are we gonna be out?"

"Why?" I ask.

"Well, you know. Sustenance."

"So I take it you're taking another night off from the ladies?"

"I don't know," he says through a smile. "Sometimes I like to make it tough on them. I mean, if she can dig me after a burger and two plates of wings, that really means something, you know?"

"I guess," I say, laughing and flagging down the waitress. "One more pile of wings, hot, please. And you'd better bring another pitcher. This could get ugly."

The waitress, slim and blond and dressed in a short black skirt, has stared at Bernie the entire time I've been placing this order, and Bernie is smiling right back up at her. I wonder if she even heard me.

"Um," I say. "Bern, is that all right?"

"Sure," Bernie says to the waitress. "Another two dozen wings, and the beer to go with. Thanks."

He winks at her, which is apparently the sign for their eye contact to end, and she walks off in search of our order.

"I don't know," Bernie says. "I think she's new."

Bernie has been making his way, for some time now, through the female service personnel in every bar on the Upper West Side. He denies this, but I swear he must have a checklist in his apartment.

According to Bernie, waitresses are easy targets. "Batting practice," he calls them. He has told me that, on nights when he just doesn't feel like putting in the effort, he'll lock in on a waitress because he knows all he has to do is stay to the end of her shift and he's got a guarantee.

It sounds twisted, sure, but remember, Bernie always treats his ladies well. I've never seen one throw a drink in his face. Bernie says this is no coincidence.

"As long as you don't make any promises, you treat them with respect, and you give them a call to let them know you had fun, it's really not that hard," he says. "Guys who don't call are worried the girl will latch on. Most of the time, I find they don't want to latch on. I pick up a girl in a bar, odds are she's there for the same reason I am—to find somebody to go home with, period."

I treasure Bernie's wisdom. I make every effort to live by it when I'm fortunate enough to collect some. Bernie is somebody to whom I can spill my guts about my love life without fear of him making fun. I can do that with Jeff too, but Jeff's not here.

That reminds me.

"Hey, is Jeff coming out?" I ask Bernie.

"Nah," he says, after a swallow of Guinness. "Anna."

"Oh . . . getting serious, huh?"

"I don't know, man. He's whipped. Says she's some kind of goddess."

"You meet her yet?"

Bernie shakes his head.

"He won't introduce me," he says. "I don't know why."

"He's afraid she'll take a liking to you."

"Ah, bullshit," Bernie says, but he's smiling when he says it, and he probably agrees.

"Anyway, she's pretty much as unbelievable as he says she is," I say. "I dropped my keys the first time I saw her."

"Dropped your keys?"

"Yeah. The two of them were hanging out in my apartment when I got home the other night, and I saw her when I walked in. I guess I was staring and I dropped my keys. Made Jeff laugh, but she just kind of shrugged it off. Like it happens all the time."

"Wow," Bernie says, mulling this. "Wow. I've got to meet her. See what this is all about."

"I'm guessing Jeff puts that off until after he marries her," I say. "Just to be sure."

"Whatever," Bernie says. "So how are things with you? Hear from your high school girlfriend yet?"

"You know, that's not funny, but almost," I say. "Girl I dated freshman year in college."

"Get out! I was kidding."

I tell him the Danielle story while he sucks another wing clean.

"So, what? This is a coincidence?" he asks.

"Not at all," I say. "She wrote something on the inside front cover—to me. Addressed to me. It's a book about all the relationships she's had in her life, and she writes, 'Jack, guess which one is you.' Is that insane?"

"Dude, this is getting out of hand."

"I know!"

"You read the book?"

"I started to. I actually got to the part with the character based on me. Not real happy with the portrayal."

Bernie laughs, and wipes his mouth as the waitress comes back with the beer. This time she stares at him some more, but no conversation has yet been initiated. Bernie's technique is measured and predictable, and he knows she's not going anywhere unless she checks with him first. Right now I'm the one who has his attention.

"So," he says. "What else is going on?"

I tell him about dinner with Connie, and I tell him about my plans to do the same thing with Amy. I tell him I plan to do Danielle's debriefing by phone, since I have no immediate plans to go to Ohio. And I admit that I have looked into the cost of a plane ticket to New Orleans, where Mary Ann lives.

"In all the zombie movies, the key to killing the zombies was always to take out the first one—the head zombie," I explain, feeling the Guinness for the first time in the night. "Way I see it, she started all this in that airport. Maybe if I go and hash it out with her, the rest of them will stop coming after me."

"I don't know about that," says Bernie, who now has had more than half the wings on the plate but is somehow no less attractive to the wait staff and the woman sitting in the next booth. "But I like the plan. I like the idea, about trying to get closure. Put the relationships behind you, you know? Clear out the trash. I like it. I hope it works."

Through all of this, it has been physically painful to keep the story of Julie Gordon concealed. But I've done it intentionally. I'm dying to tell Bernie about her. But I also want her to be the dominant topic of our conversation for the rest of the evening. So I've saved her for after the questions about the ghosts.

Now, it is time.

"But I haven't told you the best part of all this crap," I say.

"Oh yeah? What's that?"

"I met a new girl."

And I grin, and let this take hold.

"Get out!" Bernie says. "Really? Man you've been holding out on us. Let's hear the scoop."

And I tell the story. About the cab, and the rain, and the

phone number on the ATM receipt. Bernie is howling. Even he has never been so up-front bold as to accost a total stranger as she got out of a cab.

"You must have scared the hell out of her!" he says.

"That's what I thought," I say. "But she called."

"She called?"

"Yep. She called tonight. We're having dinner tomorrow night."

"No shit!"

"No shit."

"Wow," Bernie says. "That may be better than the Fairway story."

"Bern, I don't know what it is, but I'm going crazy over this girl. I've only seen her once, for about two minutes, but I can't stop thinking about her."

"What's she look like?"

"Beautiful," I say. "Just beautiful."

"Oh, man. Don't go all Jeff on me."

"Yeah, I know," I say. "But that's why I've got to see her again. To see if it's really real, you know? Like love at first sight, or whatever?"

Bernie is now actually giggling at me.

"No, I'm serious," I protest. "It just felt so cool, talking to her on the phone. So who knows? We'll see how tomorrow night goes. But man, I tell you. I'm going nuts over this one."

"You know what I see?" Bernie says. "I see a man who doesn't learn his lessons. If I were in the advice business, I might advise you to tone it down a little here. At least until you see her for a second time."

"I know you're right, but I just can't help it. Anyway, whatever. We'll see. Let's just say I'm fired up."

"Good for you, man," Bernie says. "Good for you. I hope it works out. I really do. I'm just saying, you know?"

"Oh, I know."

* * *

Duke is killing Kentucky, and we decide to play some Golden Tee. The machine is near the waitress stand, and Bernie gets to share glances with the new girl as he kicks my ass in video golf. They still haven't talked.

But within an hour, once we're back in the booth, another waitress comes over to talk to Bernie. This one's a redhead who does not appear to have qualified for Bernie's checklist. Does not appear to know him.

She does, however, know the new girl, and she apparently carries a message.

"My friend wanted to know if you're single," she tells Bernie.

Startled by the indirect approach, Bernie turns to look for the friend in question. Our waitress is nowhere to be found.

"Your friend?" he asks.

"Yeah. Sherri. The new waitress. The one who's been serving you. Wanted to know if you're single."

"Sure," Bernie says, a little mystified and looking around for Sherri.

"Okay," the redhead says, and walks away.

Five minutes later Sherri is sitting next to Bernie in our booth. Her shift is over, and she is eager to find out what the inside of Bernie's apartment looks like. It has become obvious that we will not be staying until the end of the basketball game, so I tell the happy couple that I must head home, and I leave forty dollars on the table to help cover the food and beer.

I assume Bernie will be leaving the tip.

"It's okay, man," Bernie says as I'm getting up. "I got it."

"Come on. You got lunch the other day. Don't worry."

"You sure?"

"Yeah, I'm sure," I say, sliding into my coat. "I'll call you tomorrow, all right?"

"Thanks. Take care," Bernie says.

" 'Bye," Sherri says.

And, wishing I could stay to see how it turns out, I head out the door and back home for the night. All the while smiling.

Tomorrow is Julie Day.

15

I'm in the middle of a dream when I hear the key in the front door, and for once I'm happy to have Jeff wake me up.

See, this dream was no good. Oh, it started out fine. It was a dream about Julie, and in it she and I were having a wonderful dinner at Aureole, a charming midtown French place that serves some of the best food in the whole city. We were seated at a romantic table upstairs, sharing a bottle of wine and smiling, when all of a sudden I looked over at the next table, and Amy and a man I took to be her husband were sitting there eating their dinners. They both looked at me, and I yelled.

Julie wanted to know what was wrong, but I was incapable of telling her, because I looked to the other side of our table and saw Danielle eating with Mary Ann. I screamed again, and I heard the waitress ask if everything was okay. I looked up and saw that the waitress was Connie. Another yell, and this time I may have actually yelled out loud and woken myself up.

"That you?" I hear Jeff call from the living room. "You okay?"

And I still need a moment to compose myself, but I manage to holler back, "Yeah, I'm all right. Be out in a minute."

After a few minutes, I throw on my robe and head out into the living room, where I am greeted by the increasingly familiar smell of Krispy Kreme.

"Hey," Jeff says, by way of greeting. He is stretched out on the sofa and watching cartoons. This is how I remember it's Saturday. If it were a weekday, Jeff would be watching the *Today* show, because Jeff has always thought Katie Couric was hot. I don't get it, myself, but he's not alone.

" 'Morning," I say, and head for the fridge and my orange juice. "Missed you last night."

"Yeah, sorry," Jeff says. "We stayed in, rented a movie."

"Which movie?" I ask, trying to start something.

"Ah, just a movie. You know."

"Yeah, but which one?"

"All right, all right. It was *Sliding Doors.*"

"Sliding Doors?" I ask. "That's a chick flick."

"Trust me," he says. "I know."

"Maybe Bernie's right. I think you're whipped."

"I am not," he says, but not quite as firmly as he would normally say it. "And hey, so what if I am? Least I'm getting some around here."

"Touché," I tell him, then I swat his legs away so I can sit on my own couch. "And how is the lovely Anna?"

"Pretty good, man," Jeff says, looking me in the eyes. "Pretty damn good. You know, I think I really like this girl."

"That's great, man," I say. "Great to hear. You guys going steady?"

"Bite me."

"All right. Think whatever you want to think. But I'm happy for you. I was about to offer you one of my old girlfriends, just to get one off the boards."

"Yeah," he says. "How's that going?"

And I fill him in on Julie, and he offers some of the same warnings Bernie was offering a few hours ago. I tell him of my plans to have lunch with Amy tomorrow, to get her out of the way. I also tell him that I left Bernie in a booth with a Blondie's waitress, and this is the story he finds most intriguing.

"I wonder when we get the rest of the story," he says.

"I don't know, but I'm eager to hear it."

"Let's call him," he says, scrambling for my phone and dialing. A few seconds, and he's got an answer.

"Big Bern!" he literally shouts into the phone. "I wake you?"

For some reason, Bernie does not hang up on Jeff.

"You alone?" Jeff asks. "Yes? What do you mean, yes? Our man here tells me you got picked up by the waitress. Or the waitress's friend, more like it . . . Yeah, I'm over here at Jack's. Yeah? . . . Sweet! . . . See you in a little bit."

Jeff hangs up the phone with a big grin.

"He's coming over," he says. "Says he's got a good story for us."

"Oh yeah?"

"Said he'll run down the whole thing when he gets here. I wish I'd brought more doughnuts."

"He'll probably pick up his own on the way," I say.

Meanwhile, I'm heading to the cabinet to fix myself a bowl of cereal, and Jeff is turning on the PlayStation.

"I'm going to be the Vikings again," he said. "Just can't stand to let Randy Moss go."

We're midway through the third quarter of a tie game when Bernie comes in.

"Hey, man," we both say, staring at the screen and maniacally pressing buttons.

"Hey," Bernie says, and I turn my head long enough to see him holding a bag of Krispy Kremes. "Who's winning?"

"Tied," we both say.

"Well, you might want to pause it. This is good."

This must be good. Bernie never kisses and tells. We rarely even get snippets, and we almost never get full-blown stories. The last story I remember was the one about his night with a Rockette. Guess he figured he owed that one to posterity.

"All right," I say, and pause the game.

"Dude!" Jeff says. "I was about to score!"

"So you can score later," I say. "Bernie's got a story."

Jeff is angry, but he wants the story as badly as I do. Bernie splashes down into the armchair and leans forward, like Uncle Remus.

"So, you know everything up until Jack left the bar, right?" he begins.

"Right," we say in unison.

"So anyway, as soon as Jack's gone, this girl starts kissing me. Right there in the booth. I mean, she's all over me. I was pretty surprised, and so were the people in the next booth. I mean, I'm not exactly the kind of guy who slides into these booths comfortably, even when I'm by myself. So this was like a seismic event we're talking about here.

"So, I don't want to push her away or anything, but I kind of back away from one of the kisses and ask her what's going on. She says, 'I want you to take me home. Now.' "

Jeff actually squeaks.

"So we go over to my place, and as soon as we're in the door she's taking off her clothes."

"She hot?" Jeff asks, unable to contain himself.

"She was hot," Bernie says. "Nice body. Very nice."

Jeff squeaks again.

"We don't even say three words to each other, and we're having sex. She was something else too. Screaming, yelling . . . felt like she could've gone all night."

"Bern? Some details we don't need," I say.

"Sorry. Anyway, we finish, and I pass out. Guess I had

more Guinness than I thought. A few hours later, I wake up. She's shaking me. Telling me to wake up. It's 3:45 in the morning. I'm wondering what the hell's going on, and I sit up and ask her.

"She tells me, 'I've got to go home.' And I say, 'Why?' She says, 'Just walk me home, okay?'

"So I'm thinking, all right. This is a little weird, but if it's what she wants, fine. I ask her where she lives, it's like five blocks away, no problem. I have to get dressed, and we're out the door. So on the walk to her place, she tells me the reason she sent her friend over was because she wanted to make sure I was 'up for it' last night. Wanted to make sure I didn't already have something lined up. Tells me the other girls were telling her she had to 'try me out,' that it was going to be the best she ever had. Tells me all this!

"So I'm trying to figure out what to say back, but she just keeps talking. Tells me it was great. Says it was 'everything she needed.' Then she tells me not to call her. Ever. So I say, 'Ever?' and she says, 'Never.' Of course, I ask why, and she tells me she only wanted it to be a one-night stand. Says she'd be embarrassed to run into me again, so would I mind not coming into Blondie's on the nights she works? Says if she sees me, she's not going to talk to me. We're supposed to pretend we've never met."

"I don't get it," Jeff says.

"Well, me neither," Bernie says. "So I ask for more of an ex-planation. She tells me she can't explain. That all she wanted was a no-strings, one-night thing. Just sex. Says she wouldn't have even told me her name if she didn't think she had to. Says she's always wanted to have a one-night stand with a to-tal stranger and never see him again. I guess I was a good can-didate."

"Wow," I say. "I don't really know what to say to that."

"Yeah," Bernie says. "Weird."

Thing is, he's not smiling. He has slouched back into the chair, and he's not looking at either one of us as he chews on his thumbnail.

"Are you okay?" I ask.

"Oh, yeah," he says, laughing a little and looking at me, finally, as if just now realizing I'm in the room. "I'm totally fine. Just thought it was a weird story and I needed to hear myself tell it."

"Wow," Jeff offers, then nothing.

"Anyway, there you guys go," Bernie says, slapping his palms against his massive thighs and hoisting himself out of the chair. "Your present for waking me up so early. I'm gonna go hit golf balls, if anybody wants to come."

"Yeah, I'll go," Jeff says.

"I gotta pass, guys," I say. "Got work to do."

"All right," Bernie says. "Well, we'll catch you later. And don't worry, we'll figure out a new place if I can't go to Blondie's anymore."

We all laugh at that one, but again Bernie doesn't look thrilled. He and Jeff leave, and I start to try and figure out my day.

Amy calls at noon, interrupting the scene in the book in which Ruby Gold meets the man she believes is going to be different from all the rest. Amy wants to have lunch tomorrow at noon, because "George has a thing to go to, and I don't have to meet him until three."

George . . . George . . . Oh, right. The fiancé.

Perfect, I tell her. Noon it is, at the City Café on 72nd and Columbus. I look forward to getting this one over with.

I kind of want to go for a walk, but I feel like I have to be here in case Julie calls before her appointed time of two o'clock. I don't want to miss her call. Plus, I think I can wrap up *Picking a Shade* by then and start formulating my plan for

ambushing its author with an out-of-the-blue "interview request."

Julie and I are set at Oceana at 7:45. It's hard to believe I
could get a table on such short notice, but this time fate must
be working in my favor. Yeah. Fate. Remember back when I
didn't believe in it? Well, obviously that's changed. Way I see
it, fate owed me one, and the reservation at Oceana at quarter to eight on a Saturday night in November is a pretty nice
gift.

She calls at 2:03 P.M., an hour after I have finished the sappy
final chapter of Danielle Hall's first novel, and I am glad, because a fourth minute of staring at the phone in outright
panic might have been unhealthy.

"Jack?"

"Speaking," I say, knowing for sure who it is but still trying
to play it cool. I mean outwardly.

"It's Julie Gordon."

"Oh, hey Julie. How's your day in the city?"

"It is a nice day, but it's been stressful. I'm apartment-
hunting."

"Oh, really? That is stressful. Hey, if you need the name of
a good realtor, I have a friend in the business."

"That'd be great, actually," she says. "I have no idea if these
people are screwing me or not. And what's this broker's fee I
keep hearing about? Is that for real?"

"Sadly, yes," I say. "That's for real. You're really not going to
find a decent apartment in the city without paying a broker's
fee."

"It's outrageous," she says. "Fifteen percent of the year's
rent."

It is, in fact, outrageous. But it's a fact of New York life. We
all keep telling ourselves we're paying for the neighborhood,
not the shockingly small space.

"Yeah," I say. "You can probably talk them down to twelve or thirteen percent, but you're still paying. It's basically extortion. But like I said, you gotta do it."

"Well, anyway, I may have found a place. We can talk about it tonight on our date."

I love that she's calling it a date.

"Yes," I say. "Our date. Our date is at 7:45 at Oceana, which is on 54th between Madison and Park."

"Oh, I think I walked past that today," she says.

"You were apartment-hunting in midtown?"

"I went there to see one place. It wasn't very good. Anyway, the restaurant looked nice. Seafood?"

"Yes, it's seafood. Is that all right?"

"Perfect," she says. "I love seafood. I'll see you there at quarter to eight."

"Great," I say. "And I'll bring the number of that realtor."

"Oh, that would be wonderful. Thanks."

"So, see you later, then," I say.

"Yep. See you later. 'Bye."

" 'Bye."

And I'm dancing again.

This is a real date, one I orchestrated through my own appalling bravery, and I plan to maintain the confidence I showed outside that cab. She liked it, and hopefully she's going to continue to like it. And if she does, I'll keep dancing by myself in my apartment every time I hang up the phone.

I bounce out the door of my building at ten after seven. No way I'm going to be late for this one. I've got a suit and tie on, and I hope Julie realized it's a dressy place.

On my way to the subway, I run into Paolo, the barber, who is holding hands with none other than Linda Lane, the Fairway Girl.

"Hay mun!" Paolo says. "Hayoodoong?"

"Hey, Paolo," I say. "Linda. What's happening?"

"Eh?" Paolo asks, looking perplexed. "You noehr? You noeechatha?"

"Yeah, I know Linda," I say, extending my hand for her to shake, which she does. "How are you?"

"I'm great, Jack," Linda says. "Good to see you again."

It's a little uncomfortable, considering that our last miserable date was the last time we spoke. But she does seem to be happy. She certainly looks fantastic—all in black, of course—and she and Paolo are smiling at each other like teenagers in love.

"Iz fanny, eh?" Paolo says. "Suchabeek ceety, bat lack, so smull, eh?"

"Yeah, isn't that funny?" I say. "How long have you guys been . . . together?"

Knowing, of course, that it can't be a week.

"We just met the other day," Linda says. "He saved my life."

"Excuse me?" I ask. Paolo is clearly embarrassed.

"No, no, no—" he's saying, but Linda cuts him off.

"He saved my life," she says again. "He dragged me back onto the curb before a truck would have hit me. I had my headphones on, wasn't paying attention, and I'd have been killed if he hadn't been there to drag me back."

"No, no," Paolo says. "Eet was lackey, dassuhl. Lack."

"I think it was fate," Linda says, smiling at the barber and squeezing his arm.

"Wow," I say, lost for any other words. "Wow."

"Yeah, isn't it amazing?" she says. "You never know, I guess."

"Well, I hate to do this, but I'm actually on my way to dinner," I say.

"Oh, that's okay," Linda says. "We're on our way out too."

"But I'm sure I'll run into you guys again," I say. "It was great to see you."

"Great to see you too, Jack," she says. "Have a nice dinner."

"You too," I say, already heading toward the subway.

"Ciao," Paolo calls back at me.

"Ciao," Linda Lane says, with a giggle.

And I can't help but smile at them. Isn't that great? Everybody's falling in love.

I am standing by the bar on Oceana's top floor at seven-forty. It's a small bar but, like the rest of the place, impeccable. The tables are arranged perfectly. The liquor bottles behind the bar are in perfect order. There's a large blue marlin mounted on the wall high above the bar, and the ceiling vaults up almost out of sight. It's beautiful, but it all disappears when Julie Gordon walks up the stairs in a sleeveless blue dress that I don't think I'll ever forget.

I wave my hand to get her attention, and she smiles as she walks over to join me. She has a small black purse in her hands and pearl earrings in her ears. She is beautiful, as I remembered, and there can be no more doubt. Based on the feeling in my stomach, I am, once again, in love.

"Hello," she says, giving me her right hand to shake. I have to keep remembering that this is only the second time we've met.

"Hello yourself," I say. "You look beautiful."

"Well, thank you," she says, looking me in the eye. "You clean up okay yourself."

"Oh, thanks," I say. "I thought about jumping in the shower with all my clothes on right before I left home, just so you'd recognize me, but . . ."

And this gets a laugh, and she orders a glass of wine, and everything seems to be going well.

I can't really explain what it is about Julie that has me so head-over-heels after such little exposure. Our date is fantastic. The conversation is so easy and so lively that I can't believe it's a first date. There is none of the standard first-date discomfort, no awkward pauses, no touchy subjects accidentally uncovered. She is inquisitive, engaging and unpredictable in conversation, and I'm thrilled that she's as comfortable with me as I feel with her.

Her apartment-hunting stories aren't very good. The place she found that she thought she liked sounds like a ripoff and is not within easy subway access of my own, so I decide I'm going to offer a sermon on the virtues of the Upper West Side. Chief among these virtues is my friend Will, the aforementioned realtor, who I assure her can meet with her tomorrow afternoon and show her some places in the neighborhood. (Probably should have checked that with Will, but oh well.) I also offer her my take on East Side vs. West Side, which is that the former is a great place to live, work, and hang out in bars if you're twenty-three years old and recently out of college. The crowd on the West Side is more subdued, more adult, more peaceful in a lot of ways.

"More boring, it sounds like you're trying to say," she says.

"No, no, no," I say. "Not at all." But she's laughing.

"I was just trying to see if I could get you fired up," she says.

"Seriously, though, when I go to bars on the East Side, I feel old. I feel like everybody around me is twenty-two and trying to hook up, and that really isn't my scene."

"Mine neither," she says. "But how old are you?"

I look at my watch.

"Thirty on Monday," I say.

"Wow," she says. "Bummer, huh?"

"Yeah. I'm really trying not to think about it, to tell you the truth."

"Well, why not?" she asks. "It's really not such a big deal, is it?"

"I guess not. Everybody tells me forty is a lot worse, and I'm sure it is. It's just . . . I'm going to miss that 'two.'"

"The two?"

"Yeah," I say. "You know. I've had that 'two' there as the first digit for, you know, ten years. I really don't want it to be a 'three' all of a sudden. Just doesn't seem right."

"I guess I can see your point," she says. "I've still got almost a year, so I guess I'll know what you're talking about when it gets closer."

"When's your birthday?" I ask.

"September fifteenth," she says. "You going to write it in your datebook?"

And we both laugh, but the thing is, I probably will. I find myself wishing she was still going to be around on Monday, for a birthday dinner.

We say good-bye outside the restaurant as I hail her a cab and promise I will call her in the morning to get her in touch with Will. She offers a hug this time, instead of a handshake, and as we pull apart I take her right hand in mine, bring it to my lips and kiss it.

Never did that before.

But she seems to have liked it, and as her cab pulls away, I'm already trying to figure out if I've ever had a date on which everything went so perfectly.

16

The City Grill is not very good, and I'm starting to wonder why
I picked it when Amy walks in, fifteen minutes late, and I remember that she picked it. Fair enough. At least I won't be to blame when we can't get anybody to come over and take our order.

I bounced out of bed this morning, so happy about the way last night went that I crumpled the old gray piece of paper and threw it in the wastebasket. I actually stomped down on the wastebasket with my foot to make sure it stayed in there, and I thought about calling off the lunch with Amy and going apartment-hunting with Will and Julie. But the lunch with Amy is important. If I ever want to have a real relationship again, I need to dedicate myself to the Relationship Ghost Experiment. Besides, it never hurt anybody to play a little hard-to-get. And I'm certainly not worried about Julie running off with Will, whose tastes run more masculine.

Last night was probably the best night's sleep I've had in a while. Could be because of the wine, but it also could be that a sense of calm is starting to creep into my hectic life. There were no messages on the machine when I got in—just that same 504 number on the caller ID, which by now I figure is either Mary Ann too scared to leave a message or a telemarketer who won't give up—and I drifted off with happy thoughts of Julie and her blue dress.

When I woke, a little after nine o'clock, I called Will, who was awake and (again, Fate paying me back) said he was totally free this afternoon between twelve and two. I waited an hour to call Julie (who knows how late she sleeps?), but when I did she told me she'd been up for a while and had just returned from the hotel gym.

"Wow," I said. "Good for you."

"That's the idea," she said.

"Well, anyway, I have that number for you. The real estate guy?"

"Oh, right," she said. "Let me get a pen."

I gave her the number, and she thanked me, and for a second I thought we were going to hang up without saying anything about last night. I was panicked. And then . . .

"Oh, hey, by the way," came that pretty voice.

"Yes?" I said.

"Thanks again for last night. I had a really great time."

"Oh, please," I said. "Thank you. I had a great time too. And I guess we should thank *People* magazine too, right?"

"Yes," she said, laughing. "Yes we should. Anyway, I'll call you and let you know how I made out with the apartments."

"Sounds good," I said. "And good luck."

"Thanks. 'Bye."

Hear that? She had a *really great* time. Not a 'nice' time, or even a 'good' time. No, the time she had with me was *really great*. This is a good thing. This is a very good thing. This is a *really great* thing.

I danced over to the kitchen to pour myself some cereal, and I made a mess, dancing while I ate it.

So, it was from that state of mind that I had to rouse my-self and get ready for what would assuredly be a painful lunch with Amy. Not painful in the same, emotional way the Connie dinner was painful. No, this would be painful in the old, Amy-style way—where I was the only one feeling any-thing and she was stunned that I cared at all. I was not look-ing forward to this, but I am nothing if not determined, and so here I was, at the City Grill at precisely twelve o'clock, knowing she'd be late.

Once she shows up and we're seated, I tell her the whole story, starting with Mary Ann in the airport, running right through my chance meetings with Connie, with her, with Nikki McGowan. I tell her about Danielle Hall's book and even about Linda Lane, the Fairway girl. I even tell her Linda is now dating my barber. I leave out any mention of Julie Gor-don, because that's none of Amy's business, and I sum up by telling her I've decided to meet with all these women of my past in the hopes of clearing them out of my mind, so that I can get on with a successful and string-free romantic future.

And when I finish, she just stares at me. This look she has, the one that tells me I'm making no sense to her. It still pisses me off.

"But," she says, finally, "you and I never went out."

"Oh, I know that," I say. "You don't have to tell me that. In fact, that was the central issue in every problem we ever had, if I remember right."

"But," she says, still dead serious and probably wondering how she can get the hell out of here, "that was all your fault. I didn't do anything wrong there. You always knew how I felt."

"Right," I say. "But I guess sometimes I wonder if I did a good enough job telling you how I felt. I guess sometimes I've thought back on you and wondered if everything could have been different if I'd handled things in a different way."

"What do you mean, everything could have been different?"

"Look, Amy. Somebody asks me, 'Who's your one that got away?' and you're the answer. You're the one girl, of all the girls to whom I've ever had any emotional attachment, that really sticks in my craw, you know?"

"Excuse me?"

"No, not like a bad thing," I say. "Not like I'm pissed off and bothered. It's just, when I do remember . . . us, I always have this feeling like it should have been different. Like, I always wonder what it would have been like if we'd given it a chance."

"I don't believe this," she says, pushing back her chair, standing, reaching for her coat. "I don't believe you're still not over this. It's been what? Five years, at least?"

Mayday.

"Amy, look," I say. "I *am* over it. That's what I'm trying to tell you. It's just that, there's this lingering thing, and I need to get it out of my mind. There's this lingering thing with all the women I've told you about."

"So, what?" she asks. "So, you're going to force us all to go out with you and rehash all the shit we went through together? What gives you the right?"

"Well, if I remember right, you were the one who wanted to exchange phone numbers."

And now she's pissed, and she starts to put her jacket on.

"Hey hey hey," I say, almost pleading now. "Look, don't go. You're missing the whole point."

"And what, exactly, is the point?" still standing, looking down on me now, literally.

"The point is, you and I, we had some great times together. I mean, we were great friends."

And she's staring again. But I no longer feel like she's about to run out on me.

"So come on," I continue. "Sit back down. Have lunch. I didn't call you here to rehash all the shit. I wanted to rehash the good stuff. I want to talk about Cheryl hooking up with the Big Cowboy Guy while his wife was at the bar getting them drinks."

And she smiles, for a second, then she sighs.

"I don't know, Jack. I don't get it. Maybe this wasn't a great idea."

And all of a sudden it hits me. Maybe she's right. I spent a lot of nights, during the original obsession, trying to keep Amy on the phone or keep her from leaving the room. And as I sit here now, feeling the same old exasperation, I'm starting to wonder why I'm still trying.

She's still staring at me, but this time I'm not saying anything.

"Jack?" she asks, probably expecting one of my old speeches—the ones that were designed to keep those futile conversations going.

It's not coming. Not this time.

"I'm sorry, Amy. Maybe you're right. Maybe this was a bad idea."

This being the City Grill, we still haven't been served, so it's no big deal when I get up, put on my jacket, smile at Amy one more time and pat her on the arm. I walk out, smiling, and she's still staring.

"That's it?" she asks, and I don't look back. For the first time, I don't look back.

Hey, I have to get home and make some calls.

The first call is to Angela Graves, and I'm calling on a Sunday on purpose. I have no real desire to speak to this woman—only to leave her a message telling her my name, where I work, and that I'm interested in interviewing the author of *Picking a Shade*. I tell Angela's voice mail she can call me back. I leave my home phone number, and I hang up grinning like a kid pulling a prank.

Next call is to Julie's hotel room. I know she's not there, because she's out with Will, but I want to leave a message for when she gets back. She said she'd call me, but I figure if she's digging me even half as much as I'm digging her, it'll make her happy that I thought to call.

As soon as I hang up the phone after leaving the message, the phone rings. I pick it up and, with my most chipper-sounding phone voice, say, "Hello!"

"Hello, Jack?" says a woman's voice, one I don't know.

"Yes, speaking," I say, and then I realize something.

I do know that voice.

Oh God, no.

It can't be.

"Hi," the voice says. "It's Mary Ann."

The Godfather III was a rotten movie, and a travesty when compared to the first two, but everybody knows that one Pacino line—the one that has just popped into my head.

Just when I think I'm out, they pull me back in!

It's Mary Ann on the phone. Marley's Freaking Ghost.

"Wow," I actually say into the phone, and a nervous laugh comes back along the line from New Orleans.

"Yeah, I know," she says. "Kind of unexpected, huh? Sorry about that."

"Yeah, kind of."

"Well, I've been trying to call you. I've called a few times, but I didn't want to leave a message."

That 504 area code. I knew it.

"Oh yeah?" I say, still reeling.

"I thought I saw you in an airport last month. Were you at Midway Airport in Chicago, like an early morning flight?"

"Actually, I was," I say, and wonder why I should be surprised.

"I thought so," she says.

"I didn't see you, though," I lie. "Where were you?"

"I was waiting in line for a flight home, and I thought I saw you walk past. I didn't think you saw me, and I didn't know if I should say hi or not. But then I got home, and I started thinking, and I wondered how you were doing. I tried the old number in Boston, but it was disconnected, so I looked you up in New York. I remembered you always said you wanted to move there. Guess I got a lucky break."

"Wow," I say again. "I guess so."

She's what? Stalking me?

"Anyway," she says, "how are things?"

How are things? We haven't talked in more than two years, and she asks how things are? Like, what's new? Anything happen in your life the past two years?

"I'm so sorry," she says when I don't answer. "I've caught you totally off guard, and it's not fair. Maybe I should have left a message."

"Maybe," I say, recovering. "But no, don't worry. It's okay. What's going on with you?"

"Well, things are good. Still teaching history at the high school, coaching girl's soccer. It's fun, and I really like living here."

"That's great, Mary Ann," I say. And of course, I'm not going to give her the satisfaction. I'm not going to ask her why the hell she called. I'm not going to ask her when she learned anything about soccer. She's going to have to volunteer that.

"Yeah, I'm having fun," she says. "So how about you? What's your story? Still writing baseball?"

Beep.

"Yeah, still baseball," I say. "Hey, uh. Mary Ann? I hate to do this, but could you hold on a second? Just let me get rid of this other call?"

"Sure, no problem."

And I click over to my call waiting, figuring it's going to be the girl I took to the junior prom.

"Hello?" I say, terrified.

"Hello," comes the voice of Julie Gordon, and my heart jumps a bit at the notion that she didn't feel the need to identify herself.

"Julie?" I ask. "Hi. What's going on?"

"Oh, Jack, it's great. Will has been so wonderful. I think I've found a place—perfect little one-bedroom on 78th, between Columbus and Central Park West. I love it. So much better than the other places I looked at. You were right."

"That's great!" I say, and resist the temptation to point out that it's in my neighborhood.

"So anyway," she says, "I'm calling you from my cell phone. I haven't gone back to the hotel yet, but I guess I'm near where you live? Is that right?"

"I would think so," I say. "Where are you?"

"I'm on 76th and Amsterdam."

"Yeah, you're very close. I'm on 75th and Broadway, basically."

"Well, I was thinking, since I'm leaving town tomorrow, did you want to get together?"

Control yourself here, Jackie boy.

"Sure," I say.

"Well, I was thinking we could get a cup of coffee or something, and go for a walk in Central Park. It looks nice, and of course I've never been."

I don't believe this. I really am falling in love. What a feeling.

"Sure, that sounds great," I say. "Where do you want me to meet you?"

"Well, I could just come to your place, and we could go from there, if that's okay."

"Sounds good to me," I say, looking around and suddenly panicking about the mess. I give her the quick directions to the building and tell her just to tell the doorman she's here to see me.

"All right, then," she says. "See you in a little bit."

And the lovestruck boy hangs up his phone and collapses back in his chair, smiling as hard as he can. A lot of guys might be concerned about a second date so soon, but it's just what I had in mind. I just didn't want to be too pushy.

Anyway, as soon as I hang up the phone, it rings, and I pick it up.

"Hello?" I ask it.

"Hello?" says Mary Ann's voice.

Oh, man. I totally forgot.

"Oh, Mary Ann, I'm so sorry," I say.

"Did you forget about me?" she asks.

"No!" I lie. "No, that was my office. I couldn't get them off the phone. I'm so sorry. I really am."

Of course, now I have to get Mary Ann off the phone. Julie will be here in about two minutes, and it just wouldn't do to be talking to Mary Ann when Julie comes in.

"So anyway, I guess your job is still crazy, huh?" she asks, and I realize she's given me a perfect out.

"Yeah, it really is," I say. "Matter of fact, you kind of called at a bad time. I have to run out to go to a thing."

"Oh, that's too bad," she says. "Well, I don't want to keep you. The reason I called is, you know, the airport, like I said, and I'm going to be in New York next week. I wanted to know if you wanted to maybe get together. You know, just to talk."

How did she know that?

"Sure," I say, frantically looking at the door through which Julie will soon be walking. "Why don't you just give me a call when you get in town, and we'll set something up?"

I guess I'm being pretty rude, but oh well. She was the one who called. And I've been friendlier than either of us was the last time we talked.

"Sure, that sounds good. I'll be in town starting Monday, so I'll just call you sometime early in the week."

"All right, Mary Ann, sounds good," I say. "Take care."

" 'Bye."

And just as I hang up the phone, the buzzer sounds. I press the button and hear Yousef's voice.

"Mr. Jackson? A young lady here for you?"

"Thanks, Yousef. Send her up."

Today, Julie is wearing jeans, and she looks great in them. Under her black pea coat is a navy blue turtleneck, and the pearls are in the ears again. I smile as I lean in my doorway, watching her walk down the hall.

"Easy to find, right?" I ask.

"Yep," she says. "No problem at all."

I invite her in while I get my own coat on, and she wants to see the place. I am thankful that I cleaned up recently, though the desk is a disaster. The place still looks a bit on the empty side, as a result of Connie's sudden departure, but Julie, who has been looking at unfurnished ratholes for two days, says she likes it.

"Cozy," she says.

"Yeah, get used to it," I say. "You thought those places looked small without furniture, wait till you see how little space you really have."

"I know, I know," she says. "So, you ready to go?"

I am, and we go. Yousef is smiling like a proud parent as we walk past his desk in the lobby, and he tells us to have a good day.

We head to the park, via Starbucks, and it's just another perfect day. Every time I make Julie smile, I feel as proud as if I'd just finished the marathon, and every time she does something to make me laugh it's the best laugh I've ever laughed. Her eyes never stop twinkling as we stroll through the park, past the carousel, around the horse-drawn carriages and out onto Fifth Avenue.

"What's that?" she asks, pointing to a squat gray stone building on the corner of Fifth and 57th.

"That," I say, "is Tiffany's."

And her eyes get big.

"Do you want to go in?" I ask, and she nods.

We have a nice time in Tiffany's, then head back into the park. This time we take a more roundabout way, and by the time we pop out onto Central Park West it's dark and it's almost six o'clock. She tells me she needs a cab, but she wants to give me her phone number in California first.

"So, what time's your flight?" I ask her, tucking the number into my breast pocket.

"Eight o'clock," she says. "Which is too early, really, considering we have to get to the airport two hours ahead of time now."

"Why don't you change it?"

"I tried," she says. "But they're going to charge me a hundred dollars. And since it's a free ticket, I just disagree in principle."

"I see."

"Plus, it'll be good to get home. I have to start packing. I'm moving in a week."

"A week?"

"Yeah, I move in in a week. Do you believe it? Your friend Will is a magician."

"He must be. I've never heard of somebody finding an apartment in Manhattan that easily."

"Well, you're looking at her. So anyway, next Saturday, I'll be back here, waiting for my stuff."

"Wow, that's great," I say. "Well, if you need any help . . ."

"Oh, you'll get a call," she says with a mischievous smile. "You're the only person I know in New York, since nobody else seems to have caught on to your new greet-a-cab policy."

And we both laugh, and she smiles up at me and leans in for a kiss.

It's not much of a kiss, because I've been thinking too much about how I was going to do it, and it's a little awkward as a result. She gets the idea, though, for sure, and she smiles. I kiss her again, and this time it's better.

"Wow," she says. "All right then. We'll call that a sneak preview."

"Oh really?" I ask.

"Hey, you never know," the mischievous grin again.

We step out onto the street and flag down a cab. She grabs my hand and squeezes it just before she gets in, and she waves as it pulls away.

One week.

I can do one week standing on my head.

After that little exchange, I may just try it.

17

The phone rings, and I know it's way too early for anybody who really knows me to be calling.

A quick look at the alarm clock backs me up, as it proclaims the time to be quarter to eight in the morning. I have no idea what's going on, so I start hitting the alarm clock, which is silly because it's not the thing that's ringing.

Eventually, I adjust to the planet Earth again and realize what's going on. I pick up the phone and offer a very annoyed, "Hello?"

"Jackson?" comes the voice on the other end.

"Yousef?" I reply.

"Jackson?" the voice again, confused this time, and clearly female. "Happy Birthday!"

Oh. Right. Birthday.

"Oh, hi Mom," I say, still groggy and wondering why—why quarter to eight? "Thanks."

"Did I wake you?"

Jesus Christ, Mom, of course you woke me. What do you think this is? A school day?

"Nah, that's all right," I say. "What's going on?"

"Well, I just wanted to call and wish you a Happy Birthday," she says, bubbling. "I can't believe it. Thirty years. I remember that day like it was yesterday."

"That's funny," I say, playing my part in our annual joke. "I don't remember it at all."

"Oh, don't be silly," she says. "Do you have any big plans for your birthday?"

You mean, other than going back to sleep?

"You know, Mom, I really don't know," I say. "I have the whole week off, which is nice, so I can kind of take it easy, but I don't know what I'm doing tonight. Probably go out with the guys, you know."

"That sounds nice," she says. "Okay, well, Happy Birthday again, and I love you."

"Love you too, Mom."

"All right. Here's your father."

And Dad gets on the phone, but before he talks to me I hear him say, "I told you he'd be asleep.

"Your mother couldn't wait," he says, when he finally has the receiver in his hand. "Sorry about that. Happy Birthday."

"Thanks, Dad."

"Seems like you've been busy lately," he says.

"Yeah, you know the Yankees. They've always got something working."

"Will you be getting any time off?"

"Yeah, actually, I have the whole week off," I say. "It's kind of nice. It's been a while."

"Well, enjoy it," Dad says. "And we'll let you get back to sleep. Happy Birthday, Jack. We'll talk to you later."

"Okay, bye Dad."

So begins my fourth decade on this planet.

I love my parents. Just wish they knew how to read a clock.

I roll over and go back to sleep.

* * *

My second wake-up call of the day comes at nine-thirty, and by this point it's hard to be very angry with anybody. After all, most people are at work already. Not everybody gets to sleep until noon for three months a year.

"Jack?"

"Hey," I say, knowing who it is.

"It's Mary Ann."

"Hi, Mary Ann. That was quick."

"Yeah, I'm sorry about that. And I'm sorry to call so early. Did I wake you?"

"No, no, no," I lie. "I'm up. What's going on?"

"Well, I told you I'd be in town this week, and we talked about getting together."

"Right," I say, wondering if it's a true/false quiz.

"Well, something's come up, and I'm only going to be in town for two days."

"Oh, that's all right," I say, figuring I'm off the hook.

"Well, the thing is, I'm calling from my hotel—the Grand Hyatt—and I was wondering if you could meet me for lunch today."

"Today?"

"Yes, I'm sorry it's short notice, and if you can't, I understand. It's just that I'm booked solid all day tomorrow but my meetings today don't start until two o'clock. So, I was hoping maybe . . ."

"Today," I say, knowing full well that I am totally unprepared for this particular exorcism. "Well, I guess. I don't really have any plans."

"So . . . yes? That was a yes?"

"Yeah, sure," I say. "Why not?"

I mean, after all, why not?

"All right, that's great!" she says. "Where should we meet?"

I tell her I'll meet her in the lobby of her hotel at noon, and she says that's okay. I hang up the phone wondering what the hell I've just done. Made lunch plans on the spur of the moment with an old girlfriend who can't even bother to remember that it's my birthday? Who's *squeezing me in?*

Hell, I remember her birthday. It's March twenty-eighth. Or maybe it's April eighteenth. Or June twentieth. All right, I don't remember her birthday. That's really not the point.

The point is that I'm not prepared for this one. With Connie and Amy, I kind of knew what I wanted to say when I went in there. This is going to require a two-hour cram session, and it's going to have to be a good one.

I decide I'll order breakfast delivered from EJ's—a big old stack of pancakes and a side of bacon—as a special birthday treat.

After all, you can't cram without food.

At five minutes to ten Jeff arrives, letting himself in and bearing a bag from EJ's.

"Happy Birthday, buddy," he says. "I brought you a present."

"I just ordered from there," I say.

"I know," he says. "I didn't really bring you a present."

Turns out, Jeff arrived at the same time as the EJ's delivery guy, heard him tell Yousef he had a delivery for 3C, and offered to bring it to me, since he was coming this way anyway.

"So let me get this straight," I say. "You let yourself in whenever you want, to watch TV or play PlayStation. You answer my phone. And now you're picking up my deliveries?"

"Yup," he says. "I'm a full-service pain in the ass."

Just then the phone rings, and who's on the other end but Angela Graves, public relations woman for *Picking a Shade,* the man-hating manifesto that's sweeping the nation.

"Jack Byrnes, please," she says.

"Speaking."

"Jack, it's Angela Graves, from Owen Publishing, returning your call."

"Oh, thanks for calling me back."

"You're interested in writing a review of the book, is that right?"

"Actually, I am," I say. "But first I'd really like to set up an interview with the author. I had a few questions for her."

"Well, maybe I can help," Angela says. "Maybe I can answer some of the questions."

"Well, I'm not too sure about that, Angela," I say. "My questions were kind of . . . personal. More about the basis for the book, how much of it is based on personal experience, that kind of stuff."

"Ms. Hall and I have worked together on this book for a long time," Angela Graves says. "I'm sure I can answer any questions you have about the background and the writing process."

Her voice is affected somehow, as if with that fake English accent Madonna's been using these days in her interviews. Something haughty about it. "The *bock*ground and the writing *proe*-cess."

"I don't understand," I say, determined to settle this before my pancakes get cold. "Is Danielle too busy to do her own interviews?"

"Actually, yes," Angela says. "Ms. Hall's book has been very well received by many of the critics to whom it was mailed, and we've received a mountain of interview requests just this weekend. So I'm trying to save her some time."

"All right," I say. "Would you do me just one favor?"

"What's that?"

"You give her a list every day, I'm guessing, of interviews you think she should do personally? Or to let her pick? Something like that?"

"Something like that, yes," Angela says.

"Just do me this one favor. Just put me on today's list. Just put my name on today's list. If she doesn't want to call me, then by all means, you can call me back and we'll do the interview your way. I just want the chance. I think you'll be surprised."

"Do you and Ms. Hall know each other?"

"Something like that, yes," I say. "Just please. Put me on the list, and let her decide."

"Okay, Mr. Byrnes, I'll put you on the list," Angela says. "But I have a funny feeling you're up to something."

For God's sake, lady, I'm a reporter, not a terrorist.

"Please, trust me," I say. "Just trust me."

"All right," she says. "Good-bye, Mr. Byrnes."

" 'Bye."

My pancakes are getting cold.

By ten-thirty Jeff is up to date, which means he knows about the impromptu lunch date with Mary Ann and the impending "interview" with Danielle. He's in tears, laughing at me.

He also knows about Julie, which is to say he's heard me beam and moon about Julie. I tell him that she and I got together again last night, and that she was dropping hints about bigger things to come once she moved to New York. I tell him that's happening in a week. I tell him that she has the most perfectly circular eyes I've ever seen on another human being. He tells me I appear to have stepped in something decent for a change.

"Kind of like you," I offer.

"Yeah," he says, then kind of drifts off by himself for a couple of seconds. "Anna's really something. You know, I actually went looking for rings yesterday?"

"*What?*" I shout, spitting masticated pancake onto the floor.

"Don't laugh, I really did," Jeff says. "Something about this girl, man, I just don't know. And anyway, it's no different than the way you talk about this chick you met in a cab or whatever."

And this is a good point. I'm sure I sound as moonstruck to Jeff as Jeff does to me, and perhaps I should lighten up.

Then again, it is my birthday. Can't I do what I want?

"But," I say. "You're *Jeff*. Jeff doesn't fall in love. Jack falls in love. Jack falls in love all the time. But not Jeff. No way. Jeff loves 'em and leaves 'em."

"Make fun all you want," he says, starting to set up the PlayStation. "But the fact is, I'm going to ruin your birthday by stomping your ass with Randy Moss on fifty-yard touchdown bombs."

"You're on," I say, wolfing down the last bit of pancake and deciding I'll just wing it with Mary Ann.

After all, things are going so well. Why should I worry?

Moss scores his sixth touchdown of the game shortly after eleven o'clock, sending me deeper into a humiliating defeat that no one should have to accept on his birthday. Especially when it comes with Jeff's victory dance. Realizing I've made plans to be in midtown by noon, I tell Jeff he has to go home.

"All right, man," he says. "What do you want to do tonight, anyway?"

"You guys going out?"

"Yeah, we're planning on going out. But it's your birthday. You tell us what you want to do."

"Well, this could be a rough day, with Mary Ann and now potentially Danielle to deal with. Why don't we say Down the Hatch at seven o'clock. Save me a seat."

"Sounds good, dude," Jeff says. "And if you want to head down there together, just give me a call."

"Will do," I say, and he leaves.

Now, I'm not the biggest fan of Down the Hatch, but I do like its proximity to The Slaughtered Lamb, which is where

Nikki will be plying listeners with five-dollar pitchers of Rolling Rock on this night. The way I see it, Nikki deserves an update, since this was all sort of her idea. And if everything goes well today with Mary Ann (and hopefully Danielle), there will be a lot of positive news to communicate.

And if things don't go so well, I'll need as many people as possible to drink with.

By twelve-fifteen Mary Ann and I are seated at the hotel restaurant in the Grand Hyatt. Good a place as any in this neighborhood, and she's in a hurry, so we figured we wouldn't waste time walking anywhere.

She looks good. Still got that mushroom-cap hair I spotted so easily in the airport, and she looks as if she's keeping herself in shape.

"You're still running, I guess," I say early in the conversation, figuring a little flattery never hurt anyone.

"I am," she says. "You really got me into it. I've even run two marathons—Chicago and the Marine Corps in Washington, D.C."

"Wow, that's great," I say.

"How about you?" she asks. "You still into it?"

"No, as my expanding gut-line should have told you, I am not the runner I was a couple of years ago. Amazing how easy it is to stop."

"I know it," she says. "This time of year is always hard, when it gets a little colder. But down in Louisiana we don't get too many bad days."

So I ask her if she's still enjoying living there, and she says yes. She's in town for a conference of some kind, and she says every time she comes to New York she's glad she didn't give it a shot here.

"Too big for me," she says. "I feel like I'd get lost."

I don't understand people who aren't in love with New York, but I figure I'll let this one slide. There is, after all, business to conduct here.

"So," she says, looking as if she's ready to begin something.
"Yes?"

"So I saw you in the airport."

I, of course, still haven't admitted seeing her there. Not sure if there's anything to be gained.

"All right," I say. "I must have been coming home from Arizona, after the World Series. I changed planes at Midway a couple of times."

"Right," she says. "So I saw you in the airport, and I got to thinking."

"That's funny," I say. "I've kind of been thinking about you lately."

"Weird," she says.

"Yeah, I guess."

"Anyway," she goes on. "I started thinking about us, and the way it all ended."

See now, this is getting weird . . .

"And I know this is going to sound strange, but it's like there was something . . . unsatisfying . . . about our breakup."

And so here I am, ready to cut her off. Ready to jump up from the table and yell something like *Wow! I had the same idea! Erasing the breakup! Cool!* But before I can get the words out of my mouth, the conversation takes a totally unexpected turn.

"I just felt like there was a lot more I had to say," she says.

"Excuse me?" I ask, genuinely perplexed.

"I really didn't feel like I got it all out of my system," she says. "I felt like we were holding back—like we didn't say everything we were supposed to say to each other."

"Mary Ann, we talked for four hours," I say. "International long distance."

"I know, I know," she says. "But do you really know why we broke up?"

"We broke up because you didn't want to move to Boston."

"No," she says. "That's not why we broke up."

See, I always hated this about her. She was always so contrary.

"Okay," I say cautiously. "Why did we break up?"

"We broke up because we never really loved each other," she says.

And I've got to say, this hurts a little.

Not that I'm still harboring feelings for Mary Ann. By no means am I still harboring feelings for Mary Ann. It's just, when somebody spends a year or so telling you they love you, and then a few years after you break up they surprise you with a phone call on your birthday and set up a lunch date to tell you they were lying the whole time, it kind of stings.

"What are you talking about?" I ask.

"I think you know what I mean," she says. "I think we were going through the motions a lot. I know I cared for you, but I don't think I ever truly loved you, and I think you'd probably have to say the same thing."

"I don't think I get what you're talking about," I say. "When I tell somebody I love them, I don't do it lightly."

Here's a phone number. Her name's Connie. Call her. She'll tell you.

"Jack, I'm not suggesting—"

"Well, what are you suggesting?" I bark back.

And all of a sudden we're in a fight. Which is not the reason I came here today. I came here to have a nice, pleasant lunch and to discuss the times in our relationship when Mary Ann and I got along. At this point it's going to be a huge upset if we can ever get the conversation around to that.

"So I'm sorry to dump this on you," she says. "But I figured it's been long enough that it wouldn't hurt too bad. And I know this sounds kind of weird, but I'm doing this with every guy I've ever had a relationship with."

"Really?" I ask impatiently. I actually look at my watch, hoping she'll take a hint. She doesn't.

"Yeah, I've sort of decided the concept of the breakup needs an overhaul," she says. "I don't think they're ever complete enough. I think people say certain things, or don't say certain things, because they're trying to spare the other person's feelings. And I think it's a lot healthier if you confront the thing head-on, even if you do it months or years later. Helps get it out of your system. Or so my theory goes, anyway."

It's appropriate, since this will be the last time we speak, that it will also be the last time Mary Ann and I disagree. We spent so much of our time together disagreeing.

Because lunch is on the way, and there's nothing better to do, I tell Mary Ann my own anti-breakup theory. This gets the conversation to a more amicable level, on which we are able to discuss our old times together—the times when we were happy in each other's company. But mostly we're comparing notes from our parallel quests.

"So you start out with the bad stuff?" she says.

"Oh yeah," I say. "Had one of them crying. Thought I was going to lose her."

"But then, aren't they too emotional after that?"

"No! The way I see it, emotional is good. Emotion is what we're looking for here. Emotion is what got us all into this mess in the first place. No reason to take it out of the equation."

"That's interesting," she says.

"Of course, it could be that all of your guys are jerks or just don't care enough to go back over the whole thing."

"That's what I think," she says. "But I've only got two more to try. After today, I'm a lot less likely to give up."

This is an odd twist for my experiment to take, but after Amy and now this one, I've started to realize my idealistic vision for this revolution in breaking up needs revision. See, there's never going to be a way to escape the thing that went wrong. Amy lingered because there was this thing between us that never got solved, and it still hasn't. Mary Ann left a sour taste because I realized I never really liked her, and I still don't. Connie felt like a failure because I couldn't figure out why I couldn't say "I love you," and I still don't know the answer to that.

So this is not going to be a successful search for answers, this Relationship Ghost-busting venture. But that doesn't mean it's a failure. In fact, I've got just what I want from all three so far—closure. None of these women will ever contact me again, I'm sure of it.

So we finish up, and Mary Ann grabs the check. Another expense account, what a treat. I got what I wanted out of this meal and didn't have to kick in!

We part with a slightly uncomfortable hug and—as predicted—no phone number exchange. I wish her well with her two remaining guys, and she wishes me luck with Danielle, who I guess is the only one left now.

I leave the hotel, hop in a cab and head home. Just one more ghost to go. One more to rub out of the ledger, and then it's Julie, Julie, Julie all the time. My goal was to have the ghost stuff wrapped up by the time Julie came back. Now, if Danielle calls back today, it could be wrapped up by sundown, leaving me plenty of time to celebrate my birthday.

But then I get home, and I realize it's not going to be that easy.

*　　*　　*

"What is this, some kind of joke?"

The voice on the answering machine is female, and the caller ID identifies the number as an Ohio number. Those two facts give me a strong clue as to who is calling.

The tone in the voice leaves no doubt.

"I get a message that you want to interview me about my book? I'm serious, Jack, is that some kind of a joke?"

Well, I guess it was *kind* of a joke. But not really a joke, per se. More like a prank, really.

"Let's get a few things clear here, fella. First, the inscription I wrote was not meant to be an invitation to call me. Second, it was not meant to be interpreted as in any way nice. And third, for you to call Angela and muscle her into giving me your message, as if you were some kind of book reviewer, that was just low. It was low, Jack, and I don't understand how you expected me to react."

Well, I certainly didn't expect this.

"Even if you are a book reviewer, I wouldn't want you reviewing my book. You're in it anyway, Jack. You know that, right? Wasn't too hard to spot your own character, was it? And don't bother calling me back either. I just wanted to let you know I didn't appreciate the trick you pulled on Angela. Good-bye."

It appears that time has not mellowed Danielle Hall. Maybe it's not fair to judge her based on one obviously emotional answering machine message, but she seemed an awful lot like the crazy redhead from college. She also used the word "fella," but I don't imagine that has much to do with the point.

It also appears that writing a book about her past problems with men has not been a cathartic experience.

And it definitely does not appear as if Danielle wants me to call her and talk about old times. I think the last part of her message makes that clear.

Thing is, though, isn't she the one who sent me the book?

Isn't she the one who wrote a note to me on the inside front cover? A note that ended with "Love, Danielle"?

Weird.

Maybe this is the gut-check for me. Maybe this is the cold slap of reality across my self-satisfied face. Maybe Danielle is the one that's supposed to remind me of what I can't accomplish here.

But even if it is, I've come too far to let one angry, red-headed ghost stand in my way. She would never have sent me that book if she wasn't, at least in the back of her mind, looking for a confrontation. And by God, I'm going to give her one.

Fired up, I dial the number on the caller ID and steel myself for my greatest challenge yet.

18

"Wait, wait, wait," Bernie is saying. "What did she call you?"

"I've never had a chick call me that before," Jeff is saying. "What kind of weird chick is this?"

The weirdest, of course. And, as it turns out, the thorniest of the roses I've been trying to stuff back into this vase for the past week.

I am at Down the Hatch, celebrating my thirtieth birthday with my two closest friends. But before anybody gets too drunk, I'm trying to fill them in on the day. And by "the day" I mean Danielle.

See, I did call Danielle back. In spite of her bilious instructions. I figured the book she sent me gave me license to pursue this until I was satisfied (or until she got a restraining order), and the more I thought about it, the more indignant I became. Damn it, I was going to call her back and tell her what I thought of her book, and her message, and for that matter, her publicist.

But then she answered the phone, and I found out I wasn't the only one ready for a fight.

* * *

"Danielle?" I began, selecting a traditional opening.

"Yes?" she countered, unaware of who I was, granting me an opening for an ambush.

"It's Jack Byrnes," I said, and apparently that was the wrong thing to say.

"*Jack Byrnes?*" she practically screeched. "*Jack Fucking Byrnes?*"

"Yeah," I said, as if the problem was that she hadn't heard me. "You know—"

But she cut me off.

"Oh I know who you are," she said, clearly very angry. "What I don't know is why in the world you'd be calling me. How'd you get this number anyway?"

"It was on my caller ID," I said. "Listen—"

"No, *you* listen," she said. "I thought I made it very clear in the message I left you that I didn't want you to call me. So please, *please* tell me the reason you decided to call me anyway. Because it must be a really good one."

"Well, Danielle," I said, "you did send me a copy of the book. I mean, it's not like I made the first contact here."

"God *damn* it!" she hollered, and I swore I could have heard her screaming from Ohio, even without the aid of the telephone. "Damn it, damn it, damn it!"

Thankfully, no reply was required of me. She continued on her own.

"God damn Angela," she said. "This was her idea. She wanted me to send personal copies to all of the guys I ever went out with. Said it would be a good topic for the talk shows. I knew I didn't like that idea."

At this point I was totally lost on how I was going to turn this conversation around into a successful ghost-busting venture. Danielle didn't seem amenable to such sensible, high-minded discussion. She didn't even seem lucid. But I figured, I called, so I had to make some kind of an effort.

"Look, Danielle, don't get all upset," I said. "There's no reason—"

But again, cut off.

"Jack, for fuck's sake, I don't have *time* for this!" she said, and I was trying to remember if she'd sworn so much in college. "I've got a lot going on! So great, you found me. You tracked me down. Now will you *please* tell me what you want so I can get you off the phone and get on with my life?"

"Well, if you'd settle down a little bit," I said, staggering back against the ropes with no hope of recovery. "I don't know. I just . . . I thought maybe we could catch up."

"*Catch up?*"

"Yeah, you know. Talk about some old times, maybe."

Then she started laughing. And not just giggling—I'm talking about an out-and-out roar of a laugh carrying over the long distance lines.

"Oh my *God*, Jack!" she finally said. "Please don't tell me that's why you called."

Now I'm starting to get upset. But I don't even get the chance to express it.

"Jack, for God's sake," she said. "We went out ten years ago. Ten years, Jack. Do you really mean to tell me you're not over it?"

"Of course I'm over it," I said. "I just—"

"You just what?" she said. "You just like calling up old girl-friends and rehashing all the shit you went through together?"

Well . . . sort of.

"Look, Danielle, I haven't even thought about you until you sent that book—"

"All right, Jack, all right," she said, still chuckling. "Let's pretend I didn't send the book, okay. Why don't you go right ahead and throw the book in the trash, pretend it never happened, and go right back to not thinking about me. We'll all be much happier for it."

I had no idea what to say here. She'd totally blindsided me. Even after the angry tone of the answering machine message, I still had fooled myself into believing she might be receptive to some sort of phone conversation if I actually called and confronted her. At the absolute least, I figured she'd be a human being about it.

But no.

"I take it from your silence that there's nothing else, Jack," she said.

"Well," was all I could offer.

"All right, then," she went on. "I'll agree to forget you ever called me, as long as you agree to forget I sent the book. Deal?"

"Danielle . . ." I said, trying to sound firm but fully aware that I had no chance of staying on the phone.

"We'll call it a deal," she said. "Now, like I said, I have a lot to do, and I assume you do too. At least I hope you have better things to do than this. Don't call me again, okay?"

And she hung up.

Leaving me wondering . . . well, wondering a lot of things. Especially about my plan.

The original purpose of the plan was not to eliminate the relationship ghosts from my life, but to take the angry ones and turn them into happy ones. It is my hypothesis that we are better served by remembering the positive and successful aspects of past relationships than dwelling on the negative aspects or pondering the reasons they ended.

I was never out to destroy the ghosts, just to make peace with them, with the hope that success would help me function as a better date or boyfriend in the future. If that is the case, I am three-for-four, or four-for-five if you count Nikki. But a miserable failure with Danielle, who wouldn't even submit to the all-important rehash conversation, now has me doubting not only my chances for success, but the worthiness of the plan itself.

Once she hung up, I kept the phone to my ear, still in shock, even after it was beeping angrily at me. After Danielle, the beeping noise was kind of a relief.

"I don't know, man," Bernie says, his eyes fixed on the young lady who's pouring our next round of shots. "I liked the plan. I'm not sure you should let one girl mess the whole thing up for you."

"You think?" I say.

"Oh, shit!" Bernie answers, because he has just had a pitcher of beer spilled on his black sport coat by one of our fellow bar patrons.

I don't know what's going on in here tonight. The only time I've ever seen this place this packed is on a Saturday afternoon, when they offer ludicrous drink deals like eight-for-one pitchers and shots or something like that. In fact, it was just such a Saturday that had me convinced, over a year ago, that I never wanted to come back to this place again.

It's not a particularly nice place. It stinks, for one thing, as if they only mop up the spilled beer and vomit once every couple of weeks or when the manager's feet start to stick to the floor. It's cramped and uncomfortable at any peak hour. It's dark and dingy and decorated haphazardly with college pennants and old beer ads (do they even *make* Lowenbrau anymore?), and if you don't get a seat at the bar, you're standing for the rest of the night. I think there's a pool table, or maybe foosball, across the room, but I've never seen it.

But this is Monday night. And generally that's a slow night here. We like the slow night, because we can sit at the bar and talk, drink cheap beer and not have to worry about the usual Down the Hatch insanity. We also like the fact that the place is centrally located—within staggering distance of no fewer than twenty-five other Village bars—and that the beer selection is good. But the real reason we even started coming here was the bartender.

At one time or another all three of us have had a huge crush on the bartender, whose name is Alison and who, to our knowledge, has never worn a shirt that has covered her navel. She is rude, obnoxious, forgetful, and has never given any of us a hint that she was interested in return, but we have kept coming back, mainly to stare.

When I came in tonight, I didn't see the two tour buses parked outside that said DRUNKEN FRAT GUY BUS LINES on the side, but they must be parked around the corner, because they appear to have emptied into this bar. This place is right up these guys' alley—a place where you can be as loud and as hammered as you want to be and you're not going to run into anybody who cares if you spill a pitcher of beer on their nice black sport coat.

Generally, you're not going to see too many sport coats, period.

But this time the kids miscalculated. With astounding quickness for a man his size, Big Bern is off his stool and is holding this kid by the front of his Everclear T-shirt. The kid, who can't be more than twenty-one, looks scared, and his friends don't seem to know what to do. Bernie doesn't get angry easily, and he almost never gets this close to being in a bar fight. But this time he truly looks ready to kill.

The kid has floppy brown hair and is wearing his now stretched-out T-shirt untucked over jeans. It appears to be some sort of uniform, judging from the attire of his friends, and I'm wondering what condition it will be in once they peel him from the sticky black walls of Down the Hatch.

Fortunately, Jeff is also here, and Bernie listens to Jeff. Well, in these situations he does. Jeff puts his right hand on

Bernie's left shoulder and leans in, as if to whisper to the big man.

"Hey," says Jeff, the calmest guy in the room all of a sudden. "Bern. Let's just go."

Bernie has not broken his eye contact with his new young enemy, but Jeff tries again.

"Let's just go, man," he says. "We were about to leave anyway, right? We'll get the jacket cleaned. No big deal, big guy. Happens."

And this works. Bernie lets the kid down, and as the kid staggers back against the wall, Jeff is already leading Bernie out the front door and back up the stairs to the sidewalk. This leaves me to pay the bar tab (on my birthday!), but it's clearly the best plan, because the shock is starting to wear off on the Drunken Frat Boys, and they're threatening to get tough.

"Hey, man, what the *hell?*" yells the kid whose life Jeff just saved. "I said I'm sorry, whatchu want? It was a friggin' accident!"

And he's taking a few steps toward Bernie, who's turning back around and still looks ready to shoot fire from his eyes. A security guard who's bigger than Bernie is stationed near the front door and has one hand on Bernie's chest as he eyes the kid, but Jeff is in charge here, and he's leading Bernie out, whether Bernie likes it or not.

My role is to corral this kid, which I do as I wait for my change.

"Look," I say. "Let it go, man. Just let it go. Nobody got hurt."

And he looks at me now like I'm the guy he wants to fight. And his buddies are all sort of massing around him, as if to let me know I'm outnumbered. And I actually smile a little bit.

"Look, nobody got hurt," I say again. "We're leaving, and you guys can stay and have a good time."

"Damn right we will," says another Everclear fan, and I smile again.

I really don't know why we come here anymore. It's not for grown-ups. And, much as I'd like to believe otherwise, I guess I am a grown-up now.

You can't turn thirty and fail to pick up on that.

Across the street, at The Slaughtered Lamb, I don't feel much like a grown-up. I feel like a whiny college kid, still trying to figure out girls. We've settled into a table that's bigger and more comfortable than last week's, though it's farther back from where Nikki will be playing, and we've ordered our first five-dollar Rolling Rock pitcher.

Things have settled way down. Bernie was still fuming when we got out onto the sidewalk, even though Jeff was still working on him, but we finally got him to laugh when we told him I took on all fifteen of those little college pricks by myself and avenged his sport coat. Once we paid our cover, Jeff went to the bar and got a few napkins so Bernie could wipe the beer off his sleeve, and everything seems to be back to normal now.

Which is to say, I'm doing a lot of the talking, about myself.

"I just think you're thinking way too much," Jeff says. "I want to hear more about the new girl."

The new girl, yes.

Julie.

Well, I do love talking about Julie.

"Yeah," I say. "I called her too."

"I assume that one went better?" Bernie says.

"Much better," I say, and I guess my smile is a little too big.

"Uh-oh," Bernie says. "Jack's in looooo-ooooove."

And of course, Jeff joins in, and soon they're basically

singing it to me, and people at the next table are wondering what the hell's going on.

And I don't mind.

I did call Julie, once I'd finally settled down from the Danielle call. That took a while, as I sat in my desk chair staring at my framed photograph of Bill Buckner's Game Six error in the 1986 World Series. My favorite thing in the apartment, the photo offered me no comfort as I sat among the ruins of the once-proud relationship ghost plan. I sat and stared and wondered what the hell had just happened, and I think I sat there for almost a half hour before I realized I had to get up and do something else.

Julie was home, packing up her apartment. She told me she'd given only one week's notice at her old job and that they'd told her to use her remaining vacation days for it.

"Now you can see why I wanted to get out of here," she said.

We talked for a while, and it was great. I feel the same way I felt when I was thirteen and tonight's entertainment dragged me into that dark hallway after that soccer game. I feel bullet-proof when I talk to Julie. I am the guy who can do no wrong.

There are all these rules about when you're supposed to call a girl after you get her number, or how often you're supposed to call, or how to make sure you don't scare her off, or how to look cool, but with Julie, all of those rules are irrelevant. I'm just cruising along, doing what feels right, and every single tiny little thing I do is working.

This is the speech I'm giving Jeff and Bernie as I relate the story of my call to Julie, and they're both smiling.

And then Jeff says something that changes the conversation completely:

"I know how you feel, man."

"Oh yeah?" I say. "You getting that same vibe with the lovely Anna?"

"From the very beginning," Jeff says. "And you guys, we're getting married."

The bar probably doesn't go totally silent at this news, but to Bernie and me it seems that way.

Married?

Jeff?

Already?

Just some of the formless thoughts clattering around my brain. And by the look on Bernie's face, I can see I'm not alone. The big man breaks the ice.

"You're *what*?" he asks.

But Jeff is smiling huge, as if he knew we'd take it this way.

"You heard me right, Big Bern," he says. "I bought the ring this morning, gave it to her this afternoon. We're getting married in two weeks."

There are so many things wrong with this. A partial list:

1. Two weeks?
2. They got engaged this afternoon, and he's out with us? Where is she?
3. *Married*?
4. How long have they known each other, anyway?
5. Even if it's only been a month, that might be the longest relationship Jeff has ever had.

"I know what you guys are thinking," Jeff says. "And you're right. It's real sudden. But I don't know. I'm in love with her."

"Dude," Bernie says. "What's the rush?"

"We figured, why wait?" Jeff says, still smiling.

"Wait," I say. "You got engaged this afternoon? And you didn't go out with her tonight?"

"Hey, it's your birthday," he says, looking hurt now. "I told her I already had plans. She understands. She went out with her friends. Wanted to show off the ring."

But not, apparently, the groom.

"I just don't get it," Bernie says. "Married?"

"Hey guys," Jeff says, no longer smiling. "Is there a 'congratulations' coming anytime soon?"

And I really don't know. I'm still stuck on that partial list.

"Yeah, man," Bernie says. "Congratulations. I mean, that's great, if that's what you want."

"Yeah," I say. "It's just that, you know, you kind of shocked the hell out of us here."

"I know, I know," he says, smiling again. "Sorry I didn't tell you guys before I did it or anything, but it was kind of sudden. Although I did kind of hint about it to Jack this morning."

Was that just this morning?

"Wow, that's right," I say. "What did you do, go buy the ring right after you left my apartment?"

"Yup," he says. "Went right over to Tiffany's. Met Anna for lunch, and popped the question."

"Was she surprised?" Bernie asks.

"Oh yeah," Jeff says.

Well, that's one benefit to rushing into something. You can always make it a surprise.

"Well, congrats, man," I say. "That's great. I'm happy for you, as long as you're happy."

Jeff insists that he's happier than he's ever been. He explains his thought process—that he's so certain about this girl, there's no reason to wait around, go out for a year or two, then propose. He asks us to be in the wedding. We both say yes, though I confess my heart isn't one hundred percent in it.

I mean, there's something seriously wrong with this. First of all—and no offense to Jeff—why would she go for it?

Here's a girl who literally stops traffic when she's walking down the street. She could basically have any guy in Manhattan, including the baseball players and movie stars. And she picks Jeff after knowing him for a couple of weeks? There's a real strong possibility that Jeff is marrying her to avoid losing her, and that can't be a good reason, can it?

Second, has Jeff had any time to think about what marriage actually means? It's not like deciding whether to call or send flowers after a one-night stand. Has he thought about the lifetime to which he's committing? Does he realize how much his life will change?

But then I think, what the hell do I know? Here I am in a Greenwich Village bar, thirty years old, with two other guys. In a few minutes the lesbian guitar player who's also the first girl I ever kissed is going to take the stage. And hopefully, when she's done, she can come give me romantic advice. And oh yes, I'm madly in love with a girl I've only known for a week and kissed once, and she's in Los Angeles.

So I'm going to sit in judgment on Jeff and Anna?

I don't think so.

19

I don't usually watch *Oprah*, and today's episode isn't one that's going to convert me. Yet, I can't seem to change the channel.

It is now five days since my thirtieth birthday, and it hasn't been so bad. It's been a slow week, which is kind of nice. I kind of needed a break after last week, which was Ghost Week and one of the most stressful I've ever had.

Of course, Ghost Week was also the week that brought me Julie, and for that I will always remember it well, even as the shrill and furious voice of Danielle Hall rattles around the inside of my skull.

See, I was flipping around the channels, and I got ambushed. Sitting there in the chair across from Oprah, wearing jeans and a low-cut white cotton blouse and sporting a nifty head of short red hair, is Danielle Hall.

I stopped because I heard the voice, of course. Same voice that was calling me all kinds of names over the phone just a few days ago, so it sounded familiar right away. And moments after that voice froze my channel-switching finger, my eyes caught sight of the bottom of the screen, where it read, "Danielle Hall, Author: *Picking a Shade*."

So, of course I stopped.

"It's not a man-hating book," Danielle is telling Oprah, as I gape. "I see it more as a story of keeping up hope even as things look hopeless."

"But couldn't you see where some people might take it that way?" Oprah asks. "Don't you think some of the men these characters are based on might see it that way?"

"Well, Oprah, as I told you earlier, not all the male characters are drawn from my personal experience," Danielle says. "Some are, of course, but some are a combination of different characteristics of different people, and others are just made up. It is a work of fiction, after all."

Wow. She's even snotty with Oprah.

"I think we all understand that, Danielle," Oprah says, not at all rattled. "But how do you think your book would be received by the men on whom the characters are based?"

"You know, it's funny you should ask me that," Danielle says. "One of those guys actually called me a few days ago."

"Really?" Oprah, leaning forward in her chair now.

"Yes, I couldn't believe it," Danielle says. "I don't know how he got a copy of the book, but the guy I went out with freshman year in college, he read it and he called me. Said something about wanting to talk over old times, if you can believe that."

The guy in question is sitting on his sofa in his Manhattan apartment, furious at yet another misrepresentation. He wants to phone in, to call the *Oprah Winfrey Show* and shout, *She sent me the book! She sent me the book!*

But of course he doesn't. He's still sitting in silence, wondering how the hell this book is doing well enough to warrant an interview on *Oprah*.

"Now, did this guy tell you what *he* thought of the book?" Oprah asks.

"You know, we really didn't get into that," Danielle says. "We didn't talk long, and I'm not really sure what he wanted.

But I guess some people rethink things when they're faced with the way they acted in the past. I don't know. All the guys I've ever dated, I'm at peace with the way those relationships ended. But I guess I can't say the same for them."

Oprah looks at the camera now.

"When we come back, we'll have more with Danielle, including the story of how a tragic real-life experience almost shattered her own hope for future happiness. And we'll find out about the new fellow in Danielle's life. Don't go away."

And they cut to commercial, and I'm still sitting there, wondering why I can't roll this last stubborn boulder up the hill. I try to think about Julie, but even that's not helping. So I'm left to ponder a conversation I had the other night with a different relationship ghost—a conversation that was a lot more helpful than anything Danielle has brought to the table.

Nikki was indeed back at The Slaughtered Lamb on Monday night, the night I turned thirty, and she began her first set shortly after Jeff had informed Bernie and me that he was getting married in two weeks. She came to visit during her break.

"What's going on with you guys?" she asked.

"Well," I said, "it's my thirtieth birthday. Bernie almost got us into a bar fight because somebody spilled beer on his jacket. And Jeff's getting married in two weeks, we just found out."

"Wow," Nikki said. "I don't know where to begin. I guess Happy Birthday, Congratulations and sorry about your jacket. That cover it?"

"I think so," I said.

"I'll tell the bartender your next round's on me, maybe order up some shots if you guys want," she said. "Sounds like there's a lot to celebrate."

Seeing the dartboard free, Jeff and Bernie took the opportunity to get a game going. I told them I'd be with them in a minute, but I wanted to stay and talk with Nikki for a while.

I told her what I'd done with her advice from the week before, and she laughed.

"I'm not sure I would have advised calling them all up and asking them out for a debriefing," she said.

"Well, anyway," I said, "it worked. At least on a few of them."

I related the stories of Connie and Amy, and of how Mary Ann surprised me with her totally different theory. Nikki seemed impressed that the crazy idea actually worked.

So I told her about running into Julie, and how I was loony over this girl without even really knowing her yet, and she rolled her eyes.

"Isn't that how you get into these messes?" she said.

"Yes, but I swear this is different," I said. "I swear I've never had anything like this feeling. I mean, totally awesome."

"All right," she said. "So what's the problem?"

And then I told her about Danielle. The book. The message. The phone call. And I told her I was worried the whole plan was getting flushed down the drain because one part of it was a total disaster. I told her I worried that this left the door open for more ghosts—that there were some still out there, unaccounted for, and that I had no idea when they might strike.

"See, the point of the whole exercise was to improve," I said. "To finally bury the mistakes of the past, to view my past relationships in a positive light and to be a better man for it. And if I can't pull that off with Danielle, then what value did that relationship even have? And what was the universe trying to tell me by bringing her back into my life after so long?"

"The universe?" Nikki asked.

"Yeah, it's my way of saying 'fate,' I guess."

"Thought you didn't believe in fate," she said.

"Didn't," I said, swigging the last drops of my latest Rolling Rock. "But I'm rethinking my position."

"I think that's a good idea," she said.

She went on to basically tell me I was a fool for thinking I had to complete some sort of cosmic checklist of past girl-friends before embarking on my relationship with Julie. She urged me to return, if only for a while, to my agnosticism.

"If you really don't believe in fate, then it's not hard to see the whole Danielle thing as a coincidence," she said.

Which was good advice, I thought.

But then, here it is, five days later, and Danielle's on my TV set, ripping me in front of a national TV audience.

If that isn't fate flipping me the bird, then I don't know what it is.

Turns out, Danielle's "new fellow" is a dog, which gives me a little bit of a laugh as I remain riveted. The dog, a brown cocker spaniel, has joined Danielle onstage, much to the de-light of the show's host and its oohing, aahing audience. Danielle has the dog in her lap and is rubbing it behind the ears as the show comes back from commercial.

"And who do we have here?" Oprah asks.

"This is Eric," Danielle answers.

Eric?

Eric is not a dog's name, lady. Eric is a person's name.

"Eric has been with me now for about six months," Danielle says. "And right now, all the love I need, I'm getting from him."

Okay. We're not even going to touch that one.

Oprah milks the dog angle for a while, even walking over to pet Eric (I mean, how silly does that sound?) and holding the dog in her arms for a little while. Eventually, Danielle has

Eric back in her lap and Oprah is back in her own chair, and it's time to get serious.

This is the part of the show in which Danielle informs us that the high school boyfriend character in her book is also based in real life, and that all the rotten things he did to her actually happened. This is startling news, because I thought Danielle had told me all of her dark, terrible secrets. So I sit and listen as she breaks down into tears at the memory and explains how it probably ruined her life.

And this makes it difficult to be real angry with Danielle. But then I remember that it wasn't me who was angry. It was her. She was the one who made me feel like a jackass on the phone, after *she sent me her book* and suggested with an inscription that I was one of its characters. And so, while I'd love to let all of this go and just move on with my own life, I can't. There are too many unanswered questions. I can't make it all make sense.

During the next commercial break, Jeff comes in. An afternoon visit—how unusual.

"Hey, buddy," he says.

"What's up?" I say, staring at a commercial for floor cleaner.

"Whatcha watchin?"

"Uh . . . *Oprah*," I say.

"Excuse me?"

"Yeah, *Oprah*. I was flipping channels, and there was Danielle Hall, on *Oprah*."

"Who's Danielle Hall?"

"The girl who sent me the book, remember?"

"Oh yeah," he says. "The crazy one who reamed you out over the phone. I can't keep track, sorry."

"That's all right."

"What's she doing on *Oprah*?"

"Selling her book, I guess."

"Wow," Jeff says. "It must be a big hit. I mean, when Oprah recommends a book, that's big for sales."

Indeed it is, and in the past several minutes it has dawned on me that Danielle is going to sell a pile of books. It's one thing—and a very helpful thing—to get Oprah to recommend your book to her audience. But to actually have you on the show, talking about the book and baring your innermost soul to her audience? That's a gold mine.

To change the subject, I tell Jeff we're going to play one game of Madden football (I've been practicing, since I can't seem to beat him and it's pissing me off) and then head out for the night. Tonight's plan is for Jeff, Anna, myself, and Bernie to have dinner together at Gabriela's, a Mexican restaurant on 75th and Amsterdam, and this is significant because it's going to be the first time that Bernie has met Anna. I guess Jeff figures he's engaged now, so there's less risk.

Jeff is excited about his wedding, which is a week from tomorrow. They're getting married in a church, and they're following up with a nice-sized party (about a hundred and fifty people) at Tavern on the Green.

"I'm meeting her parents on Sunday," Jeff tells me. "Well, her mom and her stepdad. I don't think she and her father are on good terms. Anyway, I'm a little nervous about that one."

"I would think so," I say. "Were they as surprised by the timing of this whole thing as everybody else was?"

"Yeah, they're a little worried, I think," he says. "But she tells me not to worry. She seems to think they'll like me."

"Well, good luck with that," I said. "Just think, a week ago you were more worried about her meeting Bernie."

"Yeah," he says. "I don't know, though. Bernie's been weird."

"Oh yeah?"

"You know he hasn't been out any night this week since your birthday?"

"Is that right?"

"Yeah," Jeff says. "He's been sitting home, reading and stuff. He told me he hasn't hooked up with a girl since that Blondie's waitress. You remember?"

"Yeah, I remember. What was that? A week ago? That's a lot of time off for Bernie."

"I'm starting to worry about him," Jeff says.

"Hm," I say. "Maybe he'll get out of his slump tonight. Are we going out after dinner?"

"I hope so," he says. "Anna wants to try some club in the Village. I'm trying to get her to stay up this way. Village on a Friday night, I'm not really into that."

"Me neither," I say. "In fact, I might beg off if you head down that way."

"No problem," he says. "I understand. Kind of like you understand that there's no way you can stop Randy Moss."

And it's true. I can't. I am losing again, this time by twenty-one points at halftime. Practice has not helped. All the PlayStation has done is help me take my mind off crazy red-headed authors on TV. But that's not so bad.

The night is an interesting one, as the lovely Anna captures our attention over chips and salsa and holds it right through the flan and fried ice cream. Even Bernie, who always tends to play it cool, is caught up. Anna is wearing a brown corduroy skirt and brown boots that come up to her knees. Her sweater is a light beige cashmere V-neck, and when she shrugs out of her hip-length black leather jacket, every man in the restaurant is staring. Jeff grins nervously through all of this, as if he's not quite comfortable with having her around so many people, and as we sit down to eat he's making a couple of jokes.

Throughout dinner, Anna directs the conversation. She wants to know all about Bernie, whom she's never met, and me, whose apartment she visited only briefly. We go back and forth between Bernie's writing accomplishments and my search for true love among the ghosts. I gush about Julie, and my ability to truly let loose my burgeoning feelings further convinces me that it really may be true love. I mean, I'm in the presence of this jaw-dropping goddess—a woman who makes men lose control of their motor functions—and here I am going on and on about a different girl. It's got to be a good sign.

Anna seems genuinely interested in my story. She never breaks eye contact, and she asks good questions about Julie and the way we met. She's as confident and self-assured as any person I've ever met, and it comes across in the ease with which she converses with people she doesn't know.

"Sounds like love at first sight," she tells me.

"I think maybe," I say.

"Just be careful," she says, sounding like my mom all of a sudden. "It sounds like you have a habit of love at first sight."

And she winks at me and touches the tip of her tongue to her upper lip. Which is probably inappropriate with her fiancé sitting right there, but it's hard to care.

Through it all, Jeff fidgets. Several times, he tries to force himself into the conversation, but it appears as if it only takes one stern look from Anna to silence him. She seems to have him on a leash, and this concerns me. Perhaps Bernie and I will adjourn to the Dublin House later, when she directs her fiancé downtown, and discuss it further.

Bernie, meanwhile, shows no traces of the trouble Jeff described earlier. Brilliantly attired in a bright, multicolored vest and black sport coat, Big Bern is at his dazzling, charming best with Anna. It's probably the ease the two of them have in talking to each other that's driving Jeff so crazy, and he starts looking around for the check before any of the rest of us do.

Gabriela's is a popular place, and it is therefore crowded on a Friday night. You have to elbow your way through the crowd at the cramped little bar just to find the host stand, and once you sit down, there's no way to avoid the feeling that you're on top of the tables next to you.

But the crowd gives Anna an audience. And when our bill is paid and we all stand up to leave, you can hear the sound of silverware hitting the floor all throughout the room. A flip of her hair and a slight stretch before she slips back into her coat, and every guy in the place has unwittingly found himself in a fight with his wife or girlfriend. The best part is, she knows it. As we walk toward the door, we overhear a woman tell a man to stop staring. Anna turns to the couple and smiles.

It is as I foresaw, and Jeff loses his argument in favor of staying local. The happy couple is headed for the Village, but they're on their own. Bernie and I are old men now, and we don't go down there to party with the kids. We wish them a good night and we head to Dublin House for a few Guinnesses with Mike.

Once inside, the conversation immediately turns to Anna. Bernie doesn't like her.

"No way does this end up good for Jeff," he says.

"How do you mean?" I ask.

"She's out of his league, and she knows it."

"Wow. That's kind of harsh."

"I know, but face facts," Bernie says, wiping the Guinness out of his moustache with his tongue. "She walks around like some Greek goddess. And God knows, she's incredible. But what can Jeff do but worship her, you know? That's all she's after."

It's a good point. Jeff does seem in awe. And while that's

not a bad thing, it can't be the only thing. You can worship the woman you marry, I'm sure, but I imagine it has to be mutual. And I just don't see the same kind of awe going in the other direction.

"Girl like that, she's only gonna get bored," Bernie says. "But why not say yes? I mean, she got a nice diamond ring out of it—gets to wear the dress and all. And you think she's worried about staying faithful? He'll forgive her for anything, and she knows it. Bad situation. I don't like it."

"Damn, Bernie," I say. "All this off of one dinner conversation."

"I know women, Jack," he says. "I can tell these things."

And while it's hard to argue with the man, I think I'm starting to see what Jeff has been talking about. This was never Bernie's personality. He was never this negative about anything—especially women. And meanwhile here we are, in the Dublin House, where the only women are the sloppy drunken regulars whose best days were somewhere in Bernie's early teen years. Why isn't Bernie out on the prowl?

"Are you all right, man?" I ask.

"What do you mean?" he says.

"I mean, I don't know. You want to go somewhere where they've got some women?"

"Nah," he says, then offers no further explanation.

So we sit for a while, silent, and drink our beers. And Mike comes over and offers friendly conversation and shots of Jameson's. And we talk a little more about Jeff and the fact that we're worried about him. But we talk no more about Bernie, and the fact that we're worried about him, because apparently Bernie doesn't want to talk about that.

We don't stay as late as usual, because I am interested in getting some rest. Julie's coming to town tomorrow, and she needs help moving. Wouldn't do to be hung over. So a little before two o'clock we stumble out the front door. At the corner of 79th and Broadway we say our good-byes. Bernie walks home, alone, and I could swear his shoulders are sagging just a little. Something's definitely wrong.

20

Being with Julie is like being on vacation. I never worry about old girlfriends. I don't worry too much about work. I even get selfish enough to put aside my worries about Jeff and Bernie.

What's there to worry about when you're looking at a smile like Julie's? How could I possibly be concerned with the silly neuroses of my everyday life when I'm staring into the biggest, brightest brown eyes anyone's ever seen and they're twinkling back at me?

I have totally fallen for this girl, and I know everybody's making fun of me about it, but this *is* different from all the other times. Think about it. Of all the times in my life when I might have been susceptible to falling in love, this is the least likely. I should be terrified of love, considering the way it keeps coming back on me and getting in my face. I should be pushing away the thought of a serious relationship and dating frivolously—something a young man like myself can reasonably do in Manhattan, where there are hundreds more single women than single men.

Instead, I'm flipping out over the new girl from L.A., and I'm loving every minute of it. The alarm bells are going off, sure, but all I hear is music, and it makes me want to take her in my arms and dance with her.

The speed with which Julie has pulled off her cross-country move is astounding. Her movers arrived in L.A. on Wednesday, packed her apartment and told her they'd be in Manhattan with her things on Monday. She also shipped her car, though she admits she's probably going to end up selling it. There's really no need to have a car when you live in Manhattan.

And here she is, in her new place, with no stuff for two more days. So really, when I say she needs help moving, it's more like she needs help shopping. She sold most of her L.A. furniture because her new place is so much smaller than her old one. When she called me this morning, she told me she wanted me to take her shopping for things for her new home, and I told her I was at her service.

The first thing she needs is a mattress. Her bed will arrive Monday, but she will need to sleep somewhere tonight and tomorrow. Easy enough. There's a Sleepy's mattress store on Broadway and 72nd Street, and within minutes she's picked out one she likes. It will be delivered this afternoon.

Off we go, then, down Broadway to the Pottery Barn, where Julie spends a great deal of time picking out things I can't imagine taking time to pick out. She buys nothing, because we're not on the way home, but she does make plans to come back and buy a desk lamp, a wall clock, and some funky-looking place mats. All I can think is that *People* magazine must be paying well these days.

A few more stops take us to 67th Street, where there's a Barnes & Noble, and Julie tells me she'd like to go in and look for a book. She finished the one she was reading on her cross-country flight, and she needs something to read while she waits for her television to be delivered.

"I don't know, something mindless," she says. "How about a baseball book?"

"Nice," I say. "Just make a big, fat joke out of my job. Go right ahead. Everybody else does."

"I was only kidding," she says, smiling a smile as big as the island of Manhattan. "Don't be so sensitive."

I am not usually a shopper. I usually feel like killing myself after about two minutes in a place like Pottery Barn. But today it all feels too good. The only thing I'm waiting for is our next kiss. Which is an interesting topic, I think. The second kiss.

We kissed the last time we saw each other, but that was our first kiss, and it was a week ago. When I arrived at her apartment this morning, she was busy replacing a lightbulb, and there was no greet-you-at-the-door situation that might have lent itself to a kiss. So today we still haven't kissed.

It seems to me that the second time you kiss is almost more awkward than the first, especially if you put some time between them. Sure, the first never goes exactly the way you want it to go, and there are always a few giggly, fidgety moments. But it's so darn *nice* that you forgive the awkwardness and remember it fondly.

The second time, unless it immediately follows the first, is a troublemaker.

In this example, the couple is back together again after a week apart. Both parties know they're expected to kiss again, but neither feels a hundred percent comfortable with initiating the ritual. There is the back-and-forth show of affection (arm in arm, head nestled on shoulder), but it's all thrust-and-parry as everybody waits for the right situation.

Often, it will end up being forced, and it can therefore stand as one of the relationship's first key tests. If it's awkward and disappointing, it can be a real red flag. If the kisser surprises the kissee, that's a pretty bad sign too. But if it goes well—if you get past the embarrassment of being the one to initiate it—then the payoff is huge.

In that case, the second time can develop. It can have a depth of feeling that the first time could never attain. It can lead to immediate third, fourth, and fifth kisses, and beyond. It can be the gateway to bigger and better things.

The whole key is to find the right spot for it, and it's certainly not here in the Barnes & Noble. Not in front of all these people. For one thing, I don't know her all that well yet. She might be the kind of person who's terrified to kiss in public. She might get embarrassed easily. No, this one is going to have to wait, possibly until we get back to her apartment or mine, which is where it should happen anyway.

As we pass the magazine rack, Julie grabs a copy of *Cosmo* and seems transfixed by the flashy model on the cover.

"She's gorgeous, isn't she?" she asks, and I peek over her shoulder to get a look.

"Oh," I say. "Sure. That's my friend's fiancée."

"What?" she asks.

"Yeah," I say, trying to sound nonchalant even as I get a huge kick out of her reaction. "That's Anna. My friend Jeff's fiancée. She's nice."

And it's true. Jeff's fiancée, Anna, is the cover model for this particular issue of *Cosmo*. There she is, in a long pale yellow dress that's cut just about down to her navel, her hair flying about as if caught in a wind tunnel, her lips pursed in an impossible fantasy come-on to every American guy who will be standing in a supermarket checkout line this month.

Julie is staring at me, waiting for the smile that's going to tell her I'm kidding, but it's not coming.

"You're serious," she says.

"I swear to God," I say. "I'm sure you'll meet them."

"Wow," she says. "You lead quite the hip New York lifestyle, don't you, Jack? Schmoozing with fashion models?"

"It's really not as glamorous as it seems," I say. "But as long as you're impressed . . ."

And she twinkles those eyes as we make for the escalator, and it occurs to me that I might not need the escalator if she keeps twinkling those eyes.

When Julie picks out her book, it's something with a pink cover. Something along the lines of *Picking a Shade*, I am sure, though not that exact one. She seems sheepish when I ask her what she's picked out, and I'm sort of glad.

"I know it's silly," she says. "But every now and then I like to read something, you know, a little silly."

"I understand," I say. "Every now and then I like to read something about baseball."

"Stop."

And I do stop, but not because I've been instructed to stop. No, I stop for an entirely different, far more terrifying reason. I stop because, right in front of Julie and me, is a huge cardboard sign with a black-and-white photo of Danielle Hall. The sign proclaims a book signing, which is apparently happening today at this very Barnes & Noble, from one o'clock to three o'clock in the afternoon. I look at my watch, which tells me it's 12:56, and I panic. I start looking around as if I suddenly realized I'm being followed.

"Are you okay?" Julie asks, somewhat alarmed.

"Uh . . . yeah," I say, still scanning the fiction section.

"You sure?" she asks again. "You look . . . I don't know . . . worried, or something, all of a sudden."

"You know, I think I'm just hungry," I say, regaining my composure a little bit. "Why don't we pay for your book and then go get something to eat?"

"Sounds good to me," she says, and we head to the checkout lines.

But on the way to the escalator that will take us to those checkout lines, wouldn't you know it?

Danielle Hall.

I see her first, which I believe for a foolish moment will save me. She's wearing jeans again, and I could swear the same cotton V-neck she wore on the *Oprah Winfrey Show* yesterday. She's got a blond woman with her, and the blond woman appears to be talking nonstop. I figure this must be Angela Graves. The two of them are walking quickly, and Danielle doesn't appear to be listening to anything Angela is saying. She's too focused on petting and making baby talk with Eric, the cocker spaniel she's carrying in her arms.

The first to chime in is Julie.

"Do you know them?" she asks, and this is what makes me realize I must have been staring.

"Uh . . ." I answer, but this is all I can get out, because before I can utter another syllable, the crazy redhead pounces.

"Oh my God!" I hear, in that too-familiar voice. "I do *not* believe this. What are you doing, Jack? Following me?"

I actually look down at my feet, and for a second I'm disappointed to find a lack of quicksand. Because, man, if I could disappear right now . . .

"Who's this, Danielle?" the blonde-who-must-be-Angela is saying.

"This?" Danielle practically shouts. "This? You know this guy, actually. This is Jack Byrnes, the lunatic who called you the other day to try and get my number."

"Oh, right," Angela says. I swear you can see the cracks in her makeup when she smiles.

"Uh . . . Jack?" comes the voice of Julie, who has faded

into the background as I've confronted this banshee from my past. "What's going on?"

"Who's this, Jack?" Danielle sneers. "Your *girlfriend*? You tell your *girlfriend* you've been on the phone with an old college flame?"

Man, she is evil. I mean, pure, liquid evil. Like a slushy, gooey, evil milk shake, dripping down the side of its evil glass.

"Look, Danielle—" I say, for about the fiftieth time in a week.

"Whatever, Jack," she says. "All I want is for you to stay away from me. Okay?"

And before I can answer, they walk away. Have to get to that signing, I guess. Angela looks back, as if she's making sure I'm not following. I'm not, of course. I have too much explaining to do right here.

Julie, bless her heart, looks more concerned than anything else. But I'm sure she's looking for an explanation.

"This is a pretty long story," I tell her.

"I'll bet," she says.

"Can I buy you lunch, and I'll tell you the whole thing?"

"Absolutely," she says, smiling now. "I can't wait to hear this."

And we pay for the book and head across the street to Ollie's, for Chinese food and a good, long ghost story.

"All right," I begin, over a cup of steaming hot tea that I'm briefly tempted to pour directly into my eyes. "First of all, I want to tell you that this is not the kind of thing I planned to talk to you about on our second or third date."

"Okay," she says.

"It all started at Midway Airport in Chicago," I say.

I then proceed to tell her the whole story. I mean, from the beginning. How I didn't talk to Mary Ann in the airport. How Connie and Amy surprised me in the city. About

Danielle and the book. Nikki and the bar. Everything. This takes a while, and she sits patiently, with a curious look on her pretty face, and listens to the whole thing. When it's over, she has questions.

"So . . . you just saw an old girlfriend in the airport and decided to call all your old girlfriends to . . . what? To redo your breakups?"

"See, no," I say, and I want her to remember the key point here. "It wasn't like that. I didn't contact any of these women. They all contacted me. All of them. I didn't initiate contact with any of them, including Danielle, who is obviously pissed off even though she's the one who sent me a copy of her book."

"Okay, okay," she says. "But I still don't get this plan where you set up one final date with all of them to . . . I don't know what it's to do."

"See, I never used to believe in fate," I say.

"Right."

"But once this all started happening, it was way too weird. I mean, it was really like the universe was trying to tell me something, you know?"

"All right."

"So I figured, there must be a way to stop this all from happening. To stop the relationship ghosts . . ."

"You really need a better name for them," she says.

"I know," I say. "But I just figured there had to be a way to stop them from popping up every time I went to the dry cleaner's, you know?"

"Sure," she says.

"So maybe it was a misguided thing, but it really seemed to be working. Until I tried it with Danielle, which has been a total disaster."

"So . . ." she says, pausing to think of her next question. "Where do I fit into all of this?"

"Yes," I say. "I left that part out. When I met you getting

out of the cab, I was actually on my way to have lunch with Connie, which was going to be the first of these meetings."

"That's weird."

"Yes," I say. "Yes it is. But the really weird thing about it was, you threw me off course."

She's smiling now.

"After I met you," I say, "I totally forgot about Connie, and I blew her off by accident. I actually went home instead of meeting her at her office, and I forgot I was supposed to meet her until she called me."

"You forgot her because of me?"

"Yes," I say, too desperate to care if I'm revealing too much. "You kind of blew me away."

Now she's blushing and looking at the floor.

"So, you see," I say, building to my big conclusion, "with you, it's all different. I just wanted them all out of the way, so you and I could . . . I don't know . . . hang out when you came back to the city."

"So you've been making plans for me," she says, slyly, and I realize I may have survived the worst.

"I guess I have," I say. "I want to show you New York."

"Well," she says, "I guess that's all right. But does the tour include any more crazy old girlfriends who might jump us in a bookstore?"

"I really can't make any promises," I say.

And she laughs at this, which is nice. But the thing is, I was serious. I really don't know what might happen the next time we go out. I have no idea who we might run into. Danielle has really thrown me off, and I don't know what to do about it.

Meantime, Julie seems happy, and so the music's playing again. We finish lunch, stop back by the Pottery Barn to pick up the things she wanted, and head back to her apartment to wait for the mattress. Based on what's happened, I figure it wouldn't really do for me to hang around her empty apartment waiting for a mattress. So I tell her upon arrival that I have some things to take care of and I will call her later, perhaps about dinner. She says that's okay, and just before I leave her in front of the door to her new apartment building, I lean in for a kiss. She kisses back, and it's a nice one. Better, even, than the first time.

"What took you so long?" she asks when our lips finally part.

"I'm sorry?"

"I've been waiting for that all day," she says.

"Me too," I say, and we kiss again.

I walk home bubbling over, the memory of Danielle in the bookstore fading already.

This girl just listened to my whole crazy relationship ghost story. And not only does she not appear to be scared off by it, she seemed to enjoy a kiss she deemed overdue. She may really be as special as I've made her out to be.

Now, wouldn't that be a nice change?

21

If there's one thing I've learned over the past few weeks, it's never to assume. Even when everything appears to be going well, never assume it actually is.

The one message that was on my answering machine when I arrived home after my kiss with Julie was a difficult one to believe:

"Jack? This is Connie. Listen, I've been wondering why you haven't called, and I just wanted to make sure everything was all right. I'm sure you're busy, but I'd really like to get together again for dinner sometime soon, so call me when you get the chance. Okay? See you soon. 'Bye."

Now, there are two possibilities here, as I see it.

The first is that somewhere between 78th and 75th Streets, I walked through a time warp, slipping back in time to a day on which Connie would actually be within her rights to call me, express concern that I hadn't called her recently, and blithely suggest a date.

And as distressing as this first possibility is, the second is much scarier.

The second possibility is that Connie didn't get what I was trying to do last week. That she thought I was trying to rekindle something rather than crush it out. If this is the case, then nothing about my plan has actually worked. It's all a failure, all the hard work of the past week and a half has been for nothing, and I am doomed to wander the streets of Manhattan with the ghosts for the rest of my life.

My machine informs me that the message came in a little before noon, as Julie and I were store-hopping down Broadway. Those were such happy times—before the Danielle incident in the bookstore and long before I came home to this insanity. Sitting, stunned, in my desk chair, I look on the wall at the photo of Bill Buckner, and for the first time I think I understand how he felt.

I certainly wouldn't want to date in front of 55,000 people. Especially if I was going to screw it all up this badly.

After consulting the photo, which serves as evidence that there was a time when the universe was functioning properly, I decide not to call Connie. Maybe it's all some big mistake. Maybe Connie has been doing a little late morning drinking. Maybe she's playing some kind of practical joke. Maybe, if I ignore this, it will just go away. Oh please, please, please just let it go away.

But of course it's not going away, no matter how hard I try to ignore it. And when the phone rings, it forces me out of this fantasy and back into the reality that is my twisted love life.

"Hello?" I ask, bracing for the worst.

"Jack?" says a disturbing female voice.

"Connie?"

"Hi!" Connie says. "I was really starting to worry about you! Where have you been?"

"I've been around," I say. "Connie, what's going on?"

"What do you mean?" she says, convincingly ignorant.

"I mean, why did you call? I thought—"

"Why did I call?" she asks. "I hadn't heard from you since last week. I just wanted to make sure you were okay."

"Connie, I thought we weren't going to call each other anymore," I say, perhaps a bit too blunt.

She's silent for a few seconds, but then goes on as if I'd said nothing.

"We had such a nice time at Gabriel's," she says. "I was so happy that you sounded so positive about us, after all our time apart. I just couldn't believe you felt that way."

"Connie, I didn't mean for—"

But she's not to be stopped.

"I mean, before that day, I didn't really know if I wanted to get back together. I thought I might, but I didn't really know. But after that wonderful dinner, I knew it was the right thing. And I was so excited that you did too."

Okay, something is wrong here. If she really got that impression from our dinner, she would have called on my birthday, right? At least to say Happy Birthday? We haven't been broken up long enough to forget each other's birthdays.

So as Connie babbles on and on, I come to the conclusion that she may have lost it. Something may have happened, and Connie may have snapped—the way she did this summer, when she had that mysterious office affair, or the way she did after the terrorist attacks. That's the only possible explanation, because damn it, the message was clear the last time we were together.

"So," she's still saying, "I thought we could go out to dinner again? Say Monday night? I have a thing tonight with my parents, but I thought next week would be a great time for our second second date."

And she giggles.

"All right, Connie," I say. "I don't know how to come out and say this, but—"

But nothing. She's cutting me off, apparently having heard nothing after "All right, Connie."

"Great!" she says. "Maybe we'll do Ruby Foo's. I haven't been there in so long."

"Connie," I say, trying to stop her. "Please let me talk to you."

"Oh!" she says. "I've got another call. Just call me Monday, and we'll figure it all out, okay. 'Bye!"

And she hangs up.

I mean, that was the weirdest phone call I've had in a long time. And that is saying something.

Reason and Mookie Wilson having failed me, I turn to the one thing in my life that makes sense right now—the one thing that's going right. I call Julie and I ask her what she's doing for dinner.

"I thought I'd order in," she says. "But I have no dishes."

"Well, then, that settles it," I say. "I'll be by around seven o'clock, with two plates, two forks, and two knives. We'll order Chinese and we'll drink soda from cans. Sound good?"

"Sounds like a date," she says. "Hey, my mattress came."

"Cool. So now you don't have to sleep on the floor."

"I was kind of looking forward to it, actually," she says. "But then I realized I don't have carpeting either. Hear the echo?"

And I do. Her voice is echoing around her empty apartment, off the bare walls and the hardwood floors. It's an exciting time for her, and I remember when I moved into my own New York City apartment for the first time. All I had was a desk—not even a chair—until my movers showed up. I couldn't even spend time in the apartment after dark, because I didn't have a lamp.

"Yes, very nice echo," I say. "Means you have an especially nice apartment."

"Well, thank you," she says.

I feel bad not telling her about Connie, but maybe I'll bring it up over Chinese. I'm thinking that, by keeping things from Julie, I'm already tarnishing the beauty of what we have, before it even really gets started. But the fact is, I don't know what to think about Connie right now, and therefore I have no idea how to present it to somebody else. Anyway, I'm sure it'll come up over dinner.

"So, I'll see you at seven?" I ask. "You want me to bring anything else?"

"Nope," she says. "Well, if you get a chance, maybe a six-pack of good, cold beer? It's been a tiring day."

"You got it," I say. "See you later."

" 'Bye."

Beer she wants. Cold beer. I mean, can you beat this?

I stuff a shopping bag with two plates and the silverware, stop in at a deli for a six-pack of Sam Adams, and head on up to 78th Street. Julie may not have any furniture, but she does not lack for Chinese food menus, four of which have been slipped under her door this afternoon.

"Yeah," I say. "That's going to happen pretty much every day."

"Very convenient," she says.

"Yes, very. Good thing about living in the city. Every place delivers."

We pick one and order, and we laugh and smooch as we sit on her bare floor, drinking beer and eating Chinese food with chopsticks. When we're finished, and the fortune cookies have been cracked open, she looks at me differently than she has at any point in our brief relationship and says—I'm not kidding here: "So, you want to check out my new mattress?"

And of course I do.

So we hit the mattress.

We both keep our jeans on, though the same can't be said for our sweaters and T-shirts. It's about an hour's worth of that breathless, exploring time, where you're always looking for permission to do the next thing and pleasantly surprised when it's granted. Lots of rubbing, kissing, sighing, and general intimacy, but not the deed itself. Plenty of time for that later.

As much as we both seem to like each other, we still haven't known each other for that long. And while I'd certainly be amenable to the idea of staying the night, I offer no resistance when she finally pulls away and starts suggesting, sweetly, that it may be time for me to go home.

"You understand, right?" she says, looking me in the eyes.

"Of course," I say, as sincerely as possible. "Of course. Hey, I'm not here to force anything on you."

"I mean, I kind of want you to stay," she says. "I mean, I *really* kind of want you to stay. But it's just . . ."

"I understand," I say. "Really."

Sure I do. We've all heard that one before. Doesn't pay to let her finish it, because she's made her decision. Trying to change her mind just wouldn't be gentlemanly.

So I clean up the Chinese food and tell her I'll be sure to throw it out on my way out the door. She stands at the doorway, her arms folded in front of her breasts, as I walk down the stairs. And just before I hit the front door, she calls out, "Call me tomorrow!"

It's almost nine-thirty when I get to the door of 3C, and I can see from under the door that a light is on inside. I can only assume Jeff is in there, and that's not a bad thing, really, because I wouldn't mind filling him in. He's been so busy with the wedding planning lately that he hasn't been around as much in the mornings.

So I open the door, walk into the apartment and ask the room, "Jeff?" before finally spotting Anna—the soon-to-be Mrs. Jeff—sitting in my armchair.

"Hello, Jack," she says, locking eyes with me, steaming up the room.

"Uh, hi, Anna," I say. "What's up?"

"Oh," she says, "not much. What's up with you?"

During this last bit, she stands up, and I have to suppress a gasp. Anna is wearing a skintight white turtleneck and a long red skirt that show off her figure perfectly. The slim skirt falls all the way to the tops of her shoes, which, I noticed when she was sitting with her legs crossed, are shiny black boots with high, pointed heels. She wears a diamond pendant around her neck, and her Tiffany engagement ring sparkles in the dim light of my apartment.

Yes, I'm in love with Julie. But that doesn't mean Anna isn't disarming. It is, after all, her thing.

Of course, once I stop noticing Anna, I notice that she appears to be alone.

"Is Jeff here?" I ask.

"Jeff's not here," she says. "He's home, sleeping."

"He's sleeping? It's nine-thirty on a Saturday."

"I think maybe I wore him out," she says, and flicks her tongue out ever-so-quickly.

"Uh," I say. "I really don't know what to say to that."

"Anyway, he went to sleep. Sometimes he falls asleep early, and he's out for the night. So I took his keys, and here I am."

This explanation is insufficient.

"Is there something I can do for you?" I ask.

"Oh, I'll bet there's a lot you can do for me," she says, and she starts walking toward me. Man, can she walk.

"Anna," I say, trying not to stammer. "What are you doing here?"

"Jack," she whispers, having now come close enough to hold my left hand with both of hers. "I don't think I ever properly wished you a Happy Birthday."

Excuse me? Is this what I think it is?

"Anna, are you drunk?" I ask.

She juts out her bottom lip and spins away from me.

"No, I'm not drunk," she says. "You hurt my feelings."

"Uh . . . I'm sorry?"

"That's better," she says, sitting on the couch now and petting the cushion next to her. "Now come over here and let's chat."

No way am I sitting on that couch right now. God knows what kind of power this woman has. I could wake up tomorrow having ruined three different lives and never even know what hit me.

"Look, Anna," I say. "I don't know why you're here, but I think you probably ought to go home to Jeff."

"Don't be silly," she says, smiling through the reddest lips I've ever seen. "I already told you, Jeff's asleep. He'll never know I was gone."

"I really think—"

"Stop thinking," she says. "You think too much. That's why you have all your problems with these women. I'm here to help."

"Anna, how, exactly, do you think . . . this . . . will help?"

"Oh, don't knock it till you've tried it," she says.

Let's take a little bit of a timeout here. We have Jack Byrnes, in the middle of two of the most emotional weeks he's ever spent and about ten minutes removed from an arousing yet ultimately unfulfilling encounter with the thrilling new woman in his life. He's confronted, in his own home, by one of the most beautiful women in New York City (and therefore the world), who appears to be offering sex and a promise that no one—not even his best friend, to whom the woman is engaged—will ever know.

I have decided not to believe in fate, or even God. But I'm pretty sure I believe in Satan.

"Anna, listen," I say. "I can't."

Good boy, Jack! Way to go! You stupid, loyal bastard, you!

"What do you mean, you can't?" Anna asks, clearly stunned.

"I just can't," I say. "I mean, don't get me wrong. I appreciate the offer. And I understand how stupid pretty much every other guy in this city would think I am for turning it down, but—"

"But you're turning it down?"

"But I'm turning it down."

"Jack, I don't get turned down."

She is still looking right into my eyes, but now her eyebrows are arched. I think I may actually have hurt her feelings, no kidding this time.

"Anna, I'm sorry," I say. "But this is all wrong."

"Why?" she asks. "Because of Jeff?"

"Yes, because of Jeff!" I say. "Because of Jeff, and because I have this new girl in my life, and because I don't know what your motivation is, but really, really, really because of Jeff! He's nuts about you!"

"Oh, come on," she says. "Do you really think he's nuts about me? Or do you think he wants everybody to see him walking around with some hot piece of ass?"

"You know," I say, "this is really something you need to discuss with Jeff. And it's really none of my business. But since you asked, if you want my opinion, yes, I think he's crazy about you."

"Pff," she says. "I think you're crazy. I'm offering you the night of your life, and you're saying no?"

Modesty is clearly not one of this woman's virtues.

"Look, Anna, I hate to do this," I say. "But if you don't leave now, I'm going to have to call Jeff and tell him you're here."

"I don't believe this," she says.

She struts over to the back of the sofa, grabs her black leather jacket, and spins to face me. Her hair is covering half of her face.

"You know you'll never get another chance at me," she says, and it's all I can do not to gulp.

She's heading for the door now. I'm holding it open.

"Good night, Anna," I say as she leaves. "And thanks again."

"Ha!" she shouts back, without turning around, and I allow myself the pleasure of watching her walk down the hallway. I figure it's the least I deserve.

As soon as she's out of sight, I race inside and dial Bernie's cell phone.

"Hello," he says.

"Bern, where are you?"

"Home," he says.

"You up for a drink?"

"Sure."

"Meet me at Dublin House. I'm going there now. Get there when you can."

22

"Dude," Jeff is saying. "You look like hell."

Considering the way I feel, it's easy to believe him.

I'm looking up at him through one eye, because it's the only one I've been able to open so far. I appear to have slept in my clothes, on my sofa, and Jeff and Anna have come in to wake me up.

It'll be a while before everything comes back to me, but the sight of Anna in jeans, a red sweater, and that black leather jacket reminds me that she was in this apartment not long ago, and that she is probably one of the reasons I now find myself in this condition.

Right now, though, she is laughing at me, as is Jeff.

"I mean, you didn't even make it to your bed?" Jeff asks between chuckles. "What is this, college?"

"What time is it?" I finally ask.

"It's one o'clock in the afternoon, man," Jeff says. "You're sleeping the day away."

It's starting to pour back into my memory. Bernie and me at the Dublin House, hammering back beer after beer, shot after shot. Convincing Mike the bartender to sing "Danny

Boy" with us. Mike finally convincing us we had to leave, as the sun was coming up.

And what the hell is Anna doing here, after the stunt she pulled last night? And is Bernie okay? And what's Julie up to today?

I need answers.

"Jesus," I say, sitting up and opening my other eye. "That was some kind of strange night."

Oh, shit. I just remembered the call from Connie. No wonder I got so drunk.

"You and Bernie hit it hard, huh?" Jeff asks.

"Yeah, I guess so," I say. "My head hurts."

Anna walks away for a minute and comes back with two Advil and a glass of water.

"Thanks," I say, unable to look her in the eye.

"No problem," she says. "Least I can do. And I'm sorry if I'm one of the reasons you're in this condition."

Huh?

"Huh?" I ask.

Anna looks at Jeff and smiles. She leans in, squeezing his right arm with both of her hands, and tilts her head so it rests on his shoulder. Jeff is smiling.

"Yeah, she told me everything," Jeff says. "I gotta tell you, buddy. I'm impressed."

I might be impressed too, if I weren't so damn confused.

"Baby," Anna says to Jeff. "I'm going to go run to the drugstore before lunch. I'll meet you there?"

"All right, sweetheart," Jeff says, and the two of them kiss. Anna struts out of the apartment, and Jeff looks back at me, still smiling.

Baby?

Sweetheart?

"What'd she tell you?" I ask.

"Everything, dude," he says. "And I gotta tell you, it was the best thing that could have happened to us."

Now I'm up and I'm headed for the fridge, hoping there's pizza. I always stop at Big Nick's for pizza when I'm on my way home at such an insane hour. Sure enough, there's one plain slice, just sitting there on the refrigerator shelf. Not wrapped or packaged in any way, mind you, just drooping there on the top shelf, next to the bottles of beer and the cans of soda. It looks delicious.

"I think you need to explain," I say to Jeff, after stuffing the point of the pizza into my mouth.

"Anna came home last night and woke me up," Jeff says. "She was crying. I've never seen her cry before. She said she had to confess something to me. Then she told me about coming over here."

"Really?"

"Yeah, I couldn't believe it," he says. "She was literally in tears, and she said she felt terrible. Said she wouldn't blame me if I wanted to leave her."

"Wow," I say, still munching.

"Now, you have to picture this," Jeff says. "I'm half asleep, trying to process all of this, and she's just going on and on. She's telling me how she hadn't really been sure she loved me, but after you turned her down she started feeling so guilty for even having come here. And she says that convinced her, because she said she never felt guilty before when she's cheated on a guy."

"She ever cheat on you?" I ask.

"No, that's the other thing," he says. "She's breaking down and telling me she always thought it was weird that she hadn't slept with anybody else since we started seeing each other, since that's generally not the way she does things. So I don't know, she wanted to try it out or something, and there you were."

"A sitting duck," I say, smiling.

"That's what she thought, at least," he says. "But she tells me now, it's like she's had some epiphany."

"Man, that is deep," I say, once again seated on the couch.

"So anyway, last night we talked, we had the greatest sex we've ever had. And, this morning, I wake up, and she's making pancakes. It's like she wants to be this perfect wife—even though she never even dreamed about it before."

"Now, watch, she'll let herself go and get fat," I say.

"That I seriously doubt," he says. "You've never seen anybody work out like this girl."

"I was only kidding," I say.

"Oh, I know. But even if she did, I don't know. I know you never believed me when I said I was in love, but I was. Now, it's like she's feeling all the same stuff in return. I always used to figure she'd come around. Now, it's like she already has, and before the wedding. It's perfect."

I guess.

"So anyway," Jeff is still chattering. "We just wanted to drop by and fill you in. I think Anna was maybe a little uncomfortable or something, but she says she wants to talk to you about the whole thing, just so there's no hard feelings. So maybe later she'll call you."

"Sure," I say. "I'll be around."

"Okay," he says. "I'm off to lunch. You need a shower."

While in the shower, much of my conversation with Bernie comes back to me. At least the parts before we got stupid and incoherent and sang "Danny Boy."

Bernie showed up a few minutes after I did, and right away I started hammering him with the events of my day. All the stuff with Julie, running into Danielle, the calls from Connie, the thing in the apartment with Anna.

"Are you shitting me?" he asked as soon as I finished with the Anna story.

And because I couldn't figure out which part he didn't believe, I gave a blanket answer.

"It's all true," I said. "It just happened. Like, ten minutes ago."

"And you turned her down?"

"I'm not going to tell you it didn't hurt a little."

"I'll bet that girl hasn't been turned down since the third grade."

"Probably not," I said. "She seemed upset."

"This totally sucks for Jeff, though," Bernie said. "She's running around behind his back with his friends? Or trying to?"

"I know it," I said. "I know it. What do we do?"

"I think," Bernie said, "that we should drink on it. And see what it looks like in the morning."

And we did. We drank and drank. I probably drank more last night than I have on any night since college—or at least since my first year in Boston. We kept coming back to the Jeff and Anna topic all night, but there was something else in the conversation that stuck with me, and I remember it in the shower.

I actually asked Bernie how things have been with women. It's a question we ask Bernie a lot, usually because we're anticipating an answer loaded with entertainment value. But on this night, things were different, and earlier suspicions were confirmed.

"You know," he said, "I've been kind of taking some time off from the ladies."

"You?" I asked. "How does something like this happen?"

And Bernie told me that the last woman he'd been with was Sherri, the waitress from Blondie's. And he told me that the whole thing had really knocked him around. He said the idea that he was some sort of sexual wind-up doll to whom women referred friends was upsetting to him.

"That's never how it's been," he said. "At least, that's never how I wanted it to be."

He told me he's been taking some time to reevaluate, and that he's wondering why he doesn't go on more second or third dates. Big Bern was as down as I'd ever seen him, and after a couple of Guinnesses I was having trouble understanding why.

"What do you mean, you're lonely?" I asked him. "You never go home alone."

"Dude, you know what I mean," he said. "Sure, it's great to always have somebody to go home with. But I'm wondering if it might not be such a bad idea to have somebody to go home *to*."

"Whoa," I said. "I think I need another beer to process this one."

"I'm serious, man!" Bernie snapped at me, slamming his pint glass down on the bar, prompting Mike to look up from the cash register.

"Okay, okay," I said. "I'm sorry. I was just messing around."

"Well, I'm not," he said. "I'm sick of messing around. I've always been some big joke to you guys—Big ol' Bernie and the ladies."

"It's not a joke, Bern," I said. "It's admiration."

"Well, it's not always something to admire. Damn it, man, I'm not a young guy anymore. Think of it this way: I'm writing a new book . . ."

"I didn't know that," I said.

"Well, I am," he said. "And I'm remembering my first book, and how the whole time I was writing it, I wished there was somebody there I could show it to. You know, as it was going along."

"You know I'd take a look if you wanted . . ."

"Yeah, but that's not the point, Jack, and I think you know that."

And of course, I do know that. And at this point I had started to realize what Bernie meant. Those of us who operate on a girlfriend-to-girlfriend basis shouldn't have a problem getting his point. Bernie has decided he wants to be one of us. He's sick of playing the field.

"Yeah, I know," I said. "I'm sorry, dude. So, what are you going to do?"

"Right now?" he shouted, changing moods instantly. "Right now, I'm going to drink away the night with my friend, and try and figure out how to save my other friend. The world's got bigger problems than me crying in my beer because some waitress wanted me to take her home."

And we didn't discuss it again. But all night, he was different. Quieter than usual. And I killed him in the video golf game, which never happens. I'm thinking Big Bern is scared. He really doesn't know what to do.

Once the clock crept past four-thirty and we were still in the bar, we figured this was going to be an epic. There were three of us left—me, Bernie, and Mike the bartender, and Mike was telling us he'd locked the door. Officially, the bar was closed, but he wanted to have a few drinks, and he wanted company. We were only too happy to help.

We drank for free for those last two hours, and by the time Mike woke up in a corner booth and decided we all had to go home, the sun was up.

My memory refreshed, I make my first phone call of the day, around the corner to Julie's place. I have made sure I am showered and alert for this call, because there's nothing good that can come of sounding hung over. Would Julie mind? Probably not. But I'd just feel weird about telling her I left her place after that tantalizing test drive of the mattress and went out drinking until six-thirty. I have to keep reminding myself we don't really know each other that well.

"Hello?" says the pretty echo.

"Aha," I say. "Still no furniture."

"What?" she asks.

"You know, you still have your echo."

"Oh, right," she says. "Hey, I'm surprised you're up and about."

Oh no.

"What do you mean?" I ask, scanning the mess on my desk, trying to remember if . . .

"Well, you didn't sound like you were in real good shape when you called me at seven this morning."

"Oh God," I say. "I didn't."

"Yes," she says. "Yes you did."

"I am so sorry," I say, my stomach churning.

But Julie is laughing.

"Oh, it's okay," she says. "You were cute."

"Cute?" I ask. "Well, that's a nice break. I mean, if you're going to drunk-dial somebody at seven in the morning, it's good to at least be cute about it."

Whew.

"Absolutely," she says. "You said the sweetest things. It was worth waking up for."

"Wow," I say, worried again. "What did I say?"

"You told me you really, really liked me," she says, giggling. "You told me you liked me soooooo much that you were glad we didn't have sex, because it was too soon and because I should get to decide. You told me you liked me as soon as you met me. You said everything about five times."

"I'm so embarrassed," I say, looking around for that quick-sand again.

"Don't be," she says. "Like I said, it was sweet. And it's nice that you're letting me decide about the sex."

"Oh, I can't believe this."

"So, listen, I'm sick of my apartment. There's no place to sit. Where can you take me?"

"You want to go out with a drunken lunatic who calls people at seven o'clock on Sunday mornings?"

"You know I do," she says. "I'm coming to your place. We'll go from there. Sound good?"

Sounds sensational, actually. Now I'm glad I already took that shower.

And as I wait for her to arrive, I stare at the picture. Sometimes I feel like Buckner, sometimes like Mookie. Sometimes it can change in a minute.

A minute ago I was feeling like Buckner, looking back between my legs, wondering how that ball got there, scared to look up. But now I feel like Mookie. I feel the way that whole '86 Mets team must have felt that night.

You know, like they'd got away with something.

Today, Julie is wearing a brown, knee-length suede skirt and brown boots to go with her cream-colored cowl-neck sweater. She has small diamond studs in her ears, and her hair is back in a ponytail, which I've never seen before. Much as I love her hair when it's down, I have to say I like this look too. Makes those big, beautiful brown eyes of hers look even bigger and more beautiful.

She has surprised me, because I'm not sure how she got past Yousef and arrived at the door of 3C without him buzzing me to tell me she was coming. Yousef, come on, man. I know you're taking an active interest in my love life and all, but how well do we really know this girl? She could be here to steal stuff.

"Not bad," she says, looking me up and down. "Not bad for somebody who passed out at seven A.M."

"Well thank you," I say. "I worked hard on it. Especially on the hair. What do you think?"

"Not bad at all. I think you'll do just fine for a mellow Sunday night date. Where are we going?"

"Well, since it's a nice day, I thought we'd walk a little bit. You want to see a movie?"

"A movie sounds great. What did you want to see?"

"Well, I figured we'd walk down there, see what's playing, buy tickets, and then go around the corner to Rosa Mexicano. You've got to try the guacamole. They make it right at your table."

"Sounds delicious," she says. "Lead on, Mr. New York."

After a few hours lazily walking through the park, we get to the movie theater at the corner of Broadway and 67th around five-thirty and find out there's an eight-thirty show. Two tickets later we're out the door and heading a couple of blocks south, past Lincoln Center, to Rosa Mexicano, where we indulge in the homemade guacamole and frozen pomegranate margaritas.

I like the movie, she doesn't, and this topic occupies our walk home. It's a little bit cool now, which isn't too surprising for late November, and Julie has both of her arms wrapped around my right arm as we wander back up Broadway. Her head is tucked onto my shoulder, and I'm just glad she can't see how huge my smile is. I must look goofy. I feel goofy.

"I don't really feel like sleeping on the floor again," she says to me, looking off into the sky, then turning her smiling face back around to meet mine. "Do you mind if I stay over your place?"

And I look down at her face, and she's smiling the most mischievous little smile I've ever seen. And all I can do is smile back.

"Cool," she says.

How well is this night going? The elevator works. We ascend to 3C, arms still locked, and as we approach the door I hear the TV on inside.

"Damn it, Jeff," I say.

"What is it?" Julie asks.

"My friend, I gave him a key so he could check on things while I'm away, and now he's over all the time."

"He's like Kramer?" she asks.

"Yes. Like Kramer," I answer, not amused. "Anyway, this isn't what I had in mind for when we got back here."

"Ooh," she says, rubbing my arm with her hands. "Me neither."

"We'll tell Jeff he has to go."

"Sounds good to me."

And I open the door and get ready to tell Jeff to get the hell out. And the first thing I see is . . . a coffee table.

The second thing I see is Connie, and my legs actually feel weak.

For a while all everybody does is stare. My mouth may be open, I'm not sure. I haven't looked at Julie, and right now I'm not sure I want to. Connie's wearing jeans and a gray sweater, and she's bustling about the place as if she just moved in.

Oh my God. That's exactly what she's done. She's moved back in.

Oh no.

This can't be happening.

The entire plan? Completely down the drain? What's next? Danielle moves in next door?

Connie breaks the silence.

"Jack!" she says. "Well, what do you think?"

What do I think? I think you're out of your mind, is what I think. I think you've picked the exact perfect time to show up and ruin everything that's going well in my life. I think I'm about ready to jump off the top of this building. That's what I think.

"Connie," I finally say. "What are you doing here?"

This is good. This should convey to Julie that I am as surprised as she is to find a strange woman in my apartment just before midnight on a Sunday.

"I thought I'd surprise you," she says. "I figure, if we're going to start seeing each other again, I might as well move back in."

"What the hell sense—" I start, but can't finish.

Now it's Julie's turn.

"I think I'd better go," she says.

"No!" I shout, maybe a little too loud. Connie has stopped decorating for a second and is looking at us, confused.

"No, really, Jack," Julie says, looking at the floor, the door, the ceiling, anything but me. "I think I'd better go. It looks like you have a lot to sort out here. I'm sorry I invited myself in."

"Julie," I say. "You can't really think—"

"I don't know what to think, Jack," she says, suddenly looking me in the eye, looking as if she might cry. "Why don't you just give me a call when you're a little more . . . I don't know . . . settled."

I feel like the worst bastard ever to walk the earth. I have disappointed this wonderful, beautiful, sweet, perfect girl, and I believe I should be locked up for the rest of my life.

Only thing is, *I didn't do anything!* I have been, for the second night in a row, ambushed in my own apartment. By a woman who has no business being here. By someone who turned in her keys to Yousef two months ago!

So, really, I can't figure out what to feel. But all of a sudden Julie's walking back to the elevator. And I'm walking after her, no idea what to say. And Connie's standing in the doorway, holding a small blue porcelain statue that used to sit over my fireplace, and watching the whole scene without talking.

I plead with Julie, but she refuses to hear me. As the elevator doors close, she's shaking her head, and my shoulders slump. I stare for a few seconds at the closed doors before I finally hear Connie's voice from down the hall.

"Jack?" she asks. "Who was that?"

23

"Hey Jack," Bernie says from across the white tablecloth. "You wanna dance?"

"Not funny," I say. "Although, you do look good in that tux."

He doesn't laugh either.

It wasn't supposed to be this way—everybody out on the dance floor but the two of us. I was supposed to be here with Julie, showing off my friends. Bernie was supposed to be fighting off bridesmaids and scoping out the girls who didn't catch the bouquet.

But Bernie is semiretired now, and my own love life went up in a big old mushroom cloud six nights ago, and so here we both are, staring at a crowded dance floor at whose center is the happiest damn couple we've ever seen.

Anna looks astounding, of course, in a sleek white Vera Wang number that shows off her shoulders. Jeff, scrawny as ever, has trouble filling his own tux, but there he is, twirling his new bride around. I think they're actually very happy. I haven't got suddenly gloomy Bernie to come all the way around to my way of thinking, but I think they have a chance to make it. I guess people can surprise you.

Take, for example, our old friend Connie from Connecticut. She threw a big surprise our way Sunday night, with that moving-back-in act. Buckled my knees and chased innocent little Julie out of there before I could get a sentence out of my mouth. Yeah, there's nothing like a good surprise, especially when it comes from an old girlfriend.

If Connie was upset about seeing me coming home with another woman, she didn't show it for long. I was still staring at the dull green elevator doors with her question—"Jack? Who was that?"—hanging in the air, and she was moving on to a different topic.

I turned to answer her (or kill her—I actually hadn't decided which), but she was gone. She'd ducked back into the apartment with her porcelain angel statue. For a second I thought about chasing Julie, but then I figured that would only further convince her that I was insane. No, Julie was better dealt with later in the night, or even the next day.

Connie, however, had to be dealt with right then and there.

"I know we used to keep this on the mantel," she said, still talking about that angel figurine. "But I think I like it better over here, by the window. What do you think?"

"Connie, what the hell are you doing?" I exploded, slamming the door behind me. "Who told you you could move back in here? Did I miss a conversation? Have you lost your mind? I was on a date, for Christ's sake!"

"You were on a date with that girl?" she asked. "But I thought you were going on a date with me this week."

By this point I had realized there must be something seriously wrong with Connie, and that the best thing for me to do was to handle her carefully, in case she was on the brink of something rash.

"Look, Connie," I said, much more calmly. "Even if our last conversation led you to believe we were going on a date this week—which I don't think it should have—"

"But you said—"

"Please," I said. "Let me finish."

Blank look.

"Even if that's what you took out of that phone call the other day, why would that make you think you could move back in all of a sudden?"

She offered no response. Just another blank look.

"I mean," I continued, "isn't that kind of a big jump?"

"I don't know what you're talking about," she said, springing back into action, unwrapping something else from crumpled newspaper. "If we're getting back together, it should be like it was before. You know, like we talked about that night at dinner."

It would be one huge understatement to say that Connie got the wrong idea at that dinner. She couldn't have missed the point more completely if she'd been one of the soup spoons.

"Connie, I don't think you understood what I was trying to do that night," I said. But she didn't hear me. Now she was dusting the end tables and the wooden arms of the sofa.

"All I know is, it'll be great to sleep in that big bed again," she said. "I always loved your mattress."

And so I was lost. Totally lost as to what to do. I didn't feel like I could scream at her, because she seemed to be in a fragile state of mind. And when I tried to talk sensibly to her, she just ignored what I was saying. I stood and watched as she started unpacking a suitcase and piling up shoes in the bottom of my closet, and I made another faint protest about how she wasn't really going to be moving back in, but she just blew it right off and asked me if I wouldn't mind helping her unpack.

"I mean, you're just *standing* there," she said.

And then the phone rang.

I raced over and grabbed the cordless receiver before Connie could get to it, and she looked stunned that I'd swiped it from her.

"Julie?" I said into the phone.

"Jack?" a man said.

"Oh. Sorry. Yeah, this is Jack."

"Jack, it's Tom Mason. Connie's father."

Sure. Why not?

"Jack, is Connie there?" he asked.

"Uh . . . yes, as a matter of fact, she is," I said.

"Oh, Jack, I'm so sorry," he said. "She said something about going back to you, and we couldn't stop her. Is she okay?"

"Well, she seems all right," I said. "Except she thinks I asked her to move back in with me, which I didn't."

I wasn't worried about Connie overhearing the conversation. She was stacking sweaters.

"I'm afraid there are a lot of things Connie is getting wrong these days," Connie's dad said.

"Excuse me?"

"Look, I'll explain everything when we get there," he said. "I know it doesn't make any sense, but her mother and I are in the car in the city, and we're heading to your place now. We'll be there in about ten minutes. Just don't let her leave."

"I don't think that's going to be a problem," I said. "She's moving in."

"We'll see you soon, Jack," he said.

And I hung up the phone and started looking around for the cameras. It suddenly appeared as if my life had turned into some twisted TV reality show where I was the only one who wasn't in on the gag.

"Who was that?" Connie asked.

"It was my parents," I lied.

"Oh, how are they?" she asked. "It's been so long. You know, my father still asks about you. He loves your job."

Somehow, I got the feeling that Connie and Tom Mason hadn't been having too many traditional father-daughter talks these days. But I had to wait about fifteen more minutes to find out what really was going on. That's when Yousef buzzed me to tell me Mr. and Mrs. Macy were here to see me. I assumed he meant Mason, but I told him to send them up anyway, because even if it was the Macys (whom I don't know), I figured it couldn't hurt to have some more people in the place.

Connie's parents arrived at my front door looking tired and panicked. I'd never seen Tom Mason so dressed-down before. In a yellow golf shirt and jeans, he looked as if he hadn't shaved in a week. Both he and his wife appeared to have aged much more than the three months that had passed since I'd last seen them, and as soon as I opened the door, Mrs. Mason dashed across the room to her daughter.

"Mom?" Connie said, as if waking from a coma. "Dad?"

"We're here, honey, it's all right," her mother told her, taking her into her arms and leading her out of the apartment and into the hallway. "Everything is all right."

But since it quite obviously was not, I turned from the touching scene and looked at Mr. Mason, who had promised answers.

He spent the next several minutes informing me that Connie had had a nervous breakdown, and a pretty bad one at that. During a recent "screaming episode," Connie had fallen down the front stairs of their Connecticut home and hit her head. Doctors were telling the parents that the symptoms she was displaying sounded like some mild form of dementia and that Connie would require regular psychiatric help.

"The only problem is, we can't keep her from running off," he said, looking across the room at his daughter huddled in her mother's arms. "We always end up chasing after her, like we did tonight, and half the time we don't have any clue as to where she might be."

He went on to say that they'd considered putting her in a hospital, where she could receive round-the-clock care, but that the idea was too painful for them to handle. He also said, however, that this night's "episode" (he liked that word) was the worst by far and that they might have to consider the previously unthinkable and commit their daughter.

"It's really been a nightmare," he concluded, his head hanging.

"I'm so sorry, Mr. Mason," I said.

"Jack, it's not your fault," he said. "I don't want you to think this had anything to do with you."

I could swear I saw tears welling up in the man's eyes, but he turned away and I couldn't be sure.

It was decided that he and I would carry out the things that Connie had brought with her to move into my place. Other than the coffee table, which neither of us could figure out how she carried there, it wasn't too much. And the coffee table fit in the back of the Masons' SUV with one of the backseats folded down.

As we carried Connie's things from the apartment to the car, Connie and her mother sat in the backseat. Connie was crying at least two of the times I walked past with luggage, and one other time she looked right at me.

"Jack?" she asked, and she looked as if she hadn't seen me in months.

The band is playing, "Jump, Jive, and Wail," the old Louis Prima swing anthem that came back with a vengeance a few years ago thanks to Brian Setzer, and one of the bridesmaids is standing at our table.

Wendy is her name, she says. She's a model, of course, since all six of Anna's bridesmaids are models, and she's gorgeous. She's got a pile of blond hair tied up in the back, sparkling green eyes, and a beautiful pair of tanned shoulders atop her very classy light blue bridesmaid's dress. If I had to guess, I'd say she's taller than both me and Bernie, but she's not greyhound-skinny like so many of the models are. Wendy has a lovely figure, a lovely face, and a lovely voice, and it's hard to believe she would ever have to ask anyone to dance with her.

Yet, she has just asked me—not Bernie—and who am I to say no?

I never took swing lessons during the recent fad, so I kind of fake my way around a bit. Wendy seems to be having fun, and when the band segues into a slow song ("Always and Forever," the wedding staple), she indicates she'd like to keep on dancing. Again, I am happy to oblige.

"You guys looked so sad over there, sitting by yourselves," she says.

I look over at Bernie, who looks even sadder now that he's alone at the table. He's staring straight ahead, clutching his beer as if it were the torpedo switch on a nuclear submarine.

"Well, thanks for coming to the rescue," I say. "But why didn't you want to dance with Bernie?"

"Who's Bernie?" she asks.

"The other guy at the table with me."

"Eeewww," she says, wrinkling her nose. "The fat guy?"

And I feel guilty for the rest of the dance, because this beautiful young woman just insulted my friend, and here I am, still dancing with her. But I continue to dance, figuring Bernie would want it this way, and when I finish I head back to the table and pull up a seat next to him.

"Not bad, big guy," he says.

"Thanks, little buddy," I say. "She's not bad, huh?"

"She sure as hell is not," Bernie says. "Anna has assembled the finest troupe of bridesmaids I have ever seen."

"I'll drink to that," I say. "So, why aren't you fighting them off?"

"Man," he says. "You still don't get it."

"Oh, you mean about your hiatus?"

"No, about why women always liked me to begin with."

"Oh," I say, and have another swig of Heineken.

"Look at me, Jack," Bernie says. "I am not what you would call an attractive man."

"Dude—"

"No, seriously," he says. "I'm fat, I'm going bald, and I'm not young anymore."

"Come on, Bern—"

"No, see, I'm not looking for sympathy," he says. "I'm giving you the facts. See, it was always this way. Women were never drawn to me because of my appearance. It was the confidence, man. The confidence. That's all it ever is."

"So, what are you saying?" I ask. "You don't have confidence anymore?"

"No, that's not it," he says. "But when you stop trying, you stop giving off that . . . whatever . . . that air of confidence. When I was on the prowl, I was always sending out signals—without even trying. And the women, man, they sniff that out. Every single time."

And I know what he means. I know it because I felt it recently. I felt that way with Julie—as confident and comfortable as I've ever been in my life. Right up until that crazy Sunday night.

By the time Connie and her parents left, it was nearly two A.M., which was far too late to call Julie. But do you think that stopped me? I couldn't go to bed without making an effort to apologize or try and salvage something. So I dialed her number quickly, before I lost my nerve, and she didn't even answer. The phone just rang and rang and rang. No voice mail. No answering machine. Nothing.

If she'd taken her phone off the hook, anticipating my call, I could hardly have blamed her. But that doesn't mean it didn't hurt. And between that and the whole Connie mess, I had a pretty hard time getting to sleep that night.

The next day, I waited until the afternoon to call. Trying to demonstrate some sliver of evidence that I still had some pride left. This time she picked up the phone.

"Hello?"

"Julie," I said. "It's Jack."

"Jack, listen—" she said, but I cut her off.

"Julie, I know what you're going to say," I said. "But you have to let me explain."

Which she did, and she demonstrated a great deal of sympathy for Connie and said she hoped it turned out well for her. But just when I was convinced she would see the whole thing as a misunderstanding and be willing to pick up right where we left off (which was on our way to the bedroom, I think), she threw me a curve.

"Still, Jack, I think maybe we should . . . I don't know . . . back off a little bit," she said.

"Back off?" I asked.

"Yeah, back off," she said. "I think maybe things are going a little too fast with you and me."

Flash to Apartment 3C, where Buckner is looking back through his legs at that damn ball again. How did that one get by? How?

"Julie, please—"

"No, I know it wasn't your fault last night," she said. "But how many times did we go out this weekend?"

"Two," I said.

"And how many times, when we were out, did we run into some old girlfriend of yours who had some issue—and who made some reference to some fairly recent contact she'd had with you?"

"That would be two," I said.

"Jack, I think you have to admit that's not a good pace," she said.

I had nothing to say in return. She continued.

"It's just that, I'm at a point in my life where I'm looking for something serious, you know?" she said. "And based on what I've seen, it doesn't seem like you're in a position to get serious."

Oh, but I am! I'm as serious as they come! I couldn't be more serious, not about you!

"Julie," was all that actually came out of my mouth.

"Jack, I really like you," she said. "A lot. It's just . . . I don't know . . . I think you have too much going on right now."

"So, what?" I asked. "So, you don't want me to call you anymore?"

"Not for a while, I don't think," she said.

"What's a while?"

"Look, you have my number," she said. "When you get things straightened out, if you're still interested, we'll talk. And we live in the same neighborhood, so who knows? Maybe we'll run into each other."

I couldn't believe this was happening.

"Are you okay?" she asked.

"I guess," I said, stunned.

"All right, then," she said. "I guess I'll talk to you later, then."

"I guess," I said again.

" 'Bye," she said, and hung up.

I'm not sure how long I sat there, but it might as well have been fifty years. I couldn't come up with a single good reason to get out of my chair and get on with my life. I'd been so confident about Julie, and now she'd broken up with me before we'd really even got started. And why?

Because of the ghosts.

Because of those damn relationship ghosts.

I just knew they were going to screw me over. I just knew it.

So that's why I'm sitting here in a tuxedo at my best friend's wedding, commiserating with another friend in a tux and unable to get excited about the interest shown in me by Wendy, a girl who was on the cover of last month's *Self* magazine. Damn ghosts.

Bernie has decided we should spend this Saturday night the same way we spent the last one—blasted. We've had a good start, taking advantage of the open bar here at the Tavern on the Green, and Bernie is off on a mission to see if he can score us some of the leftover booze once the party ends. He's spotted a cute bartender in one of the corners, and he's gone over to see if he can muster up some of the old Bernie charm.

As I sit and ponder Julie and the painful week I've just spent not calling her, I see Bernie coming back to the table with a big smile on his face. In each hand he holds an unopened bottle of whiskey.

"I guess it still works," he says.

And so we drink our whiskey until they kick us all out. And then we take what's left of the bottles and we stagger back to my place, where we pass out in my living room. Two guys in tuxes, drunk on whiskey, passed out in an Upper West Side apartment on a Saturday night.

Sad? You'd better believe it.

24

Another Sunday, another hangover, and frankly, it's getting to be too much. Bernie has become a terrible influence, especially now that we've both decided to be miserable together, and right now he doesn't smell very good either.

Of course, I probably don't smell any better. But Bernie is snoring, which, when you're sleeping three feet away from him, sounds as if somebody's doing construction work on your left eye. This is what has woken me up, and it's not a pleasant way to begin the day. On top of that, I don't think we stopped for pizza.

So it's one disappointment on top of another here on 75th Street, and I'm going to have to figure out a way to get through another day without calling Julie.

Oh, it's been real fun. About ten times I've done the thing where I pick up the phone and dial the first six numbers, then hang up before I dial the seventh. That's a good one—if you're into being utterly pathetic.

An old Mets cap is lying on the floor next to me, and I pick it up and throw it at Bernie to get him to stop snoring. It works. He wakes up.

"What the hell . . ." he says. "What time is it?"

That's a big thing with Bernie first thing in the morning. He always wants to know what time it is. I can't imagine why, since he never has anywhere to be, but that seems to be his first question when you wake him from a drunken stupor. Has to know the time.

"It's the end of the world," I say.

"Huh?" he asks.

"It's the end of the world," I say again. "Jeff's married to a fashion model who cooks for him, you haven't got laid in weeks, and all of my old girlfriends have ganged up against me to ruin my chances with my new one."

"Grrmph," Bernie says. "How long have you been up?"

"Not long," I say. "You were snoring pretty bad."

"Sorry. What time is it again?"

"It's ten-thirty."

Bernie is up now, walking around, which is more than I've done today.

"You got anything to eat in here?" he asks.

"Cereal," I say.

"Nah, screw that," he says. "I need pancakes or something. Bacon."

"Can't help you there, my man."

"All right, then," he says. "I'm out of here. And remind me to stop drinking with you. It hurts too much."

"Always a pleasure," I say, then I roll over and fall back asleep for two more hours.

This time it's not snoring that wakes me, but the phone—that horrible bearer of bad tidings. The phone—one of the conduits by which the past comes back to kick me in the nose. For a second I think about not answering it. But since I always hope it's Julie . . .

"Hello?"

"Hey, buddy!" Jeff says.

"Hey," I say, then I remember something. "Aren't you supposed to be in Hawaii?"

"Plane leaves in an hour. We're at the airport. You guys have a good time last night? Sorry we didn't get to say goodbye."

"Yeah, it was fun," I say.

"Cool. We had a blast. Anyway, I left my key with your doorman—you know, the guy that's *always* there. If you could grab the mail and check in on the cat, we'd really appreciate it."

"No problem," I say, starting to wake up now, smiling at the mention of the cat.

"Thanks, buddy," he says.

"Hey, you guys have fun. And give Anna my best."

"Will do," he says. "See you in two weeks."

I feel good now when I talk to Jeff. And I really like Anna. I think she and I have some sort of weird connection because of that bizarre night.

She came back to the apartment last week, Tuesday or Wednesday, by herself. I answered the door, and she was wearing a long wool overcoat, the weather having finally turned winter cold.

"Let me guess," I said. "You're not wearing anything under there."

"Ha!" she said. "Good one. I guess I deserve it."

And we sat and talked for about a half hour. She said she was sorry she put me in a bad spot that night, but she hoped I understood that it helped her and Jeff get to this beautiful place they're in now. I told her it was no problem at all, and that it fit right into the circus of weirdness that my life had become. She asked what else had been going on, and I filled her in on the Connie/Julie fiasco of a few nights earlier.

"And now Julie won't talk to you?" she asked.

"No," I said. "She said she wants me to get some things figured out first."

"Bummer," Anna said.

"Thing is," I said, "I have it all figured out. I know I want to be with her. It's just, I can't shake these ex-girlfriends."

Anna listened, said a few of the right things about how it's hard to be patient, that if it was meant to be, etc., etc. I appreciated the support, but I wanted to change the subject.

"I feel so bad," I said. "Here you are getting married in a few days, and all we've done is talk about me."

So we spent a few minutes talking about the wedding, and how excited she was, and how her father was flying in to give her away. That's a nice story, actually, because Anna hadn't talked to her father in three years. But after the big breakthrough with Jeff, she actually flew to Kansas to see him, tell him she was getting married, cry her eyes out and apologize for her role in their falling-out, and ask him to give her away. It must have been like some TV drama, and all I could think was what an amazing thing it was to see this woman undergo this kind of transformation.

"Sounds like it's all going to be perfect," I said.

"Oh, I hope so," she said.

"Don't you have a lot of work to do?"

"Tons, actually," she said. "But I thought I owed you a visit, since our last one was . . . you know."

"Thanks," I said, "but you really didn't have to. I'm just glad you and Jeff are so happy."

We parted with a warm hug, and the next time I saw her she was in a gorgeous white dress, crying like a schoolgirl at her own wedding. And through it all, I kept thinking that Jeff must have done something very, very good in a previous life to deserve this.

I mean, why can't we all meet a nice, sweet, kind, caring, drop-dead-sexy supermodel/homemaker like that?

* * *

Of course, I've met my own ideal woman. Only problem is, I can't call her. And by "can't," I mean I'm not allowed.

I've been a good boy, and I haven't violated Julie's dictate, but it's been almost a full week now, and I think I'm entitled to one phone call. Even prisoners get one phone call.

The first trick is to plan it right. I have to have something to say, because the odds are decent that Julie will want to get off the phone with me as soon as she possibly can.

I'll say I was thinking about her last night, because we had planned to go to Jeff's wedding together, and that I don't want to put any pressure on her or anything but I was just wondering how she was doing. Or even better, I'll say I was curious about how her first week at work went. Yeah, that's a good one. Just play it cool, like we're good friends, checking in on each other. No pressure. Don't even mention the Connie thing.

Now, the next trick is to actually make the call. Sure, it's easy to dial the first six numbers, but try tapping that seventh one once you've decided to put your heart out there for the trampling. Not exactly a piece of cake.

After a couple of fake-outs, I finally do it, and as the phone starts ringing at the other end I find myself hoping her voice mail will pick up. This would be so much easier to say to a machine.

No such luck, though.

"Hello?" says that honeyed voice.

"Hey," I say, hoping she'll recognize me immediately.

"Jack?"

She did. She recognized me. Now, the next question: Is that a good thing?

"Yeah, it's me," I say. "How are you?"

"I'm okay," she says, sounding a little hesitant.

"Good, good," I say.

And then there's a little uncomfortable silence, and I start to realize this may not have been a good idea.

Still, I press on.

"So, it's been a little while, and—"

She cuts me off.

"Jack, look," she says. "I really don't think a week is what I had in mind."

The shattering noise inside my chest distracts me, and I don't know what to say. So we have silence again until she talks.

"I know it's hard," she says. "It's been hard for me too."

"Well, if it's hard for you—"

But again—cut off.

"I just need to figure this all out, you know?" she says. "I mean, I think sometimes we forget that I just picked up and moved across the country. That's kind of a big thing there, without even throwing a new relationship on top of it."

And she's got a point. It's just that, it doesn't help me with what I want to do—what I *need* to do—which is be with her as much as possible.

But Julie is cool to all of my efforts. She doesn't seem annoyed or anything, just unwilling to bend. It's one of these stubborn female moments we are not meant to understand—where she's telling you that what she wants to do is not what she can do, at least not right at the moment. Ultimately, there's nothing we can do. You don't get to your thirtieth birthday without learning one thing about women—that you can't talk them out of anything.

"Can I at least ask you how your first week of work was?" I ask.

And she laughs, just a little.

"It's been pretty crazy," she says. "Actually, believe it or not, they're sending me to L.A. to do a story. I'll be out there for a week. Isn't that funny? I could have just left some of my stuff there."

"That is funny," I say, halfheartedly. "What's the story?"

"It's about celebrity homes. I guess they're sending a whole bunch of people all over. I wanted to be the one that went to Hawaii, but I guess L.A. isn't too bad. At least it'll be warm."

"Yeah, it is getting pretty cold here these days," I say.

"Jack, listen, I've got to run," she says.

"Well, all right," I say. "I guess I'll talk to you . . . some-time?"

"I'm so sorry," she says. "Are you going to be okay?"

"I'm not sure," I say, purposely poking the guilt needle in a little deeper. I mean, hell, why should she get off easy? She's being totally unreasonable here.

"I think you will be," she says. "And you know what? I think you and I are going to be all right."

What the hell does that mean?

"Whatever you say, Julie," I say, affecting my most hurt-sounding voice.

She either doesn't notice or decides to blow it off.

"Good-bye, Jack," she says.

And I just hang up.

Crushed.

I spend the rest of the day in my underwear and bathrobe, basically sulking. This is starting to feel like Amy, only a su-percondensed version, involving just as much agony in a far shorter period of time.

I order in Chinese food, watch *The Simpsons*, and stay up late reading a book about Japanese baseball. I fall asleep on the sofa, and I don't wake up until two-thirty in the morning, when I stagger around the apartment turning off lights, head into the other room and flop into my bed to sleep the sleep of the clinically depressed.

I wake Monday morning with an idea, which isn't always the best way to wake up. I wake also with the knowledge that I'll have to go back to work today. The Yankees are holding a press conference to introduce three of the new players they've acquired this off-season. Two new outfielders and a new relief pitcher, all of whom signed more than three weeks ago, and I will have to find a way to write something interesting about something that barely qualifies as news.

Welcome to the baseball off-season, Yankees-style.

Thing is, the plan I have will give me incentive to finish work early. It's Monday, after all, and I have to get back to The Slaughtered Lamb. It is there that my Delphic Relationship Oracle will be playing acoustic guitar amid the sound of clinking Rolling Rocks. And while it may seem outrageous to keep going to Nikki for advice every Monday night, she's really the only one who's made any sense in the last few weeks.

So, by eleven A.M., I'm out the door, bound for the subway with plenty of extra time to make it to the Yankees' noon schmooze-fest, and who would you think I'd run into?

Hint: She's dressed completely in black, looks great, and the last time I saw her she was with my barber.

That's right.

Old friend Linda Lane.

Apparently, you don't have to put in all that much time to achieve relationship ghost status in my twisted world.

"Hey," she says, stopping me. "So, I'm the Fairway chick?"

"Excuse me?" I ask, legitimately confused.

"I met a friend of yours last night," she says. "Bernie?"

"Oh," I say, and wonder if it's okay to laugh. "Bernie."

"Yeah, we met at a bar."

Bernie made it out to a bar last night?

"And we got to talking," Linda Lane says, "and somehow it comes up that we both know you, and he asks me how I know you, and I tell him, and he says, 'Oh! So you're Fairway Chick!'"

"Oh, man," I say. "I'm sorry."

But it's all right. She's started to smile.

"It's okay," she says. "It is a funny story, after all. I've told it once or twice, and I guess you've probably been the Fairway guy."

"Fair enough," I say. "So, are you still seeing Paolo?"

"No, no, no," she says. "That lasted about a day. Cool guy, but I don't know . . . kind of weird for me."

"Ah, too bad," I say.

"Actually, I wanted to ask you about your friend," she says. "Since I've got you here, anyway."

"Bernie? Bernie's a great guy. Great guy. But I'm sure, if you talked to him, you already got that idea."

"He seemed like a good guy," she says. "But he was a little shy."

"That doesn't sound like the Bernie I know," I say. "You sure we're talking about the same guy?"

"Oh, I'm sure," she says. "Big guy, right?"

"Yeah, Bernie's not small."

"Anyway, I had to talk him into letting me give him my number. But eventually he took it."

"Great," I say.

"So, I don't know. I kind of hope he calls . . ."

"You want me to talk to him for you?" I ask, finally catching on.

"Well, don't make it obvious or anything . . ."

"Don't worry," I say. "I'll be so smooth, he won't even know what I'm doing."

"Cool," she says. "Thanks."

And once again I leave Linda Lane with a smile on my face. Nice girl. I guess the timing wasn't right for her and me. Or else I was just too much of a schmuck.

*   *   *

I cruise through the press conference, slide home on the subway, and bang out a story that I'm sure the paper will bury on page eight. Don't get me wrong here—I do generally take pride in my work. It's just that I've been a little preoccupied lately. Catch me in a few months, at spring training. I'll be energized then. Don't worry.

But today it's pretty much punching a clock. I am done by six, and before I head to the Village, I want to call Bernie. First, to see if he wants to join me. Second, to see if I can get him to bring up Linda Lane.

"Hello," he says.

"Bern, it's Jack," I say. "You up for the Village tonight?"

"Sure, babe," he says. "But not Down the Hatch."

"Wouldn't think of it. Don't want you fighting any more college kids. Not without Jeff around."

"So, where then?"

"Across the street," I say.

"Aw, man," he says. "Your old girlfriend's place?"

"I think 'girlfriend' is a bit of a stretch," I say.

"Whatever. The beer's cold and cheap. I'm up for it."

We plan to meet in an hour outside my building, get something to eat up here and head to the Village. We hang up the phone without one word about Linda Lane.

I'm sure it'll come up over Rolling Rocks.

Sure enough, we're at The Slaughtered Lamb for less than a half hour when Bernie looks up from his bottle, smiles at me and says, "So I met an old friend of yours last night."

"Really?" I say. Must play it cool, remember.

"Yes. Your old friend the Fairway girl."

"No kidding," I say. "Linda Lane?"

"The lovely Linda Lane."

"Small world," I say, wondering if I look surprised enough.

"Anyway, this chick just starts talking to me out of nowhere. I kept looking around, like it was some joke like that night at Blondie's or something. But she really seemed interested. Forced me to take her phone number."

"She's an interesting one," I say.

"So, I don't know, man," Bernie says. "I figure I'll call her, right? I mean, I've been kind of taking a break, but—"

"Oh my God," I say. "Are you asking me for advice on women?"

"Stop."

"No, I think you are," I say. "I think that's what just happened here. You have a girl's phone number, and you want me to tell you if you should call her."

"Are you almost finished?" he asks.

"Almost," I say. "I wonder if this is worth calling Jeff in Hawaii. He might think it's enough of an emergency to fly home."

"All right, all right."

"Yes," I say.

"Yes what?"

"Yes, you should call her. She's a cool girl and she's interested. This could be just what you need."

"See?" he asks. "Was that so hard?"

"Now," I say. "You want to hear about my problems?"

Faithful Bernie never minds, so I give him the latest on Julie.

"She's being unreasonable," he says, in his trademark clinical way.

"You're telling me."

"So that's why we're here?" he asks. "So you can get advice from your lesbian ex-girlfriend again?"

"Basically."

"I think we need to get new lives."

Instead, we order another round as Nikki takes the stage.

* * *

Halfway through her first song, Nikki spots us sitting just off to the side, and she smiles and waves. When the set ends, she hops over to the bar, trades a smooch with the bartender, and heads back to our table holding a fresh bucket of Rocks.

"You know, I like this girl," Bernie says as he plucks a cold one from the ice. "You should have stayed with her. Then you wouldn't have had any of these problems."

"Right," Nikki says. "Just a sex change."

Small talk doesn't last long, because Nikki likes to get right to the point.

"So," she says. "You guys keep coming back for the cheap beer or the free advice? I know it can't be for the music."

"Now, now," I say. "That's not fair. We like your music."

"But . . ."

"But," I say. "Yes. Advice."

"What is it this time?" she asks, exaggerating an eye-roll as she smiles.

"If you all will excuse me, I've heard this one before," Bernie says, and he gets up to go play a video trivia game at the bar.

Left alone with Nikki, I fill her in on the latest in the Julie saga. She hears all about the assaults from Danielle, the bizarre and ultimately sad incident with Connie, and Julie's reaction. Everything up through yesterday's phone call, and the information that Julie is now on the West Coast for a week.

"Wow," she says.

"I know," I say.

"So you're sitting there thinking she's being unreasonable," she says.

"Isn't she?"

"Maybe, but there's nothing you can do to talk her out of it. If she has it set in her mind the way she wants it to be for now, then trying to talk her out of it will only make things worse."

"So, what do I do? Sit and wait? Don't even tell me to put her out of my mind. That won't work."

"Well," Nikki says, "if that won't work, then you have to do something to change her mind."

"I thought you just said I couldn't do that."

"No, no, no," she says. "I said you couldn't *talk* her out of it. She won't respond if you just try and reason with her. She'll feel like you're talking down to her. It will strengthen her resolve."

"So, what then?"

"Well, if you can't talk her out of it, you have to shock her out of it," Nikki says. "You have to do something really spectacular. A grand gesture. Something that will make her realize how cool you really are, how much you like her. Something that will make her remember why she liked you so much in the first place."

And once again I think Nikki has hit on something.

And in spite of the apparent failure of my last plan, I leave The Slaughtered Lamb with a new one, inspired by the lesbian with whom I shared my first kiss.

If this one doesn't work, maybe I'll look into that sex change she mentioned.

25

The plane touches down at Los Angeles International shortly after eleven A.M., Pacific Time, on Wednesday morning. This is another tribute to cell phone technology. I have taken a risk regarding work by leaving town, sure, but if something happens, I can always make calls from the cell.

And the flight? Three words: frequent flier miles. A beautiful perk for the traveling sportswriter. Miles racked up on flights I didn't even have to pay for. And here I am, in sunny southern California, ready to spring one of the most startling surprises of Julie Gordon's life.

The way I see it, there are three things that could happen.

1. I make a brilliant impression, she falls madly back in love with me, and all the ugliness of the past week and a half is forgotten as we live happily ever after. Obviously, we're all pulling for number one.
2. I piss her off royally. She slaps me in the face and tells me to go home and never call her again. Obviously, this is not the ideal result, but at least it would help me move on. Maybe.

3. I spend three days trying unsuccessfully to find her, searching every hotel and celebrity home I can think of, and return home a failure. She never knows I even showed up.

While number three is clearly not the ideal scenario, I must brace for the strong possibility that it will be my result. See, I have no idea where Julie is staying in Los Angeles, nor do I have any idea which celebrities' homes she will be visiting. Nor do I know how to find celebrity homes, unless those maps people are selling on the corners are for real, which I've always doubted.

I could call every hotel within twenty miles of downtown and still not find her. She could be staying with relatives. Or worse, she could be staying with friends with whom she doesn't share a last name.

Of course, I tried to do some advance work on this. I called *People* magazine in New York, told them I was Julie's boyfriend and that I'd lost the paper on which she'd given me her hotel information for L.A. For a second I thought the clerk who answered the phone was going to go for it, but just before she seemed ready to give me the number, she said she had to check with her boss. The boss must have nixed it, and quite frankly, I don't blame the boss. I wouldn't want my boss telling random callers where I was staying.

So I check into the downtown Marriott (and discover Julie's not staying here) and begin calling other hotels in the area. After about an hour and a half with no success, I realize that I am hungry, and I decide to head out to get something to eat, hoping by some miracle to run into her at a sidewalk café.

No luck there, but after lunch I spot a small local bookstore and head in, hoping to find something on celebrity homes. Maybe I could spend the afternoon cruising some of the hot spots in my rental car and spot her on the street.

So I'm poking around the bookstore, trying to figure out which section would contain books with locations of celebrity homes, when I hear an angry female voice behind me say, "Ho, lee, shit."

It's not Julie's voice, which is both good and bad.

It is Danielle's voice, and I can't believe this has happened again.

I turn around slowly, and sure enough, she's sitting at the front of a room filled with women, all of whom have turned to find out what has made her stop her speech. It's another book signing. Danielle's really getting around now. And before I even know what's happened, I appear to be Exhibit A.

"I don't believe this," she says, still looking at me from across the sea of *Picking a Shade* readers. "I don't fucking believe this."

I, of course, have no idea what to say. So I simply stand there and stare back.

"Pardon my language, folks," Danielle says, petting Eric, the dog, who is curled up in her lap. "But I think you'll understand once I fill you in."

She is speaking to her audience, but still looking at me. Looking like a bear that has a rabbit caught in its paw.

"Danielle," I finally say.

"No, please," she says. "Please, come on up here. Let these women see what the book is all about."

"Danielle, come on," I say. "Haven't you ever heard of a coincidence?"

"Ladies," she says. "This is one of my old college boyfriends. He thinks that one of the characters in the book is based on him. And to tell you the truth, he's basically right."

As a few of the women start looking in their copies of the book for a picture of me or something, Danielle continues.

"Ever since the book came out, this gentleman has pretty

much been stalking me," she says. "First, he called. Twice. Then, I started seeing him at book signings. First in New York, and now here. Where are we going next, Jack?"

"Danielle, this is ridiculous," I say.

"Damn right it is, Jack," she says. "And I'll tell you something else, if it doesn't stop, I think you just might find yourself in court."

I start to try and say something—*something like, She sent me the book!*—but it's no use. The audience has started clapping, and Danielle is ranting about me specifically and men in general. She effectively chases me out of the bookstore as the women around her become more and more energized and I become more and more terrified that I will come to bodily harm. And all I can think is this must be her revenge for the night I chased her off the floor of the dorm, screaming drunken invective until she disappeared down the stairs.

The problem here is that Danielle's book is doing incredibly well. It's at the top of the best-seller lists and has become a phenomenon as inexplicable as *The Bridges of Madison County*. Everybody's reading it, because everybody's talking about it. Frankly, I never saw what was so special about the book, but it's managed to strike some sort of chord with the female population of America, and now it can't be stopped. It has become one of several nuisances in my own personal life, and dealing with it was not the way I planned to start my L.A. adventure.

For a few minutes, as I drive back to my hotel, I ponder the idea of going home. I figure this must be some kind of terrible sign that I should quit, go back to New York, and start over, resigned to living with the ghosts and the possibility that I will never overcome them and find true love. But when I get back to my room and see the open phone book, I'm reenergized, and I spend the rest of the afternoon and evening calling hotels and anyone in the phone book whose last name is Gordon. This is occasionally embarrassing and ultimately futile, but at least by the time I go to bed I have put something between me and the latest Danielle screaming incident. That leaves me to start Thursday fresh.

Thursday starts with a brainstorm. I've decided to call Julie's old L.A. number—the one she gave me just after we first met. I figure, since she picked up and moved in a week, the best she could have done was sublet her apartment, and so whoever's there might have had some recent contact with her.

I also figure I can call early, without fear of waking anybody up, because all I am is the clueless old friend who had no idea she'd moved and is just looking for a little bit of help in tracking her down.

So, shortly before nine A.M., I dial the number and hear a sleepy-sounding woman's voice.

"Hello?"

"Hello, Julie?" I ask.

"Um . . . no," the woman says.

"Oh, I'm sorry. Did I have the wrong number?"

"No, no," she says. "It's just . . . Julie doesn't live here anymore."

"Oh really?" I ask, picking up a pen hopefully.

"No, she moved out," the woman on the other end of the phone says.

"Oh, how long ago was that?"

"Just a couple of weeks ago."

"Well, I hate to ask this, but do you have any idea how I could reach her?" I ask. "I'm an old friend and I'm only in town for a couple of days, but I was hoping I could surprise her."

"Well, she moved to New York," the woman says. "But actually, I think she's back in town this week."

"You're kidding!" I say. "What luck!"

"What did you say your name was again?" she asks, and now I'm stumped.

I could go a couple of different ways here. I could make up a name—pick a generic one out of the air and hope that Julie has an old friend with that name. Or I could give my real name, which is a generic name anyway and would lend a touch of honesty to the proceedings.

I decide on the latter, because I figure honesty is a good thing, even in sneaky times like these.

"Jack," I say. "My name's Jack. And I don't think Julie would be expecting to hear from me, so I can't really ask you to give me her new number or anything like that . . ."

"No, I really wouldn't feel comfortable," the woman says.

"I understand," I say. "But do you think there's any chance you could let me know where she's staying in town or any-thing? You know, so I could surprise her?"

"I don't really know where she's staying," the suddenly suspicious-sounding woman says. "But I'll tell you what. She and I are supposed to meet tonight at Q's. It's a pool hall in Pasadena. If you want to see her, I guess you could drop in there."

"Wow," I say. "That's a big help. Thanks. I guess I'll proba-bly see you there. And what was your name? I'm sorry."

"Katie," she says.

"Right," I say. "Katie. Well, thanks for your help, Katie, and I hope I'll see you there."

"Great," she says. " 'Bye."

Now, if Katie tells Julie what just happened, Julie might be on to me, get scared and decide to bag the pool hall. In which case, I'm likely never to find her and to alienate her forever. But it's also possible that Julie could know some other guy named Jack from college or something and will be eager to go to the pool hall to see this old friend. My ambush will then be a success.

I guess we'll have to see.

When I find the pool hall in Pasadena, the first thing I do is go to the bar for a drink. There is no way they're here yet, as it's only about seven-thirty. They're probably having dinner. But as I stand at the crowded bar and survey the canyon that is Q's of Pasadena, I wonder how I'll even find her in this place. There are at least a hundred pool tables, and while most of the room is vast and open and high-ceilinged, there are dozens of dimly lit corners and booths that will require much searching. And since I'm determined to see Julie before she sees me, I'm going to have to rely on my sleuthing skills if I want to pull this off.

Eight-thirty comes and goes with no sight of Julie or Katie (though I guess I might have seen Katie and just not known what she looked like). I've made one thorough loop of the place, all the while keeping my eye trained on the front entrance, and I am convinced that Julie is not here.

By nine-thirty, I'm starting to get bored. I have played a game of video trivia, but I didn't do well because of the couple of times I thought I saw Julie come in the door. I look up every time I see a girl with hair that could be hers, and so far I've been disappointed every time.

It's eleven o'clock when I start to worry she's not coming. By now I've been around the bar at least five times, had three or four beers, and even gone outside three times to see if I could catch her coming in from the parking lot. I'm starting to wonder just how pathetic this has to get before I call it quits.

* * *

"Last call's at one o'clock weeknights," the insanely sexy bartender in red leather pants informs me, as if she'd been reading my thoughts.

"Thanks," I say.

They do, in fact, call last call at one A.M., and shortly
thereafter I'm out the door, devastated. A long, slow drive
back to the hotel fails to calm me, and I hit the sack feeling
defeated and wondering if I'm doomed to romantic purga-
tory among the relationship ghosts.

The next night, trudging on to the plane along with dozens
of businessmen and businesswomen who look just thrilled
to be on a red-eye, I feel their depression. Of course, none of
mine is work-related, as work has hardly entered my mind in
my three days in California. The Yankees have fallen silent,
and as a result I'm basically off, so I've been able to concen-
trate on my battered love life.

I settle into a window seat in row fourteen and I figure I'll
have all three of these seats to myself, since the plane is not
going to be crowded. I pile my newspapers on the seat next
to me and open the new book I just bought at the airport
newsstand (no danger there, though I'd be lying if I said I
didn't worry for a second). And just as I start reading the
first page, the most beautiful voice I've ever heard says,
"Jack?"

And wouldn't you know it? You spend three days looking
all over town for a girl. You finally give up and decide to fly
home. And there she is, on your plane.

All right, all right. I guess I will have to start believing in
fate.

"Wow," is all I can say.

The good thing here is, Julie looks as shocked as I feel, and
it's going to be a while before either of us can put on any of

the masks we might have been planning to wear for our next conversation.

"My God, Jack," she says. "What are you doing here?"

After a few awkward seconds, I convince her to take the seat next to me, because "I have to explain something, and it could take a while." I guess she's intrigued enough, because she sits down and we get to talking.

"Okay," I say. "First of all, I don't want you to be upset about this. But I came out here to see you."

"What are you talking about?" she asks.

"Julie, I don't think you understand what's been going on with me since I met you. I mean, since the very instant I met you. When you got out of the cab, in the rain, outside the magazine offices."

I begin to explain it all, laying my heart right out there in case she wants to stuff it into an air-sickness bag and toss it in the trash. I tell her everything about how I've felt, and how much it's hurt me to not be able to talk to her. I tell her I decided to fly to L.A. to surprise her, make my movie-scene declaration and force her to look at me without all the baggage that scared her off. I tell her everything, and when I finish, I swear there are tears welling up in her eyes.

"You flew out here, not knowing even where I was staying, just to find me and tell me all this?" she asks.

"Obviously, I planned something a little more grand than this," I say.

"What are you, crazy?"

"I'm starting to think so," I say.

And she laughs. And while she's not exactly sobbing, there are definitely tears coming out of her eyes. And we manage the kind of hug two people can manage in two coach class airline seats.

No, it's not the romantic dazzler I'd been hoping for when I decided to fly to the coast, but I guess it's a pretty cool scene. At the very least, it appears to have done the job. She's not switching to her assigned seat.

After the hug, Julie doesn't say much. As the plane starts its takeoff roll down the runway, I think she's trying to process it all. We're not going to say we love each other or anything like that. For one thing, I think that was implied, at least from my end, in the outpouring of gooey sentiment with which I began this flight. And for another, I think we both understand that there's going to be time to figure all of that stuff out.

◇ Epilogue

A lot of people probably make a big deal out of turning thirty, so I don't think I was in the minority. Turning thirty-one, on the other hand, is pretty easy. But maybe that's because my life seems to be in a lot better place these days.

Julie's lease is up at the end of this week, and we've decided to move in together. We've got a nice two-bedroom in a doorman building on Broadway and 86th Street, and we've spent most of the past few weeks moving. It sounds like a big step, and it is, but we're both pretty happy with the way things are going. The only one who wasn't happy was Yousef, who cried when we told him and made us promise to visit.

We'll still be a few blocks away from Jeff and Anna, which is nice, because otherwise we'd miss Anna's cooking. Yeah, our friendly neighborhood fashion model has become a domestic goddess, turned into the wife that Jeff said she wanted to be.

The two of them still go out and party, but it's a lot more sedate than it used to be. They don't dance; they just sit at the bar and talk to each other over drinks. They're always talking. They're always happy. I've never seen them fight. And when they're home, they cook together and bake together and seem to enjoy the whole nesting thing. Go figure, right?

And good for Jeff. Women were never easy for him. Not that he ever looked real hard to find the right one, but he was always the guy who was wandering around the dating scene, not really sure what he was looking for. He basically tripped over Anna, and he knew he had something special before anybody else knew it. Looking at them now, it's hard to believe any of us ever doubted him. You don't see too many couples walking around the Upper West Side who are any happier than those two.

You might see Bernie and Linda Lane walking around the neighborhood, and that's its own story. They've been dating for almost a year, which is a personal record for Bernie and a sharp break from Linda's pattern. Thing about them is, they don't cook and clean and decorate together. The only thing they appear to do particularly well together is argue. Every time you go over to Bernie's place, you can hear the fight raging from inside the apartment before you can even knock on the door. Near as I can tell, the two of them are always trying to tear each other's throats out.

But to hear Bernie tell it, it's the happiest he's ever been. He says they have great sex and that he likes that she's "feisty" (his word). The way I figure it, Linda's the first girl in years (maybe ever) who's challenged Bernie, and that's what he was looking for. Women always came too easily for Bernie, and after a while he stopped enjoying that. Linda makes him work for it. Linda is a tougher puzzle to solve, a tougher run to drive home. Every time they fight, it's something new for Bernie. Women always used to do exactly what he wanted them to do. But not Linda, and as a result she thrills him like no one ever thrilled him before.

How it's managed to last a year, I couldn't say. How much longer it can last, beats me. They could be breaking up right

now for all I know. Of course, that would either be their thir-
teenth or fourteenth breakup of the past twelve months.
Julie used to keep a count, but we've lost track.

On the eve of my thirty-first birthday, the six of us are at The
Slaughtered Lamb, listening to Nikki Stack and drinking
those five-dollar Rolling Rock pitchers. I figure Nikki's good
enough to play some of the real music clubs in the Village if
she wanted to, but she tells me she's happy at the Lamb. She
makes her real living as a freelance writer, and she likes hanging out at the bar because her girlfriend works there. I'm not
sure I know a more content person. Maybe Anna, but then
there's no zeal like that of the convert.

The first time I brought Julie in to The Slaughtered Lamb,
Nikki made sure to claim credit for saving me from myself
and bringing the two of us together. She and Julie hit it off
immediately, and they talked through three set breaks while
I sat by and smiled like a mannequin. I swear they forgot I
was there.

Nikki, then, is a good friend, which is very nice. Some
ghosts can actually be good to have around.

The other ghosts? Not a lot to report, thankfully. Connie's actually doing well, seeing a therapist regularly. She called me a
few months ago and apologized for the whole messy situation.
We haven't talked since, but it's good to know she's all right.

Danielle we see all the time, because her book just kept
taking off and hasn't stopped. She's just published a new one
that's already selling, and you can't turn on a talk show without seeing her. Fortunately, I haven't run into her in person in
almost a year.

And, Amy, I really don't know what happened to her. And
that's as it should be.

* * *

One of the things I love about Julie? Watching her sleep. She falls asleep instantly, which astounds a lifelong insomniac like myself, and she makes the coolest little noises in her sleep. Sometimes she snores, but it's never loud and it never lasts long enough to keep me awake. My favorite is the clacking noise her teeth make when she, for some reason, starts chewing in her sleep. I knew I was a goner the first time I heard that and realized I thought it was adorable.

With Julie, it's all the little things about her, and the beautiful whole that comprises them. I love sitting up nights and talking with her about things—like which books we're reading or what happened at work that day. I love that she always kisses me good-bye in the mornings, even when I've decided to sleep in after a long game the night before and she has to get to work. I love her eyes. I love her hair. I love her smell and her laugh and the way she loves it when I tickle her feet.

I don't know where she and I are headed. Sure, I've started to think about engagement rings, and we've had a couple of conversations—in vague terms—about weddings and even kids. But we're still taking it easy, because our jobs force us into a schedule that requires it, and right now we're happy.

She makes me happy just by walking into a room. I work tirelessly to make sure she's as happy as any woman on the planet. It's nice. It's easy. It's comfortable, and it feels right. For right now, that's a beautiful thing.

Is it true love?

Truth is, I don't know. And the truth probably is, none of us really ever do. I'm guessing everybody has relationship ghosts. And even if they're not always coming back to get in your face, I'm guessing they stand as reminders of what the search for true love really is.

We've all gone looking. Sometimes you think you have it and you don't. Sometimes you think you don't and you do. Sometimes you know you don't, but you stick with it anyway, either because it's all you've got or you're having too much fun. Sometimes you spot it right away, but you still end up having to work for it. In the end, all any of us can do is do our best, learn from the good and the bad and try to be as ready as we can when the real thing hits.

Julie could be the real thing, and if she is, that means I'm ready. And if that's the case, I have to thank that crazy few weeks last fall that taught me all about the magic of fate and memories and airports and New York City.

If this is true love, I guess I have the ghosts to thank.

Imagine that.

Want More?

Turn the page to enter
Avon's Little Black Book —

the dish, the scoop and the
cherry on top from
DAN GRAZIANO

"So," the question always comes, as subtle and unpredictable as Christmas. "You get to talk to the players?"

And the answer is yes. As a baseball writer, I get to talk to the players. More to the point, though, I *have* to talk to the players. It's my job. I have to show up at the game three and a half hours early and spend time in the clubhouse chatting up the players, the coaches, the trainers, the clubhouse attendants—everybody who may someday, on the basis of casual, repetitive, afternoon pregame conversation, trust me enough to help me with a story.

After that I have to sit up in the press box, writing for three hours while at the same time watching a baseball game, write a story about the game before it even ends, so I can send it to the newspaper at the exact second the final out is recorded. Then I have to go back down into the clubhouse, ask those same players, coaches, and manager about what happened—why they won, why they lost, why they seem so angry at the media when it was, in fact, the Oakland A's or the Boston Red Sox who beat them on his night. And then, when everybody else who's come to the game for fun, beer, and camaraderie is out the door and into their air-conditioned cars, I have to go back up to the press box and rewrite the whole thing again.

What else? Well, I have to spend about 150 nights a year on the road, away from my wife and my son. That's really the hardest part of the job, because the job does have some perks, such as getting to (*having* to) watch baseball games every night. But perks or not, it's a job, which means it's hard and stressful and packed with BS just like any other job. And no, it's not nearly as glamorous as people think it is, especially when you're standing at the Tampa airport at nine-thirty, ten-thirty, eleven-thirty on a Sunday night wondering if the airplane ate your luggage and just wanting to get to bed.

That's the hardest part—the airplanes, the airports, the hotels, the rental cars, trying to be a husband and a parent by phone. That's what makes you wonder if this is what you went to college for. Being away from my family is definitely the worst part, at least for me.

Then again, if it weren't for baseball, I'm not entirely sure I'd even have my family.

This story begins on March 17, 2000, at a Tampa sports bar called the Sport Shack—a bar that's not even standing anymore. It was in that bar that I met Andrea, who changed my life.

Why was I there? To cover spring training for the *Newark Star-Ledger*. It was my first spring training on the Yankee beat. I'd just moved to New York from Florida, and I'd spent about a month in my new Manhattan apartment before having to fly to Tampa for the seven-week prelude to the regular baseball season. I had big plans, being a twenty-seven-year-old single guy in Manhattan. I was three months removed from my first New York City Marathon, looking good and full of confidence about my job and my life in general. I figured to be a terror on the New York dating scene, and it was my plan to be just that. I had no desire to enter into anything serious, especially while I was in Florida for spring training. I'd just spent five years living in Florida, and I knew for sure that it was no place for me to meet anybody special.

And then, on St. Patrick's Day, I walked into the Sport Shack in Tampa, Florida, and bought Andrea Rubin a green beer.

What was she doing there? Funny thing, it was baseball that had brought her there too. Andrea was a reporter at the *Journal News*, the Gannett paper that covers the suburban New York counties of Rockland and Westchester, and to supplement her income for the paper she was writing freelance stories for *Yankees Magazine*, the team's publication. Andrea was also good friends with one of the other guys on the beat, and so had planned a one-week vacation to Tampa, where she would hang out with her friend and pick up a few stories for the magazine. This was her first night in town, and so she'd called her friend, who, along with me and the other beat writers, were over in Orlando covering a Yankees-Braves preseason game. We all decided to meet up at the Sport Shack, mainly because it was the first night of the NCAA basketball tournament and this was one of the few places in town that had enough TVs to show all of the games at once.

Now, I'd seen Andrea once before. It was in January of that same year, when I'd attended the New York Baseball Writers Dinner—a formal annual event at which we in the New York chapter of the Baseball Writers Association of America honor those on the New York sports scene who have had particularly big years for one reason or another. Andrea was actually seated at my table that night, directly across from me, so I knew she was beautiful. But on that night, we hadn't been introduced. I was new, of course, and had to talk with a variety of other people who I believed were going to help me do my job in the coming years. She was with somebody else, and of course I didn't want to intrude. (Yeah, I really would have been something on that N.Y. dating scene, don't you think?)

But the writers' dinner had prepared me, at least, for the fact that the girl we were meeting at the Sport Shack was the most beautiful woman I'd ever seen. And when I walked into the bar, what I saw confirmed it. Never in my life have I seen a smile like Andrea's and it was out in full force on that St. Patrick's night.

The first thing you notice about Andrea is the smile, but if she happens to not be smiling, then the first thing you notice is the hair. Andrea has a head of dazzlingly straight, long, black hair that lends a glamorous touch to a face whose beauty is otherwise simple and classic. Keep looking and before long you'll notice her eyes, which are deep and rich and dark and full of sparkle. When Andrea smiles, her eyes smile with her. When she's angry, or confused, or sad, or even tired, you can tell in her eyes. There is no reality TV show or Oscar-winning movie that's as packed with true, raw emotion as Andrea's eyes. I'd pay money just to watch them. Just by watching her eyes, I think, I could tell you everything she goes through in a given day.

So this is what I had before words started coming out of either one of our mouths. I knew she was stunningly beautiful in some very specific ways. I knew she was the kind of girl that made guys stop and stare, possibly even crash their cars into the cars in front of them. In the years that followed, I would have my proof, as we'd walk hand in hand along the streets of Manhattan and I'd see men stare at her. Sometimes they'd even compliment me on my own good fortune, as in, "Way to go, buddy!" which is something somebody once actually shouted at me from the street as she and I walked together in midtown.

But it was on that night, St. Patrick's Day 2000, that I found out what really would make all of the difference in my life. That night was the first night Andrea and I talked to each other.

Thinking back on it, she remembers my asking her if she wanted a green beer as the beginning of our first conversation. Me, I don't remember a specific beginning. It just seems like Andrea and I have always been talking. We fell into a conversation so easy and natural that I don't think I can ever go back and pinpoint the words that started it, the joke I told, the thing we realized at the same time that we had in common. All I know is that our group stopped at about five different bars that night, and that she and I were sitting next to each other and talking all night.

It continued on into the week she spent in Tampa. The very next night there was a dinner, hosted by the Yankees, for the beat writers. But after it was over, we went to Ybor City—the old cigar-factory section of Tampa that's been converted into a kind of mini–Bourbon Street for the college-age boys and girls of the area. We found a bar that was playing eighties' music (so as to feel as old as possible in comparison to the rest of the people on the street), and we bellied up to the bar. Andrea and I sitting next to each other, still talking.

To this day we still laugh about that night—the one when she asked me to dance and I refused (I was trying to be polite—there was somebody else interested in her), and in an effort to make me jealous, she blatantly hit on an airline pilot who was a few seats over from us at the bar. She even got the guy's e-mail address and told him he'd be hearing from her. Poor bastard. I had to laugh. She was smiling at me the whole time they were talking.

As you might imagine, Andrea's behavior on that Friday night in Ybor City embarrassed her, particularly because of the alcohol involved. She says now that she was terrified to see me the next day at Legends Field, the ballpark where the Yankees play their spring training games. She was coming over to do some work on her freelance stories, and she feared what I was thinking of her after she'd practically thrown herself at me in a cheesy eighties bar.

It so happens that I was standing outside the elevator when it opened on that morning, and Andrea was inside, wearing a blue dress that showed off her tanned legs. I had no idea she was embarrassed about the night before. Andrea is not the kind of woman who ever looks as if she has anything about which to be embarrassed. All I knew was that my heart did a little hop when those elevator doors opened, and I made sure it was my very best smile that she saw upon her arrival at Legends Field.

I didn't get a lot of work done that week, got to be honest with you. I was a little bit too fixated on the beautiful face in the seat in back of mine in the press box. During games, we'd share glances and smiles. Before games, we'd sit in the dugout with batting practice going on and talk. We talked about everything—our families, our backgrounds, where we'd gone to school, what we liked to eat. There were no lulls in the conversations, mainly because we were both enjoying them so much we were determined to keep them going. Once, as we leaned on the railing on the balcony behind the press box, three stories up and with a view of the Tampa airport, Andrea pointed and asked me, "Where do you think that plane is going?"

Our talks would consume me. I'd try to make sure I timed my lunches around hers, so we could at least sit at the same table, even if there were others around. For decency's sake, we didn't want to make it too obvious that we were chatting and giggling with each other like schoolkids when we were supposed to be working. Really wouldn't have been all that professional of me to be falling in love on company time either. But it was something that couldn't be helped.

We'd talk for so long and so intently that I'd look up and realize that everybody else on the beat had left for one of the other fields, or the clubhouse. This is a panicky feeling for a Yankees beat writer, because if nobody else is around, it could mean big news is breaking somewhere else and you're missing it. You never know if George Steinbrenner is stomping around, making some kind of big speech that's going to be the back-page headline on all of the tabloid newspapers the next day, but you do know that you'd better be there if he is. But when Andrea and I were talking, I didn't pay much attention to the common worries and paranoia that plague the hypercompetitive ball writer. If I hadn't been wearing a watch that week, I would never have been on time for anything.

Once, in the cool evening sunshine before a rare spring training night game, I looked up from a conversation I was having with Andrea and realized (1) that we were the only people left sitting in the first-base dugout, and (2) that the Pittsburgh Pirates, not the Yankees, were taking batting practice on the field in front of us. This meant that the Yankees were working out on another field, and that I should be there. So I pointed this out to Andrea, who said she'd be happy to accompany me to Field Two. As we walked up the right-field line, past first base, Kevin Young, who was the Pirates first baseman at the time, looked over at us and gave a broad smile. "How y'all doing?" he asked, way too friendly for a ballplayer. It is because of that that we always remember Kevin Young as the first person who was on to us.

Wouldn't have taken much, really, for anybody else to figure it out. The dirtbags with whom I was covering baseball at the time would constantly offer their own insight, letting me know that they thought Andrea was into me and that I should act on it. (Thanks, guys, for the help.)

I have no idea if my work that week suffered—I like to believe I was inspired to write great stories, because when can you be inspired if not in the first frantic moments of a great love affair? But I do know that I was harder to find than I had been during the first five weeks of spring training. I didn't go out to dinner with the rest of the guys. I wasn't even always in the press box.

During one afternoon game, she and I sneaked down into the stands, where we stood in the far corner way down the left-field line while the game was in progress and we had one of our great talks. It was there that Andrea, who was carrying a copy of that day's press clippings, first read one of my stories. She tells me now that she might not have been able to go out with me if she hadn't believed I was a good writer. It is to my unending relief that my story that day was not terrible.

After spending a few innings in that left-field corner, we walked back to the press box elevator. Andrea was planning to stay in the stands, get some sun. After all, she was kind of on vacation. Before we parted, I made a fumbling, faulty effort at a first kiss. Turned out to be more of a peck than anything else—nothing to remember fondly, nothing about which to write an epic poem or launch a war.

Spring training's relaxed schedule means that many of the star players—the ones the people pay their money to see, as the saying goes—play only a few innings, then come out of the game and can actually leave before it's over. For that reason, we writers are allowed to be in the clubhouse during the games, so that we might interview these star players before they leave the ballpark. On the day of my failed first kiss with Andrea, I was in the clubhouse for the game's final few innings and beyond, as we stayed late to speak with the manager and some of the other players. Generally, if not on deadline, it behooves the baseball beat writer to stay in the clubhouse as long as possible, if only so he doesn't miss something vital. I always say it would be dumb to get beaten on a story just because you didn't stay long enough.

So, after a few hours, I was back up in the press box, and Andrea was nowhere to be found. A moment's disappointment gave way to elation, though, when I found a note tucked under my laptop computer. The note told me Andrea was sorry she'd missed me, but that she would try to stop by my apartment later that afternoon.

I don't think I've ever written a spring training story as quickly as I wrote that day's. I don't think I've ever been as upset to be stuck in traffic as I was that day, as I tried frantically to get back to my condo in case she was coming to look for me. I don't think I ever tried harder to look relaxed while watching TV as I did that day, when I had no idea if she'd already come by and missed me, if she was still on her way, or if she wasn't coming at all. This was, if you can believe it, before everybody in the world had a cell phone, and she didn't have one.

But she did come by, for a few minutes. She was on her way to the airport to pick up a friend of hers, but she stopped on the front step of my condo and leaned in for the real reason she'd come—our real first kiss. Once again I kind of botched it. It had been a while since I'd had a kiss I was looking forward to that much. It's possible that I'd never had such a kiss. So maybe it was the pressure, I don't know. It was a sweet kiss, but once again not a great one, and she went off to the airport.

From that point on we had a hard time finding time alone in Tampa. That night, we ended up at Bennigan's (yes, the one from the book), where we basically stared at each other across a table all night, wanting to revisit that kiss on the steps. In the parking lot, we had a few seconds when no one could hear us, and I managed to tell her that of course I planned to call her when we all got back to New York, and maybe we could get together, just the two of us.

"You'd better," she said.

We managed to hang out alone a bit on her last day in town, taking in a sunset from the beach outside her hotel on Tampa Bay. There was some more expert kissing done there.

That night, we went back to Ybor City, our intentions now clear. We drank too much, danced too much, and ended up together in the same room (though nothing untoward happened—we just passed out in each other's arms). The next day, she left. My hangover and I had to carpool with somebody else to Fort Myers for the longest road trip of spring training while Andrea got on a plane and went back to New York. When I returned to my apartment that night, I called her. I was in violation of every rule you ever hear about dating—I called her on the very first night after we parted. She wasn't home, so I just left her a message saying I'd had a great time and hoped to see her soon.

We talked on the phone every day after that. We have spoken to each other every single day since March 17, 2000. When I finally got back from spring training (and the weeklong West Coast road trip that began that year's regular season), we began dating, for real. Nobody there to watch over us. It was true love, love at first sight, like you read about. It was easy and natural and beautiful. And the amazing thing is that it still is all of those things.

On June 30, 2001, I proposed to Andrea, and she said

yes. On November 9, 2002, we got married. On September 16, 2003, our son was born. Along the way, we've had our share of good and bad times together. The good, like the fancy dinners at the River Café or the marathon we ran together six days before our wedding, stand out because we were so happy in each other's company. The bad, especially the day the Twin Towers went down and we spent the afternoon doing interviews for our papers, crying in each other's arms in between working, stand out too, because of the comfort we've always been able to give each other.

It's not the greatest story you've ever heard about two people finding each other, but it's not the worst either. And unlike the girlfriend-reflux madness in the pages before it, it's all true. More than that, though, it's real.

The thing about Andrea that has always made me feel so good is how real our love and our relationship are. It's never been about the effort (though marriage requires more than its share), and it's never been about trying to impress each other (though she impresses me every day, particularly now that she's a mother). It's just been about being happy to be with each other, every minute of every day that we're able to share.

That's why being away from home is the worst part about being a baseball writer—because there's so much I leave at home that I miss. But I guess in the end that's better than the alternative. I'm sad when I go away because I have something so wonderful to go home to.

Turns out, baseball must not be so bad after all.

DAN GRAZIANO

An avid baseball fan but a mediocre player, **DAN GRAZIANO** didn't play sports in college—he wrote about them instead. Since it took up all of his time there anyway, he didn't have a lot of other options than to make a career of it. Within two years of graduation he was a full-time baseball writer—a job that has taken him all over this country and all over the world. Still, no matter how many times he had deep-dish pizza in Chicago, coffee in Seattle, or clam chowder in Boston, there was never a place like New York. It was when he moved to New York that his career took off, that he really felt at home, and where he started his family, finally and thankfully putting all of the lunacy of the single-guy life behind him. A life on the road, working nights, weekends, and holidays, somehow ended up leading to a very happy, nicely peaceful home life. He's now gone suburban and moved to New Jersey, where he lives with his wife and son, and is not ever haunted by relationship ghosts.